The Thea
Development ~~Handbook~~

John Martin
Mojisola Adebayo
Manisha Mehta

Pan Intercultural Arts
32 O'Donnell Court
London WC1N 1NX
United Kingdom
Email : post@pan-arts.net

The Theatre for Development Handbook
Written by John Martin, Mojisola Adebayo, Manisha Mehta
2010
ISBN: 978-0-9550838-1-5

First Published in December, 2010

Published by
Pan Intercultural Arts, London
32 O'Donnell Court
London WC1N 1NX
United Kingdom
Email : post@pan-arts.net

Printed by
Pravin Printery
Dwarkesh, Near Royal Apartment,
Khanpur, Ahmedabad. (Gujarat) India.
Email : sales@rrsheth.com

This also available in Gujarati language published by
Vidya Educational Trust, Ahmedabad, India.
Email : trustvidya@yahoo.co.in

Pan Intercultural Arts
London

This book is dedicated to the Vidya Group Members who made it possible. They are... Bharti Rathod, Bhikhiben Thakor, Dipti Makwana, Kalu Rathod, Mehmudaben Bibi Sheikh, Raniben Rathod, Rekha Rathod, Savita Solanki, Suresh Bhatti, Vijay Prajapati.

CONTENTS

Part Three

Making an Organisation - Some Practicalities:

Part Four
KEEPING GOING

Introduction

How To Use This Book

This is a handbook, something you can use to help you on your way to using theatre in the search for change; change in your society to improve the lives of those who are not achieving their potential.

Some of you may have no experience in this field. You may want to follow the book page by page, from beginning to end. That will give you a strong framework for structuring your work.

Others may have differing levels of experience in theatre, or in development work. You can use this book just to access ideas which will enrich your own practice. We would like you to keep it in your bag or your pocket as a resource.

- This book is offered to you to help you make the best work for your community.

- It is **not** a book of rules.

We do not present it as the only way of creating excellent theatre for development work. We know that you will all need a slightly different variation depending on where you are and what your financial, cultural and political situations are.

Please dip into it,

take the ideas

and use your creativity and energy to make it your own.

Manisha, Mojisola and John, who are writing this book, were involved in setting up, training, running and developing the Vidya company in Ahmedabad in India. This has been a very successful and sustainable company and we believe that this model can be adapted to similar situations across the world. We also have wide experience of other theatre for development work. The members of Vidya have contributed their feelings, memories and experience to remind you that this work is being lived by real people who are doing it every day.

So this book is not about Vidya. Rather it is some ideas and practical examples, drawn from Vidya that we want to share, together with influences from other projects we have been involved with.

To give you a little idea of what Vidya is, and what it has achieved, here is a short version of its history.

The Vidya Story

A need was perceived. Pan Intercultural Arts (UK) and the Darpana Academy of Performing Arts (India) identified that in the city of Ahmedabad in Western India, the status of girl children was extremely low. This was seen to be even more so in the slum areas of the city where the oppression against girl children was made worse by poverty and social prejudice in wider society. Girls were frequently not put into education, were given less food than boy children and were not given available health care. As a result it was almost impossible for them to prosper and to fulfil themselves in their society.

The explanation for this lay in fixed attitudes within society that girls were worth less than boys. For example in many cases family pressure was leading to the abortion of foetuses if they were found to be female (known as female foeticide).

Vidya was formed to challenge the attitudinal mind-set which caused this.

Funding was found *for three years from the UK Lottery fund. This allowed us to employ a small group of performers, an administrator, an artistic leader, a computer and a mobile stage.*

Doing the Research. *Before any thoughts of performing we needed to know the details of the issues that we wanted to deal with. A team of researchers, drawn from the slums, visited hundreds of the slum areas in the city. They got to know people, interviewed community leaders, Non-Governmental Organisations (NGO's) working in the area, educators, health workers and municipal officers. Slowly a full and layered image was drawn up of what the group would have to deal with, and in which areas it would be most effective.*

Forming the Group. *It was decided to adopt a radical approach by forming the group from people living in the affected slum communities who knew and lived the issues to be challenged. The group was thus recruited from slum areas and was made up of people with no theatre experience. Sixteen people were chosen. The task was to train them to become actors who could speak to people like themselves about problems they knew intimately. The "peer-group" was formed, and trained. Manisha Mehta, who had already done a lot of the research and was experienced in community arts work, became the Artistic Director to guide the group.*

Making Theatre. *After three months of training, the group was able to turn their own experiences into theatre plays and begin to perform these in slums in the city as a springboard for debate and discussion. By using material from their own lives as a basis for plays, the group knew that the stories would be recognisable in the target communities. A mixture of 'straight' plays' and 'intervention' plays were used. In this second type,* *sometimes called 'forum theatre', the audience becomes involved in deciding how to change the fate of those in the play who have least power.*

Going to the audiences. *Vidya converted a minibus into a mobile theatre, complete with a fold down stage which could go into any slum area and have a highly visible playing space. From the beginning the audiences were regularly over 1,000 for each performance and the intervention plays often had 50 or more people wanting to come on stage to push the dialogue forward. This was in spite of many theatre "experts" who had said that Gujarati audiences were too "conservative" to ever participate in this way, and that this kind of theatre could not work – not these audiences! Over the years the audiences have sometimes been as many as ten thousand, and the total audiences are now over one million people.*

Community Relations. *Because of the entrenched nature of the attitudes in the community, we knew that a single visit to a slum would achieve very little. To achieve any meaningful change Vidya would have to commit to a small number of communities and work in depth with them. Eight slum areas were chosen. Each slum would be visited for a week with plays, feedback sessions, workshops and new short plays drawn from that audience's experiences. Then Vidya would move to the next slum and so on. After eight weeks they would re-rehearse and move back to the first slum with new material. Over two years this gave a deep relationship with community members and an ability to track change.*

In the second phase of the work Vidya has been involved in twenty slum communities and has also created plays on related issues in rural areas.

Developing the Idea *As the group began to know the communities they realised there were other ways to help the situation and other needs they could meet. Children's groups were set up to use theatre to imagine their futures and comment on their realities. Men's groups and women's groups were formed.*

Enrolment drives to get girls into school took place.

Sustainability. *After three years the initial funding for Vidya was at an end. Rather than go back to their old lives, the members decided to continue working and find their own sources of income. They learned how to fund-raise, gain sponsorship and get commissions from NGOs. They also looked at practical ways from within their community. Women who could sew were given work making quality products which fed the women, their families and the group. CDs of the songs in the plays were recorded and sold. Community paper bag making brings an income. A scooter-rickshaw was fundraised for and is gaining one more income.* **Even the profits of this book go back to keep Vidya alive and well.**

Still Working. *After ten years Vidya is still working, a real success story as a theatre company and an even greater success as an agent for change. This change has been thoroughly documented on personal and community levels and is recognised nationally and internationally.*

Vidya's members have also become empowered by the work. They have learned the confidence to work as leaders in the community, and have learned that change is possible.

Much of this book is based on experiences which were made in forming and running Vidya. There were mistakes, there were bad times. These were also learning experiences. Change through theatre is possible. Vidya is the proof.

Enjoy the book

Part One
before you start working –
things to consider:

Why theatre for development?

Perhaps we should first ask – **why theatre?**

Theatre takes place where live performers creatively use dramatic means to communicate an idea to an audience. Theatre is an ancient art which has taken many different forms all over the world. It can include storytelling, music, dance and puppetry. It can be used to communicate a story, a play, a myth, a message. It can take place in any environment where people are able to watch and hear it – whether it be a theatre building, a street, a temple or under a tree.

No matter where, why and how it is presented, the single most important element of theatre is **human interaction**. Without human beings present, both performing and watching, theatre cannot take place. It is this *human* quality which gives theatre its power. Theatre is a very immediate way to explore human experience, to understand life's problems, to dialogue and to find meaning. Not least, theatre can give people enormous pleasure.

Theatre also has a huge potential to engage people, because like life, it has many dimensions. Theatre can have an effect on every human sense, it can be physical, emotional and spiritual, it can be an intensely personal experience, yet have enormous social impact.

Crucially theatre is the only art which can include many other creative forms from music to movement, painting to poetry, fireworks to film, dance to drama.

Theatre is a diverse language with a wide vocabulary. Through the rich language of theatre human beings can 'speak' about issues relevant to their lives. For all of these reasons, and more, theatre can be positive and powerful in any society. This is why we chose theatre.

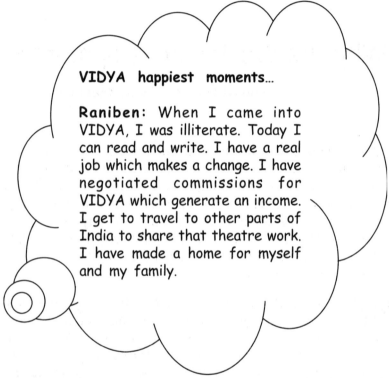

VIDYA happiest moments...

Raniben: When I came into VIDYA, I was illiterate. Today I can read and write. I have a real job which makes a change. I have negotiated commissions for VIDYA which generate an income. I get to travel to other parts of India to share that theatre work. I have made a home for myself and my family.

So why theatre *for development*?

In one sense all theatre is for development. Theatre is a communal experience in which stories are told, values are questioned and relationships are explored. Theatre can encourage debate, inform, entertain and educate. Theatre can change how you feel, think and imagine. Theatre can develop the body, mind, spirit and society.

Yet when we use the term **Theatre for Development**, we are speaking about something quite specific. Theatre for development is a way of engaging whole communities in using drama as a tool to discuss issues and solve problems.

The idea of Theatre for Development is not new. Theatre forms have been invented by many societies all over the world to discuss issues, debate problems and make change. However the term 'Theatre for Development' is relatively new, in use since the 1970s to describe the use of theatre in developing countries.

The term 'developing' refers to countries in which the majority of its people have experienced a low standard of living and a low quality of life in comparison with other areas of the world. A developing country has experienced high levels of poverty, infant mortality and illiteracy, low levels of life expectancy, education, health care, economic growth and industrialisation.

"Developing" therefore signifies it is moving from, or aspires to move from, this situation to one which is improving. However, many so called 'developing' countries are often experiencing economic decline rather than development.

Theatre for Development might also be used in so-called 'developed' rich countries. It can also be applied to countries such as those in Eastern Europe and Central Asia who have recently moved from one political economic system to another. Or it can be used in a country or territory which is under occupation or experiencing conflict. This book isn't specifically aimed at those situations but the same principles certainly apply and this book may still prove useful.

Developing countries are often those which have experienced colonialism in the past and have attained, or are attempting to achieve, national independence. This often means that the country's resources (both human and material) will have been exploited by an outside force over many years. The people may have experienced racism, prejudice and poverty, economic growth may be stunted, social infrastructures and political processes may have been left in a poor or dysfunctional state, indigenous cultures may have been suppressed or wiped out, boundaries may have been drawn up which do not reflect or respect ethnic differences, there may be ongoing international and inter-ethnic conflict and war.

To describe a country or society as 'developing' therefore largely means it is moving from this experience towards economic growth and sustainability, effective building and re-shaping of infrastructures, widening access to education, social and health care provision and re-evaluation of local traditions, practices and languages as well as establishing or improving human rights, democratic processes and national independence, a sense of national identity, harmony and peace. Yet a developing country may also be experiencing the effects of globalisation which, as well as bringing economic growth, may have a diminishing effect on local indigenous business, culture, identity and the environment.

Theatre for Development is the practice of using theatre to address issues and find solutions to problems arising from the specific experience of living in a developing situation, and to improve the lives of people living in so-called developing countries. That is why we chose Theatre for Development.

Theatre for Development may also be called, 'theatre for social change', 'theatre for human rights', 'liberation theatre', 'participatory theatre' and is part of a family of theatre practice known as 'applied theatre', which includes 'theatre in education', 'community theatre' and 'theatre of the oppressed'. All these practices have the same key elements: theatre, participation and change.

Theatre For Development means:
Entertainment
Education
Encouragement
Empowerment
Equality
Everlasting CHANGE!

The philosophy behind our practical work owes much to two hugely influential writers and their books. The first was by Brazilian educationalist Paolo Freire entitled Pedagogy of the Oppressed (1972) and the second by the late Brazilian Theatre Practitioner Augusto Boal, Theatre of the Oppressed (1974). Boal's theatre practice and writing owe a great deal to Paulo Freire. And many of the games, exercises and techniques which you will find in our book owe a great deal to Augusto Boal.

In many developing societies, people have had their languages taken away from them through colonialism. For the oppressed to develop and become empowered it is important that they become literate in all languages. Theatre is one of these languages.

VIDYA happiest moments...

Bhartiben: Now I earn an income and I am financially independent – my home is doing well.

What is a Peer Group?

What does "peer" mean?

A peer group is a very simple concept. It is a group whose members are from the community in which it works. Because of this they have day-to-day knowledge of that community, its structures, its history and the issues which are important to it. All the work will therefore be based on "equal speaking to equal" or "peer to peer" to better understand, explore and deal with problems and challenges within that community. The development of that community is of equal importance to group members and their audiences.

A "community" may be defined by its geographical location (e.g. fishing villages) or its socio-economic status (slum dwellers), or could be more geographically scattered but with common experience (people with HIV, survivors of torture, drug users etc.).

So a peer group working in the slums would be made up of slum-dwellers, a group working with survivors of violence would comprise people with experience of violence etc.

How is it different?

Theatre for Development has often been carried out by trained performers from a well-educated, middle class background. Such groups would visit communities they considered in need of help. They perform, run workshops and leave. Inevitably they remain outsiders.

Although a lot of good work was achieved with this model there was always the danger of such a group having an attitude of superiority, of "talking down" to the visited audiences ....

"We know that you have a problem and we have come to help you solve it!".

However much research they carried out, they could never know the community as well as those inside it.

A peer group model places the identification of a problem, the discussion of it, and the search for a solution to it firmly in the hands of those it affects. They have ownership and responsibility and there is no possibility of anyone resenting them as "outsiders". As the project develops the group members feel and appreciate the benefits of change just as much as those they work with.

VIDYA happiest moments...

Rekhaben: The first time we performed 'Asha' in my community. No one in my community has worked in theatre and saw it as negative. My entire family and parents were in the audience but after seeing me perform on stage, my community members began to treat me with respect.

How is it possible ?

The following chapters outline suggestions to make a peer group active, motivated and effective. It should be realised from the beginning that forming a peer-group has challenges as well as advantages. For example it will normally not be possible to find all the skills needed from within such a community. A considerable amount of training will be needed, both in performance skills and in the running of the group.

It may be necessary to start with a leadership and administration of the group which comes from outside the relevant community. These people will have the vision, skills and experience to start and develop the project. But even in such a case the medium to long term aim is to train members of the community to have these skills and take over the leadership. This can lead to the strange situation when someone from a trained development or theatre background may start up a highly successful peer group but true success is when they are no longer needed. The aim may be to make yourself redundant!

Different results – More Empowerment!

When the peer group comes to the point of being self-organising and self-sustaining we see empowerment taken to its logical conclusion. The advantages of this cannot be underestimated. As well as the fact that a community is dealing with its own challenges without outside help, the process also may provide training in many skills for those who would not normally be trained. Just as the community will undergo change, members of the peer group will also develop. The skills they learn and the experience they have in performance, workshop leading, research, evaluation and discussion-leading can increase their self expression, self confidence and their standing in the community.

In the Vidya group it was remarkable how members of the peer group underwent personal growth even in the first two years. As they engaged themselves in the analysis of their own communities, created performances to explore issues and experienced performing in front of thousands of people they became more confident, coherent and contented.

One factor which led to this is of enormous importance. Forming a peer group theatre company (when it becomes a funded project) is about creating permanent jobs and members may have never experienced this before. Having employment can bring financial and social stability not just for the individuals but for their families and their communities.

A Peer Group Theatre for Development Company is certainly a challenge but the benefits are far-reaching.

VIDYA happiest moments...

Bhikiben: The day I wore my VIDYA uniform for the first time and walked out of my house and through my community proudly.

A vision for change

Change will be an inevitable consequence of your work. Even the process of picking up this book and starting to read it has changed you.

Change is not a fixed thing, but is continuous.

Change is not a rock, but a river. Things will flow from what you do.

Change is necessary for all human development, and for development of communities. So with the knowledge that your work will change you, and your communities, what is your vision for change?

> How much change do you want?

> What do you imagine your society could become?

> Who do you want to become?

Exercise your imagination - it will cost you nothing.

Anything is possible!
What are your dreams?
What are your desires?
Be open to surprises...

In 1964 a military coup took place in Brazil, thousands of people, including theatre director Augusto Boal, were imprisoned, tortured and exiled. In 1992 this same man and his theatre company, the Centre for Theatre of the Oppressed, were elected to government in Rio de Janeiro and started using interactive theatre in communities to create ideas for changing the laws. They called this process 'legislative theatre'. By 1996 twelve laws were created in Rio through 'legislative theatre' – the desires of the people expressed through theatre, then made into law. Theatre can bring justice

In 2000 16 people born and raised in the slums of Ahmedabad, who had never performed before, were invited to form a peer group theatre company named Vidya. As we write, in 2010, they have now performed to over a million people, they travel India and the world, and are completely independent and self sustaining. Vidya is the inspiration for this book. Theatre is powerful, this is why oppressors and colonisers will always try to stop it, or use it for their own ends. Theatre is in your hands. Imagine the possibilities ! Think big !

- *Theatre for a Change* in Ghana enables 12000 young people a year to protect themselves from HIV.
- Incidents of HIV/AIDS in Uganda were proved to have been reduced as a direct result of sustained theatre-in-health education programmes across the country over the past twenty years.
- In Kenya a women's Theatre for Development company sustains itself by baking and selling bread.
- We believe theatre can help to improve the quality of people's lives and the health of an entire community.

CONSIDERATION FOUR

We offer you this to help you create your own manifesto.........

The Vidya Manifesto

Vidya's key principles:

- We BELIEVE in Change! And in artistic action for change.
- We are all artists and creators, whatever our background and education.
- People's creativity can be harnessed as a tool for change.
- Ongoing training is vital – there is always more to learn.
- Personal growth comes through artistic activity, knowledge and understanding.
- Be Down to Earth – go to people, sit with them and listen, drink their tea!
- We are all equal. We accept no inequalities in caste, class, religion, gender, disability or sexuality between group members, the company management or within the community.
- Empowerment of group members, the audience and the community is our goal.
- Sustainability of change is vital. We don't start something & walk away. We stay until change is rooted.
- Respect for each other's abilities and differences is key.

- We must be patient – allow the rhythm of others, give them space and time to communicate in their way – we don't impose our rhythms.
- We are non-judgemental about the activities of others.
- We are always adaptable to changing situations e.g. the local communal riots - which entered the stories of our work.
- We move TO the people in their environment.
- Holistic approach – What is the good of only addressing literacy if the water is polluted and there is AIDS or alcoholism in the family?
- Multi-faith understanding within the group, we welcome members from all faith groups, sects, etc.
- Transparency about all of our activities is necessary to build and maintain trust within the group and the community.
- Ongoing self evaluation, we want to learn from every situation.
- We create emotional and mental space for all, and we support each other.
- We create and maintain an open, non-judgemental, learning environment.
- We have the freedom to discuss issues with other members and with community members.

CONSIDERATION FIVE

Who is the group?

a. What makes a good leader?

Leadership can be in the hands of one person, or it may be shared or rotated between many. Different leadership structures have different qualities, advantages and disadvantages. Those who start the project will have to decide which approach they will take. The most common situation is to have one artistic leader. So who might this person be? What qualities do they need?

The most important quality is having a vision of what can be achieved through Theatre for Development in your particular situation. This has to be a long-term vision both artistically and socially. To achieve this vision considerable skills will be needed.

Vidya On Leaders

Mehmudaben : Our leader is passionate. She treats us like a family. She has forgiven us easily, even though we have made many mistakes.

Rekhaben : When the first phase of the money ran out the project could have ended. But our leader was persistent. She was brave enough to go one step further. With her bold step we became VIDYA: Educational and Charitable Trust.

Bhikiben : From 2001-2009 our leader has given her everything to VIDYA. In my research I have seen many organisations and many different leaders. Many of them think only of their own benefit first. They receive grants and do not use them for their organisations. They are corrupt. But in VIDYA, our leader did not even draw a salary for a whole year.

Dipteeben : If I could change one thing about our leader it would be that sometimes she leads with her heart and not her mind. She can get very emotional which can stop her from making those difficult decisions and taking action.

In some cases the leader may be someone who has experience both in theatre and in development work but this is rare. If you don't have such a leader don't worry because skills learned in other areas might be transferable:

- **A mother** of several children will probably have very good time management and conflict resolution skills.

- **The head of a household** will have budgeting skills.

- **A farmer**, used to planting and harvesting with the seasons, may have very good forward planning skills.

  Never underestimate what life has already taught you!

  It is worth considering the following qualities as extremely useful for an artistic leader whether they are the result of formal training or life-skills:

- **Creative skills** – the ability to imagine, think laterally and be innovative.

- **Negotiating skills** – working with other NGOs, community leaders and within the group, will need constructive diplomacy.

- **Motivational skills** – for those periods when the normal energy is flagging in the group, or the community can't (yet) see the point.

- **Conflict Resolution Skills** – there will always be frictions within the group or within parts of the community. These can be very destructive if not addressed quickly and effectively.

- **Advocacy skills** – There will come a time when you have to let people know of what you are doing and convince them of its worth. This may be to generate more work or to get that all important funding.

If all these qualities are not available at the outset, don't worry. They can be learned in workshops or even from books, where available. More importantly, if an awareness of their need is present, they will be learned from observing others or just working out how to do it through the work.

It has to be stressed that ......

an artistic leader in Theatre for Development is not a dictator or tyrant!

The essence of this work lies in sharing, working together, allowing everyone to take responsibility and power. The Director who keeps all the power to him/herself is disempowering others!

VIDYA happiest moments...

Vijay: When VIDYA would come to my community I used to feel "could I work with them?" The day (Vidya's leader) Manishaben saw me as an artist, it was a very defining moment for me.

b. What makes a good peer-group member?

Who are these special people who will make theatre to change the lives of others?

Possibly nobody in your group will have been on stage before. Equally they may have limited knowledge of development/NGO work. And they may never have worked as a member of a group where all have equal voices.

Before you choose your peer group members - make sure your project is clear, so that they understand the commitment they will make by becoming a member.

We are looking for people :

- Who want to make a change in their own lives and in their communities
- From the community you are representing/targeting
- Representative of the age/gender/faith mix of the target communities
- Willing to commit for the length of the project
- With potential theatrical skills – e.g. they can tell a story, or sing a song well...
- Who are a mix of personality types, young and enthusiastic, reliable, older or caring – a group should not be made up of identical people but complementary ones - get the balance right!
- Who may not necessarily be able to read or write
- With the potential to grow and take on responsibilities
- With aptitude to become a group member - willing to accept the equality and democratic ways of the group.
- Willing to be non-competitive in the work (and not assume that if they take on leadership it is autocratic/dictatorial)
- Able to see the group as more important than the individual.
- With self criticism and self confidence in equal measures
- Willing to change themselves and find their voices

There will, of course, be differences and disagreements. Group members must accept this and be able to deal with it.

Peer-group members will enter a process of change when they join the group. They will learn new things and work with different people. While an individual might not have all the qualities listed above, remember that the most important quality to look for is someone who wants to make a change in his/her life, in his/her family's life and in his/her community.

Be prepared for a turnover of members as time progresses. People may choose to leave the company and others may enter. Don't expect the original group to stay the same for many years.

People will come from their community and develop into role models but this process may lead to them moving on to other things. This should be seen as a success.

CONSIDERATION SIX

What do you need to start the work ?

Minimum requirements

- You need to choose a name for your group.

- Perhaps the people who are behind the project will have an idea or this might be your first creative task as a group. Write down everyone's ideas, accept criticism, consider other possible interpretations of the name you had thought of and finally, try it out on people in the community. Let them be part of the decision making.

- Theatre for Development, like so much work in the community, does not need huge resources. It does not need big buildings and corridors of offices. Of course some groups will develop to have buildings, vehicles, computers and more, but to start the work very little is needed.

- You will need a safe space to prepare your work. This may be inside or outside, depending on your situation but should be safe in the sense of:

- not likely to cause injury during training

- safe to express feelings & thoughts without being judged You will also need to consider:

- legality – in your country do you have requirements for working conditions, laws about health and safety, employment contracts, a need to obtain insurance for those working with you?

- sufficient money. You may be able to operate with very little money, but make sure you have what is necessary before you start. This may only be what it takes to get a legal certificate, or to pay travel costs. It is worth taking the time to find that money before you start so that you do not have to interrupt the work to go and find it later. (see Funding – below)

- transport, refreshment, nourishment: these are just a few basics. You may have more. If you have a large grant or commission you need to allocate money to basic human needs. If you do not have the money, how can you provide these elements through other means ?

Some new organisations (Vidya is an example of this) started life within a host organisation. When it was mature enough it moved out and became fully independent. Could this be a growth-strategy for you? Is there a college, an arts centre, community centre, who could give you some of the above to get you started?

Part Two
The Process

STEP 1

Research

You know why you started this process – there was a burning need that you wanted to address. That is a strong subjective motivation. But now you need to substantiate that need through a thorough research process. By doing this you will have more than an emotional drive. You will have evidence.

The reason why we started the project was because we knew there was a need for change, but we have to be absolutely sure of all the local conditions before we start our creative work.

We have to research:

- the issues which cause the need
- the communities and how they are made up
- who are key people in the community
- any other projects in the area,
- which NGOs are working there
- possible places to perform

All this will give us a "baseline" from which to progress with our work, and from which we can measure the results.

Remember that when talking of a community this may have many forms. A community may be geographical, it may be people of shared interests, shared experience. Vidya's community is mainly one of shared location, the slums of Ahmedabad, India.

VIDYA happiest moments...

Geetanjali's father was an alcoholic and would get very angry when VIDYA would perform in his community where alcoholism and gambling were big issues. VIDYA would perform plays that focused on alcoholism and gambling and how these relate to the oppression of women. After seeing VIDYA's performances, Geetanjali's father realised the dangers of his alcoholism and now is pro-active in helping his daughter with her education.

BEWARE !

Sometimes the fact that you are researching in a particular area might upset people who don' t want change, or factions who want money. They could see your activity as threatening their power-base, and may try to dissuade you, even threaten you. So you may need to be careful and make sure you have a support structure – your trustees, a good lawyer, a local activist etc. Don' t try to act entirely on your own. Use others who can support you.

The Vidya Research Model :

- Select peer group researchers – local people, very important in terms of trust and understanding. You might use a local NGO network to find them.

- Give clear instructions to researchers and specific goals to focus on your objectives. Rehearse their initial introduction of the project, clearly stating its target area (e.g. girl child or HIV affected or water usage etc), its duration and its goals.

- Conduct initial research in more communities than you will finally focus on. Part of the research is to find the optimal areas for this work (Vidya researched two hundred communities in order to choose eight)

- Collect statistics and data according to your issues. This can be done informally, going from family to family e.g. 50 families in each area. Then compare this with corporation and NGO data.

- Talk to local bodies, e.g. NGOs, corporations related to that community. Is there anybody working in a similar field to yours? Invite suggestions of collaborative work.

- Host a community meeting – with the peer researcher. Present the project. Explain why it would be good in this community. Identify those who are eager for the work (e.g. youth groups, women's groups etc.) and involve them in the process.

- Contact the "head" of the community to convince them of the project's worth. They may have great (even controlling) influence about what goes on. Sometimes these are elected leaders, sometimes self-appointed (because they have more money, more friends or even more power – muscle or even guns).

- Contact any local authority leader (district commissioner or similar) who will know more than you!

- Identify possible places for performances – Will you need power for microphones, lights etc. Where could it be sourced?

- Ask if permission would be given for performances (police, local authorities) NB. different countries will have different rules.

- Create a relevant questionnaire according to the local situation. This should not be a visible questionnaire on a clipboard pushed into people's faces. It should be learned at home, and left there, to be filled in after a day in the field. The manner of asking questions should be as informal as possible

- There is always a danger that people give you the answer they think you want to hear, so research should try to go beyond this.

- You will probably need more than one visit. We suggest 3 visits over your research period. The first might be to contact leaders, NGOs etc. The second might go into families. The third might be to call a community meeting.

When all this research is completed you will have a lot of data and a lot of anecdotes. Now you need to sift this to find where your work is most needed and where it will be most possible. If you balance these two your choice will become easier. But you may also wish to have a spread of different types of communities e.g. some with different religions; some with migrant labour, some with fixed populations; some with more infrastructure, some with less. And so on.

STEP 2

Selection of peer group

The time comes when you are ready to select those people who will become your theatre for development practitioners, the actors. This is a vital, and exciting time. But where do you find these people if you are in an area where there are no trained actors?

Here is a possible route.

- Issue an invitation to all the communities where you are researching that you are looking for performers – your peer researchers can inform people during their research.

- Interested people can be invited to attend an initial meeting. A brief form can be filled in by each person. Support people in reading and writing if necessary.

- Read these through and shortlist those who interest you for interviews.

- The Interviews: Ask interviewees why they would like to join, what they understand of the project, how committed they are to changing things, what job are they doing now (if at all). You might find some who are not good for the peer group but may be good in your office or as volunteers.

- Short-list from the interviews a reasonable number (perhaps 3 times the number you will finally choose) and invite them to auditions.

- The Auditions: How do you audition people who are not performers? Get as close as you can to their performance possibilities. Ask if they can sing you a song, or tell you a story. Can they be heard at a reasonable distance?

- Invite a number of people from these auditions to a training period. Invite a number which is greater than those you wish to finally engage. There will be some who drop out when they see just how difficult theatre work really is!

> With the VIDYA project's peer group selections, the first question we were asked was "how much do we get paid?". People have households to support. Be ready for such questions during the auditions!

Bhartiben : When I joined VIDYA as a teenager I never thought I could be financially independent at the age of just 16.

Sureshbhai : I never had a theatre background. I did not dream I would be able to perform in front of thousands of people. When I did my first performance I felt so nervous but so happy I could hardly speak!

The Training: Your final selection will be based on how people react during the training phase (see below), how they work together, how creative they are, how confident they are etc. We discuss the training below, but plan for it to be as long and as thorough as possible.

What is the ideal size for a peer group?

You can have five people in a group or you could have twenty.

With hindsight the Vidya group was perhaps too big.

We had sixteen people.

If we were doing it again we think we would choose nine.

This choice will also depend on your resources.

Throughout the audition and selection process, be prepared to think long-term for the life span of the project. The peer-group members will undergo a process of change, as they encounter many unknown elements. Some may move onto other things.

Savitaben: The best thing about our group is that even if there is a conflict, when we go to perform we are all united and we give our very best. We don't let our problems affect the performance. We have been united now for nearly ten years.

Raniben: If I could change one thing about our group it would be that we learn to listen to each other. Everybody thinks their point of view is the most important. And the whole issue we are debating becomes unclear.

STEP 3

Why Training?

All Theatre for Development groups need training.

Vidya trained in theatre skills for two months, full time, before starting to think about the plays they would create.

We recommend that you also take as much time as you can afford in training before you go on to create plays and lead workshops in the community.

Training involves **games, exercises and theatre making techniques**.

Games are a very important way of re-discovering a sense of play which many of us lose as we get older.

Exercises are a way of developing and refining a particular skill.

Theatre-making techniques such as improvisation, storytelling, devising and interactive theatre give us the tools which we use to communicate in our target communities.

In this training section we are going to give you just a few examples of our favourite games, exercises and techniques which help to get us working as a creative team, get us physically and vocally playful and expressive, awaken our imaginations, get us making images, building characters, expressing emotion, developing stories, scenes and interactive, problem-solving plays.

Much of this work owes a huge amount to the people who have taught and influenced us over the years and their many names are acknowledged later in this book.

There is not room enough to include all of our techniques, nor is there need. What is important is that you use this book for ideas, but go ahead and invent and develop your own games and exercises and draw from your own cultures.

Adapting the work

Be aware that the games and exercises we are suggesting sometimes need to be adapted to suit people's different physical abilities, age and impairments. We recommend that you always invite the participants themselves to adapt the work to suit their own bodies.

Theatre behaviour

Many of the games and exercises may require you to work beyond what you normally do in your ordinary life, or even in your own culture. Theatre is an art form which looks at the everyday, but not necessarily in an everyday way. Whilst it is important to draw from your own cultural heritage, it is equally important to realise that theatre is a culture in itself. It is a form which is capable of presenting and addressing all human situations. An actor needs to have the skills to be able to represent what may not be usual for him or her. For example in training for Theatre for Development, participants may touch and make more eye contact than they normally do at home or on the street.

Rekhaben : In a game during the training I was so embarrassed when I had to touch someone nose to nose. But now I know how important it is in theatre training to break down barriers.

Group agreements

As well as allowing a certain freedom from the ordinary, theatre works within quite strict boundaries of acceptable behaviour.

Therefore, as part of your training, ask the group to sit together and create a group agreement about how you are going to work.

This may be a list of rules or requests. You may also want to include how you will respond if someone breaks a rule or does not observe a request.

Here is an example of an agreement from the Vidya group:

Vidya Group Agreement

- Don't do anything you don't want to do
- Don't stop anyone else from doing their work
- Support each other without aggression
- No competition – only try to be better than yourself
- No violence and no pain
- Be on time
- Turn off your mobile phones
- There should be unity in all work
- Each actor should be able to perform each character in all the plays so that, in case one person is not there, another person can perform the role
- Each month a new leader is selected by the group
- A leader has to be transparent, democratic and nonjudgmental
- Self discipline is important
- Respect each other's boundaries
- Know each person's likes and dislikes
- Before each meeting, re-read any decisions already made
- Each member is committed to theatre and bringing awareness through theatre
- Create physical and mental space for each other so each person can share their story
- Listen to each other.

Training - Team Work

Now you have created your group agreement you will be ready to begin your practical work. Theatre is a practical team activity which requires great skill. For any theatre team to function well there needs to be :

Communication & Co-operation

Collaboration & Participation

Trust & Support

Questioning & Listening

Giving & Receiving

Sharing & Respect

Tolerance & Patience

Energy & Invention

Spontaneity & Creativity

Passion

All theatre groups need to train to develop their team-work skills.

This training can involve breaking down barriers between people and building the team, getting to know each other better, group problem solving, decision making and ultimately learning to create theatre together.

Here are a few games and exerises which work well in the very early stages of creating a theatre team. You do not need to play them all. You may also know games which would be useful to play to encourage team work. Try to think of games which are non competitive, which do not always have winners (and therefore losers !).

This chapter ends with some examples of how a team building training day might look. Later steps in this handbook will give you plenty of guidance on how to run and plan sessions like this.

1. Building the Team

Name Circle

Aim : To learn everyone's name
Mood : Moderate energy
Level : Basic
Number of people : 5-30
Time : 5-20 minutes

Directions:

- The group stands in a circle.
- One at a time each person says their name. The rest of the group listen carefully.
- The aim of the game is to move into someone else's space in the circle.
- You cannot move until you have made eye contact with someone across the circle and said their name.
- Only one name is said at a time.

- Once you have made eye contact and said the person's name you can start to walk towards them to take their place in the circle.

- This person must then look at someone else and say their name before the person walking towards them gets to them.

- Once the group is playing this well, you can move from walking to running.

> *After each game or exercise it can be useful to ask the group to draw out observations, or make comments yourself, about how this work connects to theatre for development. Each game or exercise can be a very useful starting point for discussion, or indeed creating a scene or making a play. Within each and every one of these games and exercises there is the possibility of drama.*

In the 'why did we suggest this?' sections we will indicate just a few of the points we have learned from playing these games, over the years. You, of course, will discover more.

Why did we suggest the 'name circle'?. ..

'Name circle' is one of many possible games that help you learn people's names. The significance of names is huge and cannot be overstated. Saying your name in a circle requires you to build up a good deal of confidence if you have never done it before. It might be the very first step towards performing, asserting yourself, and taking your place in the team. The next stage in this game is making eye contact and saying someone else's name. In this you must acknowledge other people in the group. Perhaps the second most significant step you will take in training to be a theatre maker.

> *You will notice that many of our games and exercises begin in a circle. Negotiating the creation of a circle is very much part of the group's task. This may take some time at first. Gradually the group will improve. Forming circles is significant. A circle is a symbol of equality. In a circle every one is at the front. Only rarely do you meet situations where even this might be too exposing for people. Always encourage your group to notice the different kinds of shapes and patterns that are made during their work. Theatre is an art which communicates through the shapes and formations that bodies make in space.*

Here is an exercise which does not start in a circle, but starts with one person chasing the other group members. Notice how the dynamic is very different.

Name Tag

Aim: Warming up the body, learning everyone's names and calling for help when you need it!

Mood: High energy

Level: Medium

Number of people: 5-30

Time: 5-10 minutes

Directions:

- The group moves freely around the room.
- One person is the chaser.
- The chaser tries to tag one player at a time in the group, by touching them gently on the shoulder or on the back. Everyone in the group tries to keep away from the chaser by moving quickly.
- If the chaser tries to tag a player, the player can avoid being tagged by calling the name of someone else in the room – loud and clear! – *before* they are tagged. The person whose name has been called then becomes the chaser.

- However, if a player is tagged before they have called someone's name in the room, they become the chaser. The chaser must identify themselves by calling loudly 'it's me!'.

Stuck-in-the-mud

Aim: Warming up the body, building a supportive team

Mood: High energy

Level: Basic

Number of people: 5-30

Time: 5-10 minutes

Directions:

- The group moves freely around the room.
- One person is the chaser.
- The chaser chases the group members around the room and tries to touch as many of the players as possible.
- If a player is touched they become 'stuck' in a position in the room, as if they were stuck in mud. They put their legs and arms apart to indicate that they are stuck.

Stuck-in-the-mud

- The aim of the game is for the players who are not stuck to free the stuck players by crawling under their legs (or arms).

Variations:

• Have more than one chaser.

• Use various different body positions to be stuck in.

Why did we suggest 'stuck-in-the-mud'?

This game is a good ice-breaker, meaning it can mix people well and help to break down barriers between people. The aim of the game: 'if someone is stuck, help them out', conveys an important team building message without resorting to words. We learn by doing.

Questions to think and talk about after playing
games and exercises...
What did you discover?
What surprised you in this game?
How did you feel in this exercise?
What has changed since we started this game?
What made the game pleasurable?
What skills do we need to develop to make this
game work well?

Pass the ball

Aim: Team work, group focus, name learning
Mood: Moderate, building to high, energy, fun
Level: Basic to intermediate
Number of people: 3-30
Time: 5-20 minutes
What you will need: 1 soft (preferably foam) ball – no smaller than a football

Directions:

- The group is in different places in the room – not in a circle.
- Players throw the ball from person to person, standing still.
- Each player calls the name of the person to whom they are throwing the ball.
- Players must make eye contact with the person to whom they are passing the ball.
- The players should pass and receive the ball with care and kindness, not aggression.
- There should be no feeling of competition.
- Once the group has achieved this they can move on to passing the ball from person to person whilst travelling in the room, starting with walking and building up to running.
- Eye contact must always be maintained.
- After a while the name calling can be taken out, so the game just involves eye contact, giving and receiving the ball and moving in space.

Variation- Keep it Up!:

- Start as above.
- This time the aim of the game is to keep the ball in the air without letting it touch the ground for as long as possible through touching the ball with the fingers in an upward motion and directing it to another player (a little like volley ball, but with less force).
- Each player can touch the ball twice - once to control the ball and once to pass it.
- Each time a person has touched the ball, the group counts – this way a group can see how it has improved each time they play.
- You might want to set a target for yourselves, perhaps 50 on the first day, 100 on the second and so on. You might be surprised how difficult It Is until the group starts working together, giving and taking, directing carefully.
- The Vidya group is now up to 5,112 in this game!

Ball connection

Aim: Deep focus and concentration

Mood: Calm focused energy

Level: Intermediate

Number of people: 5-20

Time: 10-20 minutes

What you will need: Small balls – preferably tennis or soft balls

Directions:

- The group stands in a circle in silence.
- The facilitator makes eye contact and then throws the ball to a player.
- The receiving player makes eye contact with another person and throws the ball to them and so on from person to person.
- Once there is good eye contact and focus the facilitator throws another ball to another player.
- This continues until there are several balls being thrown from player to player, always getting eye contact before a throw.
- The aim of the game is to get as many balls being passed as possible without a single ball being dropped.
- If a ball drops at any point, the balls come back to the facilitator (or whoever is starting the game) and the game starts again.

Why did we suggest these ball games?. ..

In our work, these games have shown us the following:

- Like these games, theatre involves no sense of competition.
- Eye contact is important in theatre.
- Passing and receiving the ball is like delivering a line and listening to a line of text – each is equally important and connected.
- When the ball goes to the ground, there is a feeling that energy has dropped, this can happen in theatre too. So in theatre, just like in the game, keep the group energy up. If

something goes badly, don't worry, don't blame each other, pick up the ball, pick up the energy, and keep going.

- Learning to use your breath to support your activity is essential in physical games and in theatre.

In our experience, ball games work very well with most groups. However some people may have had a negative experience with ball games in the past through competitive games at school for example. It is important to emphasise that our work is non-competitive, it is not about how well you catch, but how we work as a team. If there are members of the group with visual or hand impairments the game may need to be adapted. For example balls can be passed through rolling the ball,using the feet, or through balance. Always use a soft ball!

The 'do nothing' game

Aim: To get the group observing and imitating each other

Mood: Gentle, building to moderate, energy

Level: Basic to intermediate

Number of people: 6-30

Time: 10-15 minutes

Directions:

- The group stands or sits in a circle.
- Each person in the group is assigned someone they will watch for the duration of the game. The person they are watching will be watching someone else.
- Each person will watch the person 3 people along from them in the circle.
- Alternatively you can give each person a number. So that in a group of 10 people for example, number 1 will watch number 4, number 4 will watch number 7, number 7 will watch

number 10, number 10 will watch number 3, number 3 will watch number 6, number 6 will watch number 9, number 9 will watch number 2, number 2 will watch number 5, number 5 will watch number 8, number 8 will watch number 1.

- Everyone stands or sits as still as possible.
- The instruction to the group is to 'do nothing'. Each player watches without doing anything.
- However, if a player sees the person they are watching making even the tiniest movement, they must copy them exactly.
- Keep repeating the instruction 'do nothing, only copy what you see'.
- The smallest movement will create a 'ripple effect' of movement around the circle.
- You can begin to add instructions. Do nothing, but if you see your person do anything at all, exaggerate it by 10%, 50%, 100% etc – things can become very lively at this point! Now minimise what they are doing by 20% etc.
- Ask the group to make observations about what happened during the exercise.

Sometimes the things a group does not like about an exercise teach us the most. For example if a player says 'I felt uncomfortable in this game' you might, as facilitator, ask who else felt uncomfortable? What does that feeling remind you of? Let's imagine a scene where a character feels uncomfortable too, who is this character? Where is the scene set?... Or 'I found this game difficult'. What was challenging about this game? What do we need to improve in order to be better at this game?...

Why did we suggest the 'do nothing' game?

Hopefully you will draw your own conclusions from the group. For us this exercise has demonstrated the following:

- It is impossible for human beings to do nothing, we are constantly in action, we are constantly communicating and sending out messages, even without words.

- Each of our actions will have an effect on every other member of the group – just like in the exercise. Therefore it is important in a team to know the impact our actions are having on other people.

- This exercise is also an excellent tool for getting a group performing if they have never performed before. It highlights three key skills an actor needs for their work: observation, imitation and awareness.

- If you are working with a group which is resisting your work and wants to 'do nothing'. This is a perfect game to play with them too!

Walking group

Aim: To develop group awareness of the space and each other

Mood: Moderate energy

Level: Intermediate

Number of people: 2-30

Time: 10-15 minutes

Directions:

- The group begins by walking in the space. The group will keep walking throughout the exercise unless they are instructed to stop. They walk in different directions, not touching each other, keeping their eyes alert.

- The facilitator calls out certain instructions for the group to carry out quickly, in order to heighten the group's awareness of the space. For example: Touch three walls, touch the floor and the ceiling, touch one cold object, touch one hot object, touch 3 man-made objects, touch 2 nature-made objects, touch one object which might cause an injury, touch one object which is soft etc.

- Now the group are more aware of the space, and potential hazards in the space, the group returns to simply walking.

Extension:

- The group must cover as much of the ground as possible, not following each other but keeping the space balanced (evenly covered).
- The facilitator calls out stop! The group must stop instantly. Observe whether the group has covered the floor space. Where are the gaps? Are there many people all in one area? The aim is to keep the space balanced.
- This can be repeated several times until the group's spatial awareness has improved.

Extension :

- The facilitator can add to the exercise by gradually reducing the size of space the group is permitted to use. This will encourage the group to have closer physical contact with each other, without thinking about what they are doing.
- The group continues to walk and keep the space in balance. But now their awareness switches to each other.

Extension:

- The group must try to walk at exactly the same pace, without anyone leading.
- The group must try to stop walking at exactly the same time, without anyone telling them to stop.
- The group must try to start walking again, at exactly the same time, without anyone telling them to stop.
- The group continues to walk at any pace. The facilitator now calls out the name of one of the group members. Everyone must now walk at their pace. Continue until the group has walked at the pace of everyone in the group.

Counting group

Aim: To increase the group's awareness and sensitivity towards each other

Mood: Intimate and focused

Level: Intermediate

Number of people: 3-30

Time: As long as it takes!

Directions:

- The group sit, stand or lie down in a circle The group will now count up to ten, one person at a time.

- No one knows who will speak first, second, third etc. The ordering of who says the numbers must be completely random without signalling to each other, without anyone leading the group or taking control or indeed being passive.

- The group play by using their senses and it is the whole group's responsibility to get to 10, to choose when to speak, and when to be silent.

- If two people speak at the same time, even for an instant, the group returns to number one.

- The game is played several times depending on the skill of the team. The number can be increased from 10 to 20 etc.

- Try the reverse; counting from 10 to 1. Is this easier?

- Now repeat it with closed eyes.

Rhythm of the group

Aim: Rhythm skills, learning to accept other people's ideas, express your individual ideas and form collective ideas

Mood: High energy

Level: Intermediate to advanced

Number of people: 5-30

Time: 10-20 minutes

Directions:

- The group stands in a circle.

- One person makes a rhythmical movement and sound that the rest of the group can copy. The movement must be something which can be carried out whilst travelling around the space.

- The group copy the rhythmical movement and sound exactly.

- When you are satisfied everyone is in rhythm and is moving and making sounds which look exactly the same the facilitator calls – 'leave the circle and go around the room!'

- The group continue making this same movement and sound whilst they are travelling in the room.

- The group can meet each other while they are travelling, but they must keep the movement and sound exactly the same.

- The facilitator calls out 'change'!

- Each player can now change the movement and sound from the one which was given to them to whatever they want to do.

- The players go around the room repeating their movement and sound. There are now many rhythms and sounds in the room. The players can meet each other.

- The facilitator calls out – 'return to the circle!'.

- Each group member returns to the circle. There is now a circle of many different movements and sounds.

- The facilitator calls out – 'unify!'

- Now all of the players' movements and sounds must merge into one new movement and sound until everyone is moving and vocalising in exactly the same way.

- When you are satisfied everyone is in rhythm and has copied exactly the facilitator calls – 'leave the circle and go around the room!'

- The cycle continues in the same way again – 'change', 'return to the circle', 'unify'… This cycle can be continued two or three times until the group has improved.

Why did we suggest 'rhythm of the group'?

As we will explore further in this handbook, rhythm can be used to great dramatic effect. The 'rhythm of the group' exercise is also particularly good for building a team as it develops and demonstrates the skills any theatre group will need to form a strong team. The team will need to observe and imitate, they will sometimes need to do things that someone else has given them to do – whether they like it or not! The team will also be encouraged to express themselves as individuals as well as team members, the members will also sometimes have to surrender their ideas in order to create something new, something surprising and unexpected. There is a high level of difficulty in doing this work and it will require listening, patience and acceptance. The cycle that the exercise takes is very much like the journey the theatre company will take – from the group, to the individual, back to the group.

> From your playing of all the games and exercises in this book, draw out your own observations and learning points. Invent your own versions of the games, create new ones !.

2. Getting to know each other

All of the games and exercises in the 'Building a Team' section above will enable the group to get to know each other through very expressive and playful means. However you may also want to give the group exercises which bring a more personal and intimate level of sharing. If so, the following exercises are for you.

You can use these exercises at a very early stage of working together. They are very simple ways of getting a group to start sharing about themselves, gently. This work will also enable you, as a facilitator, to get to know the group better. You will start to be able to identify what the group members have in common, what the relevant issues are for their lives, and this will provide you with many ideas for future creative work and play-making.

As we have discussed earlier, names have enormous significance. So when it comes to getting to know each other, they are a good place to start:

The story of my name

Aim: To learn each others' names and their significance

Mood: Gentle and intimate

Level: Basic

Number of people: 2-30

Time: 2 minutes per person

Directions:

- One at a time each team member says their name. Alternatively the players can sign their name on a large piece of paper with colourful pens, once each person has signed it, the paper can become a beautiful wall hanging to decorate your space.
- After saying or signing their name, each person will tell a small story about the background to their name, or say how they feel about their name.
- The rest of the group simply listen to each short name story.
- Once completed, thank the participants for sharing the story of their name.
- From this point you could even go on to name an imaginary character who will be at the centre of a play you are going to create... What is the story of her name?

Examples:

- **I am named after my grandmother, she was my best friend as a child, I often dream of her.**
- **My first name is from Ghana, my middle name is from India, my last name is from Jamaica – these names are where I am from.**
- **Everyone shortens my name and I hate it ! I want everyone to call me by my full name.**
- **My name means I was born on a Monday. I hate Mondays but I like my name.**
- **I don't like my name. It means nothing to me. If I were born again I would name myself Shanti...**

My journey to here

Aim: To share and hear how the group members arrived at this place in their lives

Mood: Moderate energy

Level: Intermediate

Number of people: 2-15 (if working in a group of more than 15, split the group into 2 with a facilitator per group)

Time: Minimum 5 minutes per person

Directions:

- Place an object or mark an X in the centre of the space where you are working. This represents the here and now.
- One at a time each group member will choose a spot in the room which represents where they were born. If they were born very close to the mark for example, they will start fairly close to it. If they were born in a foreign country or another district, they will be further away.
- Starting from the place which represents their birth place, one at a time each group member will take 5 minutes (or more if you have time) to tell the story of how they arrived at the theatre training course (or workshop). As they are telling the story they move to different places in the room

according to where they went in their lives. As they are speaking encourage them to demonstrate their story through actions. Each person's journey will finally end at the mark in the middle of the room until everyone has arrived there.

Why did we suggest 'my journey to here'?

This ritual-like exercise will symbolically create a sense of unity in the group and a focus on the present moment. Wherever the group members have been in their lives, and whatever they have experienced in the past, they can feel secure in the fact that now they are together, working as equals, in a theatre group. Many elements of these stories and actions may give you rich source material from which to create plays, dances, stories and songs to perform later.

My journey to here - Vijay

I was born in a small village in Uttar Pradesh located in Northern India. I came with my family to the community Bhagat Na Chapra, Ahmedabad, to work. I worked at various jobs, such as travel agencies, hospitals, courier companies but was not satisfied.

I knew how to play the harmonium, drums, keyboard and mouth organ. So, I also worked part-time at night in a band as a keyboard player.

One day, I met a researcher from VIDYA, Bhikiben, and filled out the selection form for the peer group member. I was interviewed and even selected as a good candidate but had to go back to my village.

Then, I returned again to Bhagat Na Chapra and saw VIDYA perform in 2004. Money was tight so I had to sell my keyboard. Kalu introduced me to Manishaben so that VIDYA could purchase my keyboard. Instead of offering me money, Manishaben offered me the opportunity to perform and play in VIDYA.

Anyone who...

Aim: To mix the group and find out more about them.

Mood: Moderate to high-energy fun

Level: Basic

Number of people: 5-30

Time: 10-15 minutes

Directions:

- The group sits in a circle on chairs, seats or mats.
- There is one person without a seat who stands in the middle (to begin with this can be the facilitator).
- The aim of the game is for people to change seats. The last person without a seat stands in the middle.
- Participants change seats by responding to a sentence from the person standing in the middle.
- The person in the middle says the phrase 'anyone who...' and completes the sentence with something which is true of themselves. For example, 'anyone who... loves chocolate', anyone who... plays football', 'anyone who... is a father', 'anyone who... is afraid of loud noises', 'anyone who... wants to be a theatre for development worker' etc.
- If the statement is also true of anyone in the group, they must change seats as quickly as possible. The person in the middle will also try to get a seat.
- The person who does not get to a seat in time, then stands in the middle and says a new sentence beginning with 'anyone who...' and the game continues in this way.
- The facilitator can also play. It is often a useful opportunity when the facilitator is caught out and must stand in the middle, as they then have an opportunity to steer the questions a little towards information they would like to know about the group for example the roles they play in their lives, the subjects they care about, the things they want in life, the things they fear...

2 truths and 1 lie

Aim: To find out about people, challenge perceptions of each other and to start acting

Mood: Gentle

Level: Basic to intermediate

Number of people: 4-12

Time: 10-30 minutes depending on numbers playing

Directions:

- The group gets into pairs with someone they do not know very well.
- The pairs place themselves as far as possible away from the other pairs in the room, they are going to talk in secret.
- The people in each pair label themselves A and B.
- B is instructed to tell A two interesting facts about themselves; 2 things that no one else in the group will know.
- A must listen carefully and remember what B has told them.
- B is then instructed to invent a lie about themselves. Again A listens carefully and makes sure they remember the two truths and 1 lie they have been told.
- A and B swap over.
- When all the pairs are ready they all rejoin the circle.
- We will hear from the pairs one at a time.
- One at a time A & B introduce each other. They each tell the rest of the group the 3 pieces of information about their partner, the 2 truths and 1 lie.
- BOTH PARTNERS MUST BE SKILFUL AND NOT REVEAL WHAT IS TRUE AND WHAT IS A LIE.
- The rest of the group must try to guess which pieces of information are lies.
- Only after the group has decided which piece of information they think is the lie, do the pairs confirm what was true and what was false.
- The group discusses issues raised such as perception and performance

Why did we suggest '2 truths and 1 lie'?

This is an excellent game for people who have no concept or experience of acting. It can ease them into working with each other and, before they are aware of it, they are acting. Anyone who can lie, can act, we can all lie, so we can all act! This game also presents a framework in which to learn a lot about the participants. The lies we tell often reveal our deepest desires, or our biggest fears. Most of all this game encourages us to challenge our perceptions about each other, and be prepared to be surprised by each other.

The chair of truth

Aim: To get the group to share some of their beliefs and attitudes about various subjects and start to debate some of the issues, with dramatic spatial awareness

Mood: Dynamic debate

Level: Intermediate to advanced

Number of people: 5-30

Time: 30 minutes

Directions:

- Place one chair or object in the centre of the space.
- This chair is the 'chair of truth'.
- The participants walk around the space in different directions.
- The facilitator will call out statements around issues relevant to the work (the facilitator can start with a couple of statements which are just for fun, to start with).
- In reaction to the statement called out, the participants will place themselves in relation to the chair.
- If they believe the statement that the facilitator has called out is absolutely 100% true, then they stand as close to the chair as they can. They can even sit on the chair. If they believe the statement is 75% true then they place themselves a bit further away. If they think the statement is nonsense then they place themselves as far away from the chair as possible.

- The facilitator should invite the group first to reflect on how the bodies have been placed in the space. Even this will heighten the group's awareness of how placing yourself in a space can heighten a dramatic message.

- The facilitator can then invite people to comment on why they have chosen to stand where they are. Some debate may then be entered into.

- It is important however that no one is shouted down, and differences of opinion are valued and the right to believe different things is respected.

- The facilitator asks the group to move around again, and calls out another statement.

- This process continues until a good level of debate around various issues has been achieved.

- The facilitator can then hand over to various members of the company to call out statements and 'chair' the debate.

Why did we suggest 'the chair of truth'?

It is important to furnish an atmosphere of debate where differences are welcomed, valued and respected. This exercise helps the group to practise this difficult skill. It is also a very useful way of assessing attitudes in a group and for everyone to be challenged to think about their beliefs.

3. Solving Problems

It is inevitable in the life of any theatre team that they will experience problems. Whilst there is no way of preparing for every eventuality, games and exercises can be a fun, positive and confidence-boosting way of understanding the strengths, weaknesses and differences in a group, overcoming challenges and solving problems together. Applying yourself to a team task can be a great way of breaking down barriers between people.

Blob Tag and Group Knot

Aim: To get everyone involved, create a problem and solve it together

Mood: Fun, moderate to high energy

Level: Basic

Number of people: 6-30

Time: 10-15 minutes

Directions:

- As a preparation, start with one person chasing the others in the space.
- The chaser attempts to catch someone.
- When the chaser catches someone the two now hold hands and must not let go.
- These two attempt to catch more people together. They must catch others by using only their outside hands.
- When the next is caught they hold hands with one of the chasers to make a chasing group of three, then four and so on....
- Eventually the whole group is caught.
- The two ends of the line join hands so that a circle is formed.
- The group then makes many knots in the circle by moving in and out, under and over each others' arms, and through each others' legs.
- When they have made a really knotted circle they attempt to undo the knots.
- The group must not let go of each others' hands or change the grip until the game is complete.

Savitaben: My favourite game is circle of knots. It teaches us how we deal with conflicts and problems and how we resolve them.

Newspaper game

Aim: Team problem solving

Mood: Thoughtful, challenging, moderate energy

Level: Intermediate to advanced

Number of people: 3-30

Time: 15-45 minutes

What you will need: Lots of old paper, or newspaper

Directions:

- Lay out one big area of paper on the ground, taped into one piece.

- Tell the group you are going to give them a clear instruction which will not change during the exercise, you are not going to answer any questions so they must just listen and work together.

The instruction is this :

- "Touch the paper without touching the ground". The group must work together, they cannot use any object, and they must all be touching the paper without touching the ground at exactly the same time.

- Actively observe the group while they work together to do this task.

- Usually the group will begin by talking and looking at the paper.

- Eventually the group usually decides to all stand on the paper – but do **not** tell them this before hand!

- As they work the workshop leader gradually takes pieces of paper away, or tears pieces from the large sheet of paper, so that the group has to work with less and less paper and find more and more ways of touching the paper without touching the ground.

- Usually a group will get into lots of different body shapes and angles as the paper gets smaller.

- Eventually you will leave the group with one very small piece of paper, which will be about the size of the palm of a small child's hand.

- The usual outcome of the exercise is that the group all holds the paper and jumps in the air together! But do not tell them this - this is up to the group to discover!
- After the exercise invite the group to describe their process. Ask them to observe the different approaches to solving the problem in the group. Every group is different.

Why did we suggest the 'newspaper game'?

This is a very useful way of discovering together what the character of the group is like, what are its strengths, how it makes decisions and which skills for team work the group needs to develop. This next exercise follows on very well from the 'chair of truth' game above.

Perspectives

Aim: To learn to see things from someone else's perspective and to learn how conflicts can start

Mood: Moderate energy debate

Level: Advanced

Number of people: 5-30

Time: 15-20 minutes

Directions:

- The participants sit in a circle.
- One volunteer sits in the middle. The volunteer is told they are going to be described by the rest of the group, but not to worry, it's only a game.
- The participants in the circle are asked to describe the person in the middle only from the perspective of what they can see, and stating what they can see to be absolute fact. For example, if someone can only see one ear they say 'She has only one ear'. Someone else will then contradict what that person has said from their perspective for example, 'what are you talking about, it's quite clear that she has one and three quarter ears'. Some one else may say 'I don't

know what you are talking about, she hasn't even got a face!' and so the debate continues into a kind of improvisation.

- Then the person in the middle is invited to change position in their seat. The debate / improvisation continues.
- Then all the participants are invited to move from their seat and sit somewhere else in the circle.
- The person in the middle then rejoins the circle. The debate is over. The group now reflect on the many meanings of this exercise and what it has demonstrated.
- The group is invited to remember this exercise whenever they are facing conflict within the group.

Image Theatre and Intervention/Forum Theatre are also excellent problem solving tools which will be expanded upon in great detail in steps to come. Group dynamics and dealing with conflict are explored in further detail towards the end of this handbook.

4. Making Decisions

Your group will need to think about what kind of process they will use to decide on issues affecting the group. The following three games and exercises demonstrate three very different models of decision making, each of them is also an image of much bigger political processes and is designed to provoke a reaction. The games are also suggested as fun ways of getting your group to question how decisions are made, and to start to make choices. The craft of theatre itself requires a capacity for continuously making detailed, confident and informed choices, and so, through these exercises, your group will learn how demanding theatre is.

The following exercises work very well as a sequence.

Invisible Sword

Aim: To warm up, test reflexes and start to think about power in decision making

Mood: High energy
Level: Basic (though physically challenging)
Number of people: 5-30
Time: 5-7 minutes

Invisible Sword

Directions:
- The leader stands in front of the group holding an invisible giant sword.
- The group stands in a row opposite the leader.
- The aim of the game is to jump out of the way of the leader's attack with the sword.
- The group should also invent sound effects to express as they jump.
- The leader can be replaced regularly.
- The leader has 6 strokes that they can use with the sword:
- Aiming for their heads slashing from left to right or right to left, the group must duck.
- Aiming for their legs slashing from left to right or right to left, the group must jump.
- Aiming for their belly with a thrust to the middle, the group jumps backwards.
- Aiming for their left side with a clear thrust, the group jumps to the right.

- Aiming for their right side with a clear thrust, the group jumps to the left.
- Aiming to slice them in half from the head to the belly the group jumps right if they are on the right hand side and left if they are on the left.
- Now form two opposing lines facing each other.
- Each line has a leader and each has an invisible sword.
- The two leaders do battle using the strokes as before (make sure there is plenty of distance between them).
- Each leader has a line of followers behind them who react to the blows their leader is receiving.
- They fight to the death!
- Discuss how the game felt, and what kind of decision making process this was, what were the strengths and weaknesses in this decision making process, if the game was a political system what would it be?

This and That

Aim: To get to know the group's opinions on certain issues, to explore voting and provoke debate

Mood: Moderate energy with debate

Level: Intermediate

Number of people: 6-30

Time: 10-15 minutes

Directions:

- If you choose to play this game after the 'invisible sword' game above, the group remains in the lines.
- The groups are in two parallel lines facing each other. One line is called "This", one line is called "That".
- The leader calls out two choices. These should be relevant to your group and should provoke a reaction. As examples – 'love marriage or arranged marriage?', 'vegetarianism or meat eating?', 'living with family or living alone?', 'cricket or

football?", 'university or work?', 'stay at home with baby or go out to work?', "East or West?' etc...

- Each time two choices are called out, everyone has to vote on which one they want to choose by moving and going to stand in the this line (the first proposal) or the that line (the second proposal) , or remaining where they are in the one they support.

- Participants have no other choice but to stand in this or that line. If people do not stand in this or that line in this exercise, their choice, their vote, does not count.

- The leader can be rotated so that different members of the group get to call out opposing choices.

- The leader may invite comments from the players in why they chose to stand in this or that line.

- Discuss how the game felt, and what kind of decision making process this was, what were the strengths and weaknesses in this decision making process, if the game were a political system what would it be?

Group Yes

Aim: To decide actions by collective decision making, to begin to improvise as a group

Mood: Entirely depends on what the group brings to it

Level: Advanced

Number of people: 3-30

Time: Depends on the group, 30 minutes is usually adequate

Directions:

- The group starts to walk around the space wherever they like.

- After a few moments they make a circle.

- Anyone in the group can make a suggestion at any time of something the whole group could do. They make the suggestion by saying 'Let's all..' For example 'Let's all hop on one leg', or 'Let's all lie down' or 'Let's all sing a song' etc.

- If the participants want to do the suggested action they must reply with an enthusiastic 'Yes let's' and then begin to do the action until another is suggested.

- However, if anyone in the group does not say 'Yes let's' and says 'No thanks' then no one in the group can carry out the suggested action. So the group are making decisions by 100% consent.

- Discuss how the game felt, and what kind of decision making process this was, what were the strengths and weaknesses in this decision making process, if the game were a political system what would it be?

- Group Yes can also be used as an excellent group improvisation game.

Post 'Making Decisions' Discussion

After you have carried out these exercises, make sure you leave plenty of time to discuss them. The exercises are deliberately provocative so people should be allowed to express themselves afterwards.

What kind of politics did these exercises reflect? When have you ever been in a situation where you were asked to make a decision in one of these ways? Which exercise felt least / most satisfying ? What are the pros and cons of these ways of making choices ? And finally, how is our group going to make decisions? Is our group going to use something like the exercises demonstrated, or are we going to invent our own?...

How VIDYA group makes decisions as a team. We...
Listen to each other Understand each person's point of view Respect each person's input Discuss the best solution/idea and if it is possible Look at each point's good and bad sides, and then..... Vote!

5. Creating together

After you have carried out exercises to build the team and have looked at how you might solve problems and make decisions as a team, there is no better way to develop a theatre group's team work skills than by carrying out creative tasks together. We have found that storytelling and singing are excellent areas which both develop the team's theatre making skills and create a sense of group cohesion.

Here is a fun and easy exercise which can be used to prepare the group for both storytelling and singing.

Conductor circle (with sounds, words and tunes)

N.B. the word "soundscape" means a sound picture; evoking a scene through sound.

Aim: Making and listening to sounds, words and tunes, following visual instructions

Mood: Gentle

Level: Intermediate

Number of people: 3-15 (with a bigger group split into 2)

Time: 10-15 minutes

Directions:

- The group sit in a circle.
- One person is the conductor (this can be the facilitator who can demonstrate to begin with).
- Each participant is going to make their own individual sound when they are conducted to do so.
- The conductor invents a series of clear actions which will indicate when s/he wants the participant indicated to start, stop, keep going, make the sound louder, quieter, longer or shorter etc.
- The conductor brings all members of the group in (and out) at different times.
- In this way a soundscape will be created.

- The group can comment on what the soundscape felt like, what stories, images and emotions it suggested.
- Experiment with the sounds a few times with different conductors.
- Once this version has been explored, the conductor can do the same with words. The group can explore how words, when played with, can have many meanings.
- Do the same with short phrases from songs – those known from before and new creations.

Storytelling

Here are a few storytelling exercises which are excellent tools for developing team work skills. There will be plenty more suggestions of how to create stories later in the book.

Story Pairs

Aim: To tell a story, to develop listening and sharing skills
Mood: Gentle
Level: Advanced
Number of people: 2-30
Time: 5-10 minutes
Directions:

- Ask the group to get into pairs and link arms.
- The pairs are each going to tell a story together by speaking just one word each at a time. The story must be original, it must make sense, it must have sentences, stops etc. Neither participant knows where the story is going to go. They must be open and listen well.
- The pairs start by walking around the space arm in arm and telling the story, just one word at a time.
- As the pairs gain confidence they can be encouraged to start a new story, this time not only to walk around the space but to start to act out the story.

- The pairs can practise storytelling in pairs in front of the rest of the group.
- Discuss what this exercise needs from the players to make it work well.

VIDYA Plays Story Pairs:

Kalu and Bharti

Kalu : I
Bharti : went
Kalu : to
Bharti : the
Kalu : vegetable
Bharti : market

Kalu : I
Bharti : banged
Kalu : into
Bharti : a
Kalu : cart

Bharti : I
Kalu : fell
Bharti : on
Kalu : top
Bharti : of
Kalu : the
Bharti : vendor

And it went on a lot longer

Shared Experience Story

Aim: Listening, clarity of speech and movement, storytelling

Mood: Gentle through to high energy

Level: Advanced

Number of people: 6-30

Time: 30-45 minutes

Directions:

- Ask the group to get into pairs with someone they have not worked with before.

- The pairs label themselves A and B and stand opposite each other.

- A is going to tell a story. To begin with, this story might be something as simple as what they did when they got up that morning.

- A must speak very slowly and very clearly.

- B copies exactly what A says at the same time as A says it. We should almost not be able to tell which player is telling the story and which one is copying.

- After some time, pause the exercise. Ask the pairs to briefly reflect on how this went, and what skills you need to make the exercise work well.

- Now the pairs swap over. B begins a new story. This time however B must bring physical action into the story by moving around the space and describing the story with their body. A must now copy B's words *and* their movement.

- Pause the exercise briefly, and give a short time for reflection if desired.

- The players stay in the same pairs. A now begins a story through slow clear speech and in action. B copies what A is saying and doing and where they are travelling to in the space. This time at any point the facilitator may tap B on the shoulder. When B is tapped on the shoulder, s/he must continue the story from where A left it. A must now copy B.

- Now, any time when the facilitator taps A or B on the shoulder, they must continue the story and the other one must follow in words, actions and space.

- Encourage the pairs to exaggerate the clarity of their speech and the movement of their bodies so the exercise becomes quite dynamic.

- Pause the exercise briefly. Now either A or B will begin a new story. At any point throughout the rest of the exercise if anyone is tapped, they must continue the story. Also, now at any point the facilitator may take the pairs and bring them into another pair's story. If a pair is brought into another pair's story, they must immediately copy the words and actions of that pair. They may be thrown straight into a story they know nothing about, they must just immediately listen and copy. They may also be quickly tapped on the shoulder and expected to continue a story which they do not know much about. Therefore everybody's concentration must be at a high level and players must be open to surprises!

- The words and action should be so synchronised that it should be very difficult to tell from the outside who is leading. The transitions from storyteller to storyteller should be smooth.

- The facilitator brings the pairs together so that there are bigger and bigger groups.

- Finally the entire group should all be together telling a story, there are no longer any pairs. At any point the facilitator may change the leader by tapping them on the shoulder. The storytellers must take responsibility for where and how the story ends.

Why did we suggest the 'shared experience' storytelling exercise?

This very challenging exercise is an excellent way of getting the group to listen, concentrate, speak clearly, move clearly and take responsibility for collective creativity. If it is facilitated and played well it can also be enormous fun, and by the time you get to the end, when the entire group is speaking with one voice and moving with one body, it can be extremely exhilarating and uplifting.

Story circle

Aim: Listening, accepting and building on ideas, creating a story together

Mood: Gentle

Level: Intermediate to advanced

Number of people: 4-20 (if you have more participants split into 2 groups)

Time: 15-25 minutes

Directions:

- The group sits in a circle. They are going to create a story together through saying one sentence each.
- One person begins the story with a sentence. The next person continues the story with a sentence and the next and so on.
- The story must make sense.
- Encourage the group to listen carefully to what has been said before, who the characters are, where the story takes place, which objects feature in the story. Encourage the group to keep within the parameters of the story and to bring all the elements together by the end.

Songs

Singing songs can be a rewarding and uplifting way of bringing a group together. Singing requires togetherness, harmony, and this is what you want from your group. It can be an excellent way of starting or ending a day. If there has been stress or conflict in the group, singing can help to reconnect people and give a sense of unity and direction, especially if the words express the working ethos or mission of the group. Good singing also requires that the group listen carefully to each other, and to themselves. Singing songs in a round can really challenge a group's listening skills, improvising songs together can help to develop the group's sensitivity toward each other. It is also a great way of strengthening the voice – an important tool in theatre.

You will find steps later in this handbook for creating your own songs together

---

A VIDYA song

This song is about learning and the importance of education for girls and women.

Dharti se udke jaungi
Mein sab ko padhaungi
VIDYA

Har ghar mein geet rahe
Nari ki jeet rahe
VIDYA….

I will fly from the earth
Sharing knowledge (vidya) with everyone
Every home has songs about knowledge and using this
knowledge.
Women can get ahead

Later steps in this handbook will give you lots of guidance on how to plan and run training sessions and workshops. On the following pages are just two examples of the order in which some of these exercises might be used. These examples are not recipes to be followed exactly. They are just provided to give you ideas...

TRAINING SESSION EXAMPLE 1

A physically active theatre team-building training day, aimed at a new peer group of 10 to 30 people:

Introduction
(including - who is who, aims of the session, how we are going to work, questions and requests...)

Preparation: (also called a 'warm up'):
Name tag

Pass the ball

Stuck-in-the-mud

Exploration: Walking group

Short break

Group knot

My journey to here

Rhythm of the group

Teach a song

Mealbreak

Ball connection

Invisible sword

This and that

Group Yes

Short break

Creation into Presentation:

Story pairs

Shared experience story

Conclusion:
Feedback discussion

Repeat the song to close

END

WORKSHOP EXAMPLE 2

A 3 hour, less physically active, theatre team building training session for a new peer group of 6 - 12 people:

Introduction (including who is who, aims of the session, how we are going to work, questions and requests...)

Preparation:
Name circle

Anyone who

Exploration:
Do nothing game

Story of my name

3 truths and 1 lie

- Short break -
Chair of truth

Perspectives

Newspaper game

Creation / Presentation:
Story circle

Feedback discussion

Conclusion:
Counting group to close

Bodies

This chapter outlines a training you can do on a regular basis. It is not a series of games which can be played once or twice, discussed and left behind. Rather it must become part of your everyday activities to prepare you for work and make you more expressive and more able to make excellent theatre. Like an athlete who trains every day to maintain their physical readiness, so you should ensure that bodies and voices are always at their best.

What do you use as your first method of communication as an actor? What does the audience see when you are on stage? Your body.

It is a fantastic instrument with which you can express so much. Your audience can "read" if you are old or young, strong or weak, angry or in love, hesitant or determined, just by looking at your body. If you look around you will see so many different body types and positions on the street, in the market, in the fields. We are "reading" them all the time.

Our job is to prepare our bodies so that we can communicate whichever state is necessary for the play we are performing.

It is not just being gymnastic or flexible; we have to know and feel the states we put our bodies into. You can't just walk on stage and say your lines with your everyday body. You need an "extra-ordinary" body, larger and more expressive than in daily life. Look at the body of a martial artist, wrestler, yoga practitioner or anyone who has that degree of control and energy. We need to obtain those elements and use them in our theatre.

The following exercises are some which can help that process. It is a fascinating study, right at the heart of theatre.

Start with a warm-up.

You can use any game at first, which helps you leave your worries on the doorstep, get focused and know where you are. Warm up games can be local games you have played since childhood, or you can create new ones. Nothing too complicated so everyone can take part. When the blood is flowing and you are a little loose and warm (that's why we call it a warm-up!) we can start on our bodies as our tools.

N.B. try to avoid games which eliminate people and where one person "wins", use games everyone can play all the time.

1. What Is My Body? What Shape Am I?

You don't have a musical instrument, or a paintbrush, or a paper and pen to make your art – just your body. So you better know what it is, and get to know it. This is a quiet, gentle introduction:

- Stand easily with your feet slightly apart.
- Close your eyes.
- Focus on the surface of your skin, from the tops of your feet, slowly up the front of your body, over the arms, over the head, down the back of your body and down to the soles of your feet. Just concentrate on your skin.
- Now try to feel it all together – your skin – that is your shape. At the moment it is not good or bad, it is just you!
- Imagine that shape is now an empty, hollow pot – you are an empty pot.

- Start to breathe consciously and fill up that pot with air. As you breathe out, empty the pot completely. The breathing gives you the feeling that you are gently washing out your body with air. And the air slowly gives you plenty of oxygen to turn into energy.
- You should feel a little energised as all that breath enters you.
- Open the eyes but keep that feeling.
- That is you, your body, the instrument you will be using.

2. The Ready Body

Now you have an idea of your body shape, it is important to prepare it for action, to be ready for expressing different characters, emotions etc. Even before you start to perform a role the body must have the energy in place. It is like the sprinter just before the race. He is not in the body he uses in everyday life, but he is not yet racing. He is in a state of readiness for action.

- Stand with feet parallel, shoulder-width apart.
- Feel the feet in a firm contact with floor. Working barefoot is good for this.
- Check that your weight is equally distributed between the two feet. This will give a strong base for the body and avoid you looking "off-centre"
- Check that your weight is not too far forward, and not too far back. You can rock gently between the weight over the balls of the feet and the weight over the heels, so that the body discovers its front and back limits, then slowly reduce the rocking until you find the middle point.
- Feel your weight going down into the ground through the feet – then feel the pull of your spine up and into the air – as If you are a conductor between earth and sky. If you get

these two forces you will have established a strong vertical body.

- Try to imagine the energy flowing to the feet and to the top of your head.
- Keep the eyes looking out to the horizon. If your eyes are looking down you may look depressed or self-absorbed. If they are looking too far up you may look over-hopeful.
- Now your body is well positioned, not giving any messages you don't intend. It is like a blank piece of paper before drawing on it, a good piece of clay before sculpting.
- We often call this state "Neutrality": a live readiness.

Neutrality Check !

- Work with a partner. Let them look at your body and gently correct anything they think is not neutral (head not straight, shoulders too tense, weight too far back etc. etc.). Then you check them for neutrality.
- Try the same exercise again. When you have established neutrality in the other person, ask them to start walking at their own speed around the space. Watch to see if their walk is neutral, or are they projecting some un-wanted messages?

3. Energy - you need it – where do you get it?

All actors need energy to carry out the hard work involved in making and performing theatre. The energy on stage is what allows you to have that presence which people will want to look at. Just as we love looking at children and young animals because they are full of energy, so the audience will be drawn to the actor with energy. It does not have to be "acrobatic" energy, in fact a still energy, like a cat just before it pounces on a mouse, is fascinating. The study of energy is a deep one but here are some good starting points to get the performers more energised:

- Power Shower. Use your hands to rub your face vigorously, even slap it gently, until you feel it a little more warm and alive. Then rub the hands into the hair as if washing. Continue this brisk washing action over the back of the neck, shoulders, arms and hands, down the torso, down the back and front of each leg to the feet, and as much of the back as you can reach. This will get blood flowing to the surface of the body so it feels more alive.

- Massage your abdomen (just above and below the navel) vigorously with two hands. Then start to slap that area gently, then more strongly. These are the breathing muscles and you are waking them up.

- Continue that massage and slapping round to the base of the spine, as if warming and waking it. These two positions are really the front and back of what is often called "the centre" from which energy radiates to the body. You may find this energy–centre referred to in martial arts, meditation or dance forms. Identifying it will help you when you walk neutrally (see last exercise).

- Breathe! The oxygen you draw into the body with each breath is your principle source of energy. Each breath floods the body with oxygen to burn.

- The best breathing is breath to your abdomen, your belly! All babies breathe this way naturally – you can see the rise and fall of their abdomen when they are asleep. As the abdomen expands, air is drawn into the lungs. As the abdomen falls, the air is pushed out.

- To discover this breathing, and all the energy it can give you, place your hands on your abdominal muscles – just above the navel – take a breath in, then push firmly on your abdomen to push out the air. Hold the hands in that position and, as you breathe in, try to let the hands be pushed back to the starting position. This may take some practice but once you have got it you will feel that the deep in-breath gives you a rush of energy you can use in your movements and voice. In fact if you breathe in like this and hold your breath for a few seconds you will feel you have energy just waiting to explode into action.

- IMPORTANT – as you are developing this breathing make sure the only movement is in your abdominal muscles. If there is a little movement in your lower ribs, that is good, but you should have no movement at all in the shoulders. Shoulder movement makes you look tense and can block the voice.

- Breathe in to your centre – hold the breath – breathe out slowly and powerfully.

- Breathe into your centre as you take one hand back and behind you – breathe out as you swing the hand forward and up (as if throwing a ball). The breath gives power to the movement.

- Stand with the legs wide apart:

Centred low position

- Breathe in deeply to your centre as you bend the legs and sink the centre about 20-25 cms. Breathe out as you jump into the air and land in the same low position. You will feel the breath "powering" the jump.

- Breathe in while standing still. As you breathe out, start to walk in a straight line across the space until you reach the end of your breath. Breathe in and turn to face a new direction. Breathe out as you walk etc. etc. etc.

- All these exercises are drawing breath into your centre and energising your movements.

- Experiment with other actions, put a strong breathing onto them to see how they gain more purpose and intention.

4. Walking in Space

It seems really simple to walk but on stage we have to think about where we walk, where we are facing, how close we come to other actors, whether we walk in direct lines or hesitating ones, and where we position ourselves on stage so that we are visible to the audience and not blocking the vision of fellow actors.

- The whole group walks calmly around the space, in all directions not in a circle, stopping, changing direction, just being aware of their own, neutral, energy-filled bodies.
- Continue walking. Be aware of other people, but try to keep as much distance between yourself and everyone else as possible. Try at a faster pace. How does that make you feel?
- Continue walking. Try to pass as close to other people as possible without touching them. Try this at different speeds. Try it with eye contact. Try it without eye contact. How is it different from the last way of walking? What situations does it remind you of?
- Continue walking. Choose one person to be the focus. That person is also walking but everyone looks at that person as they move. Try to keep a clear line of vision between yourself and the focus-person as you move. Choose another person, then another as focus-person.
- Continue walking. Let three people stand at one end of the space with a few metres between them as if they are a watching audience. As everyone else walks they focus on one of these three for as long as possible. Try to keep a clear line of vision to at least one of these three all the time. This way the focus is to one side of your space – you are getting used to being aware of your audience.

- The same as above but play between looking at the three people and deliberately breaking that contact, re-finding it, breaking it again. This way you can relate to the audience when you want to, and then break the contact.

- Through these exercises your bodies start to become conscious of the stage space and the space you create with and around other actors. Your body starts to be comfortable with, and in control of, the space.

5. Open and closed bodies

As an actor you will need to use your body in different ways to show the audience different characters and different states (emotions, reactions etc). These changes in your body depend on how you use the energy. By using it in different ways you feel different and you also communicate different states to our audience. Try this series of ideas to see how you feel different and how others look different when doing them.

- Stand in your neutral energised position with good deep breathing.

- Take a breath in. On the out-breath try to feel the energy flowing outwards from your centre in all directions. Down through your legs to your feet it strengthens your standing. Upwards let it travel through your torso to the shoulders and the arms and to the finger tips, stretching to the most open position possible. Also feel it through your neck, face and head, opening your expression into space. Stay in this open position for a moment to appreciate how it feels to be in this open-energy body. **Who are you when you are like this?**

- Take another breath in. On the out-breath feel the energy flowing inwards from the extremities towards the centre. Slowly close the whole body down to the most closed position you can make. Stay there and feel what it is like to be in this closed energy body. **Who are you when you are like this?**

- Move several times from open to closed, each time on a slow full outward breath, feeling the changes in how you

open and closed bodies

feel. Imagine a story which makes you change from an open-energy person to a closed-energy person.

- Now, when you have stretched the body to an open-energy position, start walking around the room like that. **Who are you? What are you doing?**

- Now change the body slowly to the closed energy position and move round the room. **How does your movement change? What do you feel like in this position? What type of character are you becoming?**

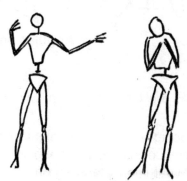

open and closed characters

- Repeat the walking exercises but add gestures; when you have open energy, add opening gestures – ones which go outwards to the space or to other people. When you are walking in the closed energy position, add closing gestures, which come inwards to you.

- Working in this way gives you possible characters through your body. We often talk of people being "open" or "closed". This is a discovery of such states through the body.

6. Angular or flowing bodies

Other uses of energy will give different character types – in fact we are discovering that the body is always saying something to those who watch. This is what we call body-language, and we are beginning to communicate with it.

The following use of energy can also be used to define character-types:

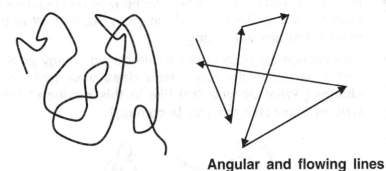

Angular and flowing lines

- Everyone takes a place in the room, with as much space as possible.
- You are all going to walk in straight lines only, starting, walking a distance, stopping, changing direction, walking again in a straight line..... and so on

- Start at a medium pace, your eyes focusing on where you are heading, walking a short or long distance. Make sure your stop is definite – you have arrived where you wanted to go, not run out of energy! Then make a clear turn with the head and body to face a new direction. Start walking. You should feel that you are drawing straight lines in the space with a clear angle at each stop and turn.

- Try varying the speed – but not so fast that you bump into other people.

- **How do you feel using your energy like this? What kind of person uses their energy in this way?**

- Now you are going to explore the opposite use of energy. Instead of the angular straight lines with starts and stops you are going to follow a flowing, curving line which has no straight lines and no stops.

- Start walking in curving lines; long slow curves or tight circles, around the room and around other people. Remember - no stops.

- Your eyes do not need to focus on a fixed point so they can travel and follow what they like.

- You can vary the speed of your walk.

- **How do you feel different, using your energy like this? What kind of person uses their energy in this way?**

- Change frequently between the two ways of using your energy.

- When you are clear about both energy uses you can start to speak quietly as you move, almost to yourself. Just say the first words which come. They might be describing your movement e.g. "I am going straight over there. Now I shall turn", or what you can see e.g. "Ahah, let's look at that door, very nice. Now we'll follow that person", or even better, how you feel e.g. "ah, that's good, I'm enjoying myself" or "I am determined to do this today" etc etc.

- As you change from the angular movements to the flowing ones, notice how the words change. It is all linked. And you are starting to generate text!

7. Isolation of body parts – Everything speaks!

As you are already learning, the body is an incredibly expressive instrument. Every slight change in the body's position or tension communicates something. As we get control of this wonderful range we can use it to change character or express a reaction or change of mood. Every part of the body can be used. Here are some important ones:

The head

- stand as neutrally as possible with a steady breathing pattern. Roll the head to loosen the neck muscles. Bring the head upright. Now push the head as far forward as possible. Look around. Notice the difference in the others in the group and in yourself. Start to walk around like this. How do you walk in this position? How do you view the space? How do you view others? How do you feel? What kind of character are you becoming? Allow a voice to come out of this walk, first just sounds, then words. Note what sort of words you bring out of this character.

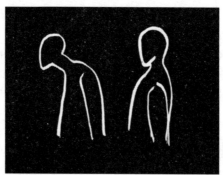

head forward, head back

- Return to neutral and now pull the head back and the chin in – look around and experience the discovery of this body-shape, through walking, meeting others, making sound, making words. Just with the adjustment of the head position you have found two personality types.

The shoulders

Shoulder positions up/down

- Roll the shoulders in a big circle up, back, down, front. Then reverse the direction until they are free of tension. We hold a lot of tension in the shoulders so this may take a little time.

- Now pull the shoulders up as far as they will go, right to the ears.

- Look around. Notice the difference in the others in the group – what atmosphere is in the room? Start to walk around like this. How do you walk in this position? How do you view the space? How do you view others? How do you feel? What kind of character are you becoming? Allow a voice to come out of this walk, first just sounds, then words. And what sort of words are you finding in this character?

- Pull the shoulders right down as far as they will go – repeat the discovery process of a character through a body position.

- Pull the shoulders as far back as they will go – repeat the process

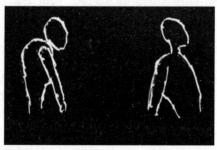

Shoulder positions forward/ backward

- Pull the shoulders as far forward as they will go and again repeat the process.

The chest

- Pull the chest forward, not the shoulders, just the rib-cage. Feel that the chest volume has increased. Look around and notice how you feel about other people. How do you walk? Meet? Speak? Who have you become?
- Pull the chest in, as if the lungs have collapsed and there is much less lung capacity. Look around and notice how you feel about other people. How do you walk? Meet? Speak? Who are you?
- Walk around the room and change between these two positions. Note the inner story of your change of position.

The pelvis

- Stand neutrally and focus your energy in the pelvis.
- Swing the pelvis in as wide a circle as you can to loosen it up, changing direction from time to time.
- Push the pelvis as far forward as you can as if all the energy were projecting from there. Follow the process of discovering what this position suggests as a state or as a character.
- Now pull the pelvis back behind the line of the body, almost hidden away. Look around and notice the difference, in others and yourself. How does this affect your body, thoughts and character?

The feet – throwing the weight

- Do all people walk the same? Of course not. By concentrating the energy in different parts of the feet we get different weight distribution in the body, which gives different rhythms, speeds and associations. Try some of these:
- Walk with your weight right at the front of the foot.
- Walk with the weight on the heel.

- Walk with the weight on the "pad" of the foot.
- Walk on tip toe.
- Walk with the weight on the inside of the feet.
- Walk with the weight on the outside of the feet.
- Walk with the feet lifting slightly more than normal.
- Walk with the feet dragging slightly more than normal.

Try all these and examine how you feel different, are different and have different associations in each position.

8. Stopping and starting

Watching animals is always fascinating as they have wonderful and varied control of energy and rhythm. They can also be the basis for developing characters. In particular we can learn how they hold their energy, how they stop and start. They always seem to be perfectly in control, and using the correct energy for what they intend to do. Some are better than others. The cat-family is a great example, which is probably why we are so fascinated by them.

- Everyone walks around the space in all directions, not in a circle. Be alert, taking eye contacts, looking at things in the space.
- When a leader calls "Freeze!" try to stop in exactly that moment – like when a cat suddenly sees a bird or a mouse.
- Make sure that the whole body stops, from eyes to toes, not just your legs with the arms still swinging. Think how a cat sometimes stops with one paw lifted – everything frozen and ready.
- Practise this until you can stop instantly with your energy held in your body. A stop is not when your energy runs out. It is when you hold all your forward energy from moving. So a stop has double energy – the forward energy and the energy which holds that energy back. When a cat stops and

is perfectly still, looking at a bird, there is no movement but we can all see the energy held in the body, waiting to jump.

- As you start to walk again, feel that the held energy has been released so you suddenly burst into movement. Not a slow, lazy acceleration, but a full energy start. Such starts are great for entrances on stage. They have energy and intention, and that makes the audience look at them.

- Now when you walk feel that you could stop at any moment. Now you don't need a leader to shout "Freeze". You can stop at any impulse: seeing something or someone, hearing something, smelling something, thinking of something. Try it, stopping on your own impulses. This is the level of energy control which will make your acting alive.

- Now try it moving at different speeds between the stops.

- Now try it walking with some of the body shapes you tried above.

- Now try it varying the amount of tension in the body. Walk with a lot of tension, like somebody very stressed, the stops and starts should be quite easy.

- Walk with a very lazy tension, like someone who is tired or in the heat. Even with this you should be able to do the stops and starts precisely.

Observation and copying

Start copying people you see around you. With the work you have just covered you should be able to look at someone and analyse how they hold their body, and copy it. You will find hundreds of different types from extreme to subtle. Try reconstructing with your body a shape that you have seen and notice how different you become. Try to find words which come from this "new" body shape.

AND......

Later you will see how the body can be modelled into new shapes to be used in making images.

Get a VOICE

When you are out there, on the stage, trying to get your audience involved in the dialogue, or leading a workshop with a lot of noisy people, you need a strong, audible voice.

Having a good voice is not the same as shouting. Shouting might get you heard but you won't have a voice for long, just a sore throat.

Training your voice to get those words across to the audience with clarity, meaning and emotion is a process of breathing, opening the throat and projection. The voice is a physical action and when we know which parts of the body help voice production, it becomes much easier.

Some actors take years to train their voices but you will probably need to get your voice to an effective level in quite a short time. So daily training is necessary, but not for hours and hours because the voice can get tired easily. Probably one hour per day is enough.

Here's how you might start work on your voice.

1. Breathing for Power.

If you remember the abdomen breathing we discovered earlier

(*above*) then repeat it now because the breath is the base for the voice. You can develop it further by practising a quite fast in-breath and a slow controlled out-breath. If you breathe in and then count with a soft voice as you breathe out you are helping your control. Start with counting to 5 on the out-breath, then 10, then 15, then 20. Can you go further? Don't strain anything, and don't move the shoulders – it should all be powered from the abdomen.

2. Yawning – for Openness

Many of the voice's problems are because the throat is too tense. It is vital to open the throat and keep it relaxed. Yawning is a fantastic way of opening the throat. Don't be scared of yawning – just let it come and don't cover your mouth. In fact stretch the body like when you wake in the morning. You will feel the automatic reaction of the throat in the yawn to stretch to its maximum openness.

As you yawn let the voice gently come through the open throat, quite relaxed, probably on a falling tone.

This is the position we must re-create for our stage work. SO.....

Breathe in and try to find that same position of the throat as you breathe out, and let the voice come through it. You may start yawning, even though you don't want to. Slowly take control of those muscles until you can create that big open sound easily.

3. Finding the sound

With the abdominal breathing and the open throat you can now engage the breath with the vocal chords (or vocal folds as they are also known). This creates the sound. Again we want to avoid tension in the voice. If you feel tension then go back to the yawning for a moment.

- Stand in an easy position with the feet slightly apart. Take a deep breath in and breathe out without making a sound. Do this several times.

- Repeat this but make a very breathy **"Ha"** sound as you breathe out. Do this several times.

- Again take a deep breath in. As you breathe out let the air gently touch the vocal chords to make a very soft, breathy **"aaaah"** sound. Feel as if the air is caressing the vocal chords, not attacking them.

- Repeat that, but each time try to let a little more air through the vocal chords to vibrate them and make sound. You should concentrate on feeling the mechanism of the voice – Breath – Air – Vocal Chords – Sound.

- This voice will be relaxed and quite a low tone because it is so relaxed.

- Produce that same tone but jump gently while making the sound. The movement of the body will push air up through the throat and open it. As you land you will hear a slight volume increase in the voice. Keep the mouth open and you will feel the effects of the jumping better.

- Other ways of increasing the volume on that basic tone are to raise and drop the shoulders as you produce the tone, or to gently beat your fists on your chest, lower ribs and abdomen to "massage" the voice out of you. You can also do this to a partner. Watch that your partner keeps the mouth open and the shoulders relaxed as they produce the sound.

4. Humming for amplification/volume

To give the voice the power it needs is not a matter of pushing. We need to use the body to amplify the volume. Just as a guitar has a sound box behind the strings to resonate their vibrations, we have parts of the body which naturally amplify our voice. By being aware of them and maximising them, we can find richer and louder tones to use.

The two main areas for resonance are the head and the chest. Here is how we can feel their resonance and increase it:

- Start to hum with the lips closed. Choose an easy note where you are comfortable and relaxed. Breathe deeply (abdomen only).

- Try to feel the hum on your lips. If you can't, slightly relax the lips and vary the note you are humming up and down until you feel your lips starting to "buzz". If you gently bring the teeth together behind the lips you may feel that they are also "buzzing" with the sound.

- Now place your hands on your face, let your fingers give a little pressure around the nose, under the eyes, on the forehead. Vary the pitch of your hum to try and feel these parts resonating with the sound. When you can feel it, try to relax those areas – perhaps by massaging them – to increase the resonance.

- Do the same with the top and back of your head. These are useful resonators, using the structure of the skull to amplify sound. Again vary your note from high to low and back again, until you feel the "buzz" here.

- These are the head resonators. See if you can feel them all working at the same time.

- Now place your hands on the front of your chest and continue humming. It should be easy to feel the vibration here, perhaps on a lower note than in the head.

- Take the hands to the lowest ribs, and to the side ribs. Try to find a note to resonate here. You may need to gently massage the fingers into the ribs here to feel the resonance. If it is difficult try to imagine that your mouth is in the place you want to resonate – that the voice is coming out of your body at that point. This can help sensitise the area.

- When you have explored all these areas, try slowly to open the lips so that you are making a "Mmaaah" sound, and try to maintain the resonance while you do it.

- Work on this regularly until your resonator/sound-box is fully helping you.

5. Calling for communication

People who work in the fields, in the hills, on the shore, often have ways of calling long distances – sometimes in a song – which is clear and unforced. It is a technique with an open throat which can help us discover the potential of our voices, and is useful when we are performing in big spaces. Here is one way to discover it for ourselves:

- The group stands in as big a circle as possible; feet apart and knees very slightly bent.
- You swing your "throwing arm" back and forward in unison with everyone else, as if in an under-arm throw. As you swing back, take a deep breath in. As you swing your arm forward breathe out and release the hand as if letting go of a ball which will fly up and forward.
- Check that your throat is open (like in the yawn), especially for the out breath.
- Now use the out breath to throw a sound – as if calling someone who is across the river, across the playground, up a mountain etc. It is good to start with the sound **"Hey"** as the **"h"** helps to keep the throat unblocked.
- Each time you swing the arm forward let that call fly out with your mimed throw.
- Check everyone is doing it without tension by letting everyone try it one by one. Point out any tensions you can see or hear in their voices.
- Try it with two syllables and two notes, e.g. **"Hey,ho!"** **"Hoh-Yah"** etc. All together, then one by one.
- Try it on three syllables, four etc.
- Try putting words to the call e.g. **"Hello – are you there?"**, **"Do you need help?"** etc. making sure that each word is called and not swallowed.

6. Lips, Teeth and Tongue for Clarity

So far you have all the elements to make a big clear sound which projects through space to the very back of your audience. But you will be using words and these must be heard in every detail. To do this we have to use much more precision than in our everyday speech, and we may have to speak a little more slowly. After all we want the audience to understand what we are saying. The most important factor in achieving this clarity is the use of all the muscles in and around the mouth. There are many of them and these exercises will help feel where they are so we can train them, just like we would train any other body muscle:

- Chewing Gum – imagine putting a very large and very hard piece of gum in your mouth. Try to chew it. It takes a lot of muscles and a lot of effort. Chew it slowly. As you chew, it gets softer and you can chew faster, and faster, and faster. This will get a lot of your muscles working.

- Start saying the sound **"Baaa"**. Use the lips to explode the **"B"** sound in to a good open **"aaaa"**. Start slowly then accelerate. Make sure the sound is not blocked.

- Different languages have different sounds but almost certainly there will be sounds made from the lips (e.g. **Baaa, Paaa**), sounds made with tongue and teeth (e.g.**Taaa, Thaa**), with tongue and palate or dental ridge (e.g. **Naaa, Laaa**), and sounds made further back in the mouth (e.g. **Kaaa, Gaaa**).

- Try each of these one by one trying to use your muscles to get a strong start to the sound and an open **"aaa"** sound afterwards. Start slowly then speed up to make the muscles work at speech pace..

- Try different sounds after the consonant – **Boh, Boo, Bee, Bay** etc. Notice how the mouth changes shape to produce those sounds.

- Create a more complex phrase to get all parts of the mouth working from front to back, e.g."**Ba Na La Ka Ga**". or "**Po Do Ro Ho Go**". Start slowly, then accelerate keeping the sound free and open.

- Finally, and to bring it close to direct theatre use, take a phrase of five or six words – perhaps a line from a play – and work on it slowly, making the muscles of your mouth get the maximum definition of sound – every part distinct and clear.

- Hear other people's phrases and let them know if there are unclear parts.

- Run to the other end of the space and speak your phrase with breath, open throat, resonance and clarity to your colleagues.

7. What Tone shall I choose – high or low? Vary your pitch

Even when voices are well trained some actors do not use much variation in pitch. This can lead to a monotonous voice and lack of expression. In some cultures women tend to speak socially in a very high voice which is not their natural tone and does not carry well from the stage. It is worth watching out for these factors and exploring other possibilities. Often performers are very surprised when they find they have other voices, or vocal ranges, they can use.

- Take a simple phrase – like that in the last exercise. Speak it a few times in your "normal" voice – as clear as you can

- Now speak in the lowest voice you can find which is audible in the space. Repeat several times to get the maximum from it.

- Now speak it in the highest voice you can find without straining. Check that others can understand it. Repeat it several times.

- Now try to move slowly from your lowest voice to your highest, pitch by pitch There should be at least ten pitches between the two.

- When you have tried it for yourself, present these different levels to other members of the group. Let them choose which levels are most effective.

- Ask yourself how you feel different at different pitches in your voice.

8. Observation – Listening and Copying – Explore the Voice

Now you have a basic knowledge of how it all works, use your ears and listen to people around you. Start copying voices you hear, and analyse angry voices, loving voices etc. The more flexible your voice becomes, the more characters and situations you can communicate to your audience.

VIDYA happiest moments...

We performed in front of nearly 500,000 people at one performance. It was the first time we saw our performance being shown on screens placed in different locations around the big field while we were performing. It was incredible.

Play, Expression and Imagination

So far we have looked at building the team members and strengthening and conditioning their bodies and voices to make them more expressive for performance. This next section will offer games and exercises for awakening individual sensations – touch, sound and sight, heightening awareness, recalling body memories, stretching their imaginations and making the group more expressive and playful together.

Hug tag

Aim: Breaking down barriers, play and mutual support
Mood: High energy
Level: Basic
Number of people: 5-30
Time: 5-10 minutes
Directions:

- The group moves freely about the space.
- One person is the chaser. The rest of the players run away from the chaser.
- The chaser attempts to touch (tag) the players.
- The players can avoid being tagged by hugging one other person in the group (or linking arms) for no longer than three seconds. When they hug (or link arms) they are safe and cannot be tagged by the chaser.

- However, if they are tagged, they call 'it's me!' very loudly so that everyone knows who the new chaser is.

Duels

Aim: Breaking down barriers between people, nurturing playfulness, exploring how a clash of desires creates drama

Mood: High energy

Level: Basic

Number of people: 2-30

Time: 10-15 minutes

Directions:

- Ask the group to get into pairs.
- Both players face each other, and place one hand behind their back with the palm showing and with the other hand one finger is stretched in front like a sword ready for a duel.
- The aim of the game is for each player to use their finger to touch the palm of their opponent's hand (which is held behind their back) without being touched themselves, as many times as possible.
- X wants to touch Y's hand.
- Y doesn't want X to touch her hand.
- Y wants to touch X's hand.
- X doesn't want Y to touch his hand.
- Encourage the pairs to be as creative, inventive, expressive and playful as possible in this game, and to get their bodies into as many different shapes, using as many levels as possible, using as much of the space as possible, both in defending their hand and in trying to touch the other's hand.

Variation 1:

Ask the group to get into new pairs. The game has the same principle as above, but this time the pairs are going to use their hands to touch each other's knees, and defend their own knees.

Variation 2:

Ask the group to get into new pairs. The game has the same principle as above, but this time the pairs are going to use their toes to touch each other's toes (gently!), and defend their own toes.

duels hands to knees

duels toes to toes

duels fingers to hands

- The pairs mix all three games at the same time.
- The whole group plays together – no longer just in pairs.
- Play music – the game can become a dance!
- Ask a pair to play in front of an audience. When the pair gets into a really dynamic shape, the facilitator can shout 'freeze!' – which means the pair should immediately hold the pose they are in. Ask the other participants to imagine and describe what this scene could be, what does it look like? From here you can even start to build a short scene based on these suggestions.

Why did we suggest 'duels'?...

Every game we play in this work has an element of theatre within it. Just like the duels game, drama is all about the clash of strong 'wants', the passionate conflict of desires. For example Y wants to go to school. X doesn't want Y to go to school. X wants to marry Y and Y wants to marry X but Q doesn't want X to marry Y, and so on. When a human being has a strong desire, a powerful want, their body will show it in the shape of their body, the distance between their body and someone else's, and the levels in space that they use. In theatre, just like in the game, we show drama, the clash of wants in a much more expressive way, a much bigger way than in everyday life. To make a scene dramatic and dynamic, we need to use our bodies expressively and imaginatively to show the character's wants in the scene, and to make the story clear for our audience.

> Whenever you see someone who wants, and someone who doesn't want, a story comes to mind...

Person to person

Aim: Body knowledge, breaking down physical barriers
Mood: Moderate to high energy
Level: Intermediate
Number of people: 8-30 (an even number is required)
Time: 15-25 minutes
Directions:

- The group gets into pairs.
- At any time the facilitator can call 'person to person'. When 'person to person' is called the players must get into a new pair as quickly as possible.
- Once the players are in pairs, the facilitator calls out the names of two body parts, which the players must make contact with. For example 'right leg to left elbow', then one player's right leg must make contact with the other player's left elbow.

- The players must keep the body parts in contact throughout the game, they must stick like glue, unless the facilitator calls out 'person to person'.
- The facilitator calls out more body parts, for example 'head to ear', knee to back' etc.
- After six or eight body parts the players will be very tangled.
- To increase the level of difficulty and playfulness, music can be played whilst the players keep the body parts in contact and move around the room.
- Once the game is established, different players can call out the instructions.

elbow to leg

and head to head

and knee to back

Why did we suggest 'person to person'...

This game can be a fun way of enabling the group to get to know their bodies and to get them into positions and moving in ways that they may not have known were possible. Performers need to have good knowledge of the potential of their bodies for expression. This game helps draw attention to that. Theatre is also an art form which sometimes needs people to be in close physical contact, in ways which may be unusual in their every day lives and in many cultures. So this game provides a way of breaking down inhibitions and physical barriers between people and is a good preparation for challenges to come.

Groups and Shapes

Aim: Expressive task-based group work, getting to know each other better

Mood: High energy

Level: Intermediate

Number of people: 5-30

Time: 15-25 minutes

Directions:

- Ask the group to move around the space, tell them you are going to call out groups which they must get into as quickly as possible.

- When they are in those groups you are going to tell them a shape or object which they must make as a group. They must find the most dynamic way of making that shape, using different levels, with attention to detail etc.

- For example 'Get into groups of 6, make a circle', 'Get into groups of 3, make a star', Get into groups of 7, make a bowl of fruit'...

- As you progress, the groups and tasks should get more challenging. For example 'get into groups of people with the same colour eyes as you, make the word theatre', 'get into pairs with a person who is most different in height from you, make a bird on a pond', 'get into groups of people with the same size feet as you, make a bicycle'...

- You can also start to introduce themes or issues you want to explore through the kind of group they are in, and the task: 'get into groups of 12, make a factory paying low wages', 'get into groups of people born in the same month as you, make a family who have received some good news'...
- After a while you can ask groups to look at each other's pictures and talk about what they see.
- The groups can introduce sound and movement to the shapes they have made, so they start to become potential scenes which you can develop.

Why did we suggest 'groups and shapes'?

This exercise is a useful way of the group finding out more about itself, and for working together quickly and creatively as a group.

Points of contact

Aim: Developing physical expression in a team

Mood: High energy

Level: Intermediate

Number of people: 5-30

Time: 15-25 minutes

Directions:

- Ask the group to get into groups of about 5 people.
- Tell them how many points of contact they can have, as a group, on the floor at any given time.
- Start off with an easy instruction, for example 9 points of contact on the floor (so in a group of 5 people with 2 feet each, if one person raises a foot off the ground, the group now has 9 points of contact on the floor).
- Continue changing the number of points of contact on the floor.

- The group should discover more and more inventive ways of contacting, and not contacting, the floor.

Variation:

As above. Then call out different body parts that can have points of contact on the floor. For example 5 feet, 2 hands, 3 elbows, 1 knee, 1 hip, 2 shoulders...

Why did we suggest 'points of contact'?

The group will make some fascinating stage pictures during this exercise, they will use different levels (some high, some low, some on the ground, some climbing on others etc) and they will start to use their bodies imaginatively and dynamically. The group will start to make physical contact without thinking about it. This exercise is also a great way to get a group working as a team.

Sounds and hands circle

Aim: Awakening the senses and the imagination, group trust and cooperation.

Mood: Moderate energy

Level: Intermediate to advanced

Number of people: 8-30 (an even number is required)

Time: 15-25 minutes

Directions:
- In a circle give each person a number 1,2,1,2,1,2...
- Ask the Number 1s to face the person on their right hand side.
- The Number 1s create a sound which they can repeat. Number 2s listen to that sound and try to remember it.
- Number 1s turn back to their original place in the circle.
- Number 2s now stand next to the person on *their* right i.e. not the same person as before.
- Number 2s create their own new sound for the person they are facing.
- Number 2s turn back to their original place in the circle.
- Now ask everyone to hold hands with the person either side of them and really feel the hands – they will have to recognise those hands very soon!
- The group lets go of hands. Now everyone must close their eyes and not to open them until the game is over.
- The facilitator now mixes up the group with their eyes closed, by leading them by the hand to other parts of the room.
- Ask the group to all make the sound they made before, to listen for the sounds of their partners and to feel for the hands they touched.
- The aim of the game is to re-create the circle as it was at the start by listening for the sounds they heard and feeling for the hands they touched.
- Let the game go on until the circle is back where it started.
- Ask the group to reflect on the experience, what kind of environment did they imagine they were in, what kind of emotions came up etc...

Sound Pairs

Aim: To heighten the senses and develop trust
Mood: Gentle

Level: Intermediate

Number of people: 2-30 people

Time: 15-20 minutes

Directions:

- The group gets into pairs.
- In pairs, one person has their eyes closed, the other has their eyes open.
- The person with their eyes closed folds their arms in front of their body or keeps their arms by their sides so that no one is injured during the exercise.
- The person with their eyes open leads the other around the space through making a sound which their partner will follow by listening.
- The person with their eyes open must guide their partner through the space safely, through sound.
- The leading partner may only use gentle touch if their partner is in danger of hurting themselves or another player.
- Once a good level of trust has been built up, the leading partner can start to experiment with volume, stops and silence, they can play with the distance from their partner.
- Swap over so the leader is now led.
- Reflect.

Why did we suggest these sound exercises?...

Closing eyes and listening for sounds can really sensitise the participants throughout their whole body. Sound is particularly powerful for awakening the imagination, generating stories and evoking memories.

For the exercises to work well, a certain level of trust is developed. Trust is also a crucial feature of working together in a theatre group. Here is an exercise that helps us develop trust and our imaginations…

Imaginary journey

Aim: To heighten the senses, develop trust and awaken the imagination

Mood: Gentle to moderate energy

Level: Advanced

Number of people: 2-30 (an even number is required)

Time: 20-30 minutes

Directions:

- The group gets into pairs.
- One person has their eyes open, the other has their eyes closed.
- The person with their eyes open will guide their partner on an imaginary journey.
- The guide will 'describe' the journey without using words at all. They must create the whole journey for their partner by making sounds of the places they are going to, by manipulating their body and using objects and touch sensations if they wish. For example if the guide is taking their partner through a muddy swamp, they might make squelching sounds and lift their partners feet and legs in a heavy laboured way, creating the feeling of resistance in mud. If they are taking their partner in a battered old car they must make the sounds of the car door creaking opening, the feeling of the car seat, the sounds of the engine and the traffic etc.
- At the end of the imaginary journey the person who has been guided opens their eyes. The guided person describes the journey they have experienced, how it felt, what they saw in their mind's eye etc. The guide listens, then describes where they imagined they were taking their partner. They discuss what they experienced.
- The partners swap roles.
- Once everyone has been on a journey, the group can sit in a circle and share some of their stories. This exercise may give you ideas of locations in which to set a scene or a play.

VIDYA EXAMPLE: Imaginary Journey:

Kalu took Rekha on an Imaginary journey :

One cold, shivery night, Rekha was taken to a jungle. She walked through the jungle at night listening to the various animals that came out to hunt. The animals were sniffing her and she was very afraid. She even heard a lion roar. She was taken up a mountain and had to hide in a cave. A few moments later, she heard sparrows and small birds and thought it was morning, she was guided further up the mountain where she felt thirsty. She approached a small lake where she finally drank some water.

Touch story

Aim: Evoking memory and imagination through touch stimulus

Mood: Gentle

Level: Advanced

Number of people: 2-30

Time: 15-25 minutes

Directions:

- We recommend you play a warm-up game featuring touch such as 'hug tag' or 'person to person' at some point before starting this game as it requires a level of trust and sensitivity.
- The group gets into pairs.
- One person has their eyes closed, the other has the eyes open.
- The person with closed eyes stands in a still relaxed position.
- The person with open eyes will provide their partner with physical sensations through gentle touch to various body parts, making certain sounds and touching their partner's body with different objects and textures.
- In response to each touch, the person with their eyes closed allows certain memories to be stimulated.

- The memories are spoken quietly. There may be just one sentence or word per stimulus. Sometimes no memories will come. The person providing the stimulus must work slowly and gently, giving plenty of time for the person with their eyes closed to think, feel, react and speak. Do not rush it.
- After a few minutes of working in this way, the facilitator instructs that the one with their eyes closed no longer only has to speak memories, now they can start to make up small stories, describe pictures in their minds, and invent scenarios.
- After 10 minutes or so, they can open their eyes and reflect on the experience.
- Swap over.

Why did we suggest 'touch story'?...

Augusto Boal has said that no one remembers without imagining or imagines without remembering. An exercise which opens up the memory can also be a wonderful starting point for stretching the imagination. In Theatre for Development work, many of the plays we create are based on our personal experience, but are enriched through creative collaboration. Exercises such as 'Touch Story' help to make that important transition from memory to imagination, biography to fiction, as well as heightening physical sensation.

VIDYA EXAMPLE: Touch Story

The trickle of sweat under the stiff collar of my new school shirt.

Leila's grandmother's hands were as soft as peaches and as wrinkly as old apples...

...holding on to the branch of the tree when I was stuck at 7 years old.

The man stood at the cliff's edge, he noticed a bird's egg at his feet, and changed his mind.

The environment game

Aim: To use bodies and voices in a group to create an environment

Mood: Creative focused team task

Level: Intermediate

Number of people: 10-30 people – this game works particularly well with children

Time: 20-40 minutes

Directions:

- Do some work preceding this exercise which will get the group working well as a team, physically and vocally expressive such as 'groups and shapes' and 'sounds and hands circle' (above).

- 3–5 people volunteer to leave the space. They are 'the investigators'.

- The rest of the group quickly decides upon an environment they are going to create through their bodies and in sounds, but not words.

- The group uses the entire space, their bodies and their voices in different levels and shapes, to create the environment, for example a rain forest, a train station, a dairy farm.

- The investigators come back into the room. They walk around the environment, looking and listening.

- After they have spent a few minutes moving around the environment they describe what they have seen and heard.

- Finally this group tries to guess the environment they were in.

- Play the game a few times with different investigators.

- The environments might suggest good settings for a play that you go on to create. For example, who is the girl sitting in the train station? What is she doing? Which train station is it? Why is she there? Where are her parents? etc

Eyes and Eye Contact

Eye contact game

Aim: To make your eyes expressive and to discover playfulness through them

Mood: Playful

Level: Easy

Number of people: 2-30 people. Even numbers as you will be working with a partner. If you have uneven numbers, a different person can drop out at each stage.

Time: 20 minutes

Directions:

- Move around the room freely, just looking at the floor in front of you.

- As you feel you are approaching someone look sharply up for a very, very short eye contact. It will take a little time to get the eyes "switching on" and "switching off". Don't stop when you make the eye contact. Keep moving!

- Next, move around, find an eye contact with someone, hold it for a count of three, break it and move on, and another, and another. Keep moving during the eye contacts, but note how your movement might change when in contact with different people.

- Now do it and keep the contact for ten seconds – play with the distance between you. An eye contact is like elastic between you. It can be 50cms or 5 metres. Play with it.

- Now keep the eye contact for 30 seconds (the leader might have to call out the time to start and stop each contact). At this length of eye contact, let your body react to what is happening. Let yourself play. You may be pulled towards your partner, you may be slowed down or speeded up, you may find yourself in competition with them or developing a game with them. Let these things happen. Just don't break the eye contact!

- If all is going well, you can keep the eye contacts going for a minute or even more. Allow yourselves to play with levels, speeds, power-play between you and whatever emerges. Just don't stop, when you are moving the body can react and change more easily.

Why did we suggest this eye contact game?

This is a very basic sort of improvisation in which we discover that ideas can suggest themselves to us very easily. You start without knowing what will emerge and by following the basic rule (make an eye contact and keep moving) you find yourself creating moods, relationships and emotions which finish as soon as you break the eye contact. The game also makes your eyes really alive. Your audience won't see the same power if you have "dead" eyes.

Break the eye contact game

Aim: To explore the power of eye contact and how it can be used

Mood: High energy, playful

Level: Intermediate

Number of people: 3-30 people

Time: 15-25 minutes

Directions:

- Get into groups of three
- The aim of the game is for two people to maintain eye contact whilst the person in the middle does whatever they want to do (without causing physical pain) to break their eye contact and get one or the other to look into their own eyes.
- Encourage the middle person to take risks and keep trying to find different ways to break the eye contact, to come up with many different approaches to this challenge, to improvise.
- When eventually a player has broken the eye contact by looking into the middle person's eyes, they must themselves go into the middle.

- The game is played several times so that each person gets to experience both roles.

- Once the game has been played to satisfaction, discuss how it felt. What emotions came up? What situations can you think of where eye contact is used, or not used, to affect another person's behaviour, to communicate or to oppress? This discussion may bear fruit for scenes and plays you may wish to develop in your Theatre for Development performances.

**Break the
eye contact**

Here are two example training sessions based on some of the exercises in this section. Of course when you are planning Theatre for Development peer group training sessions and community workshops you can also use exercises from the 'Making a Team', 'Bodies' and 'Voice' sections, as well as using your own local games and exercises. We offer these example workshops just to put the work in a context. Later in this handbook you will find advice on planning and running workshops like these :

Example training sessions to release play, expression and imagination

Example 2-hour workshop for a group of 15-30 people at an early stage of training:

Introduction – aims, objectives etc

Preparation (or warm up):
Hug tag

Points of contact

Exploration:
Groups and shapes

Sound and hands circle

Creation:
The environment game

Choose one of the environments you created for a scene. Decide
who the characters are, what they want and where the conflict
between them is. Rehearse the scene.

Presentation:
Present the scene.

Conclusion:
Discussion

Hug tag to close

A 2-hour workshop for a smaller group, 4–8 people, who have some theatre training and who want to make a performance on the theme of trust and risk.
Introduction – aims etc

Preparation (or warm up):
Person to person

Exploration:
Sound pairs

Touch story

Creation:
In pairs write song lyrics arising from the sound and touch exercises on the theme of 'feeling safe' and 'taking risks'.

Swap song lyrics with another pair. Improvise a very basic tune to go with the lyrics the other pair has written.

Presentation:
Present the songs to each other in pairs.

Conclusion:
Discussion of how these songs might be used in the future performance.

1-hour workshop for an established group to create dramatic material as the basis for a play exploring power and oppression:

Introduction – aims etc

Preparation:

Duels

Exploration:

Stop and freeze the duels game – decide who people might be, what they want, where the power lies, what the conflicts might be.

Eye contact game

Briefly discuss how the eyes can be used in different ways to communicate meanings.

Break the eye contact game

Briefly discuss situations this game reminds you of. Make notes.

Creation:

In groups of 3, create short 30 second scenes based on the games we have played. For example one person is being ignored by two other people and wants to be looked at, or one person is being looked at when they do not want to be looked at. Where are we? Who are the characters?

Presentation:

Present the short scenes

Working with Images

Now that everyone is working as a team, creatively expressing themselves vocally and physically, the group may be ready to go forward and develop their skills as makers and readers of images and stage pictures.

If a film is a series of photographs, theatre can also be seen as a series of dramatic pictures all connected together to communicate a story. We have found that image work is an essential element in training a theatre for development group. Image work not only introduces a technique for understanding and making theatre, it also equips people with the skills they will need to analyse the world around them, to look in detail at oppressive situations and community issues, and to reflect upon them, interrogate them and change them.

Mirrors

Aim: Observation and reflection

Mood: Gentle

Level: Basic

Number of people: 2-30

Time: 10 minutes

Directions:

- The group gets into pairs and name themselves 1 & 2.
- They stand facing each other.
- 1 starts to move very slowly, carrying out an action.
- 2 reflects the action, as if in a mirror.
- Swap over.

The next exercise is a great development of mirror work. You have to be observant, precise AND allow your associations to guide you.

Mirror and change game

Aim: Observation and reflection

Mood: Gentle to moderate energy

Level: moderate

Number of people: 5-30 people

Time: 20-30 minutes

Directions:

- Stand in a circle.
- One person enters the circle and makes a strong physical position.
- The next person enters the circle and mirrors the first person. This mirror can be in front of, behind, at the side of the other person.
- They hold this position
- The first person leaves the circle.
- The second person slowly changes position to another strongly defined picture trying to develop the meaning, mood or character they find themselves in (this could be done to a count of 8, for example).
- The third person enters, mirrors and holds the second person's position, second person leaves.
- Third person slowly changes position to another picture and so on.

Why did we suggest mirror exercises?

In this work the whole group's observational skills will be sharpened. Copying another person is also fantastically useful for an actor – this work will develop it. In the more advanced exercise 'Mirror and change game' above, you find yourself in the mirrored position but you have to do more than just physically copy it, you must "interpret" it and develop it. For these few moments you are creating a new "moment".

As actors we have to speak, move and "be" in a larger, clearer way than we are in ordinary everyday life. As theatre is being viewed by hundreds, perhaps thousands of people, we cannot be ordinary, we have to be extra-ordinary. Acting might look like everyday life but actually you have to use many skills to make it look like this.

Spot the difference

Aim: Observation and memory skills
Mood: Gentle
Level: Basic
Number of people: 2-30
Time: 5-10 minutes
Directions:

- Ask the group to get into pairs, naming themselves 1 and 2.
- 2 turns her back to 1.
- 1 makes a shape with her body, and calls 'ready!' when she has finished making the shape.
- 2 turns around and studies the shape 1 has made for a few seconds.
- 2 turns her back to 1.
- 1 changes 3 small things about the shape she has made, then calls 'ready!'.
- 2 studies the shape again and says which 3 things have changed.
- Swap over.

The following exercise leads very well from 'Spot the difference'

spot the difference

Image line

Aim: To test the group's observation and imitation skills

Mood: Moderate to high energy

Level: Intermediate to advanced

Number of people: 4-30 people

Time: 20-30 minutes

Directions:

- The group gets into pairs and name themselves A and B.
- The As and Bs now each form a line. The partners named A and B should stand opposite and facing each other.
- Line A close their eyes.
- The facilitator counts down 10 seconds in which the players in line B all individually make a still image with their bodies. Line B must hold this image until the end.
- After 10 seconds the players in line A open their eyes, they have 10 seconds to look at the image their partner B has made.
- Line A close their eyes.
- Line A now has 10 seconds to re-create the image their partner in line B made. Line A must all keep their eyes closed whilst making the image!
- Line A opens their eyes.
- Line A can now see how closely they copied line B.

- Line B gives them feedback on how accurate the image is.
- Swap over. Play the game as above this time with line A creating the image, and B closing their eyes and copying.
- Once the pairs have practised once or twice, the exercise gets more challenging. Play the game as above, only this time 2 players in line B work together to make an image, which involves both of them. The opposite two players in line A have to work together with eyes closed to recreate the image.
- Then 3 people, then 4 people until at the end of the game the whole of line A is a reflection of the whole of line B and vice versa.

Variation:

- You can suggest locations for the images. For example 'Line B make an image of a street scene' or 'line A, make an image of a market' or 'line B make an image of a courtroom'... etc. From here you can build discussion and stories for scenes. For example what is happening in the courtroom? Who is the judge? Who is on trial? What are they on trial for? Are they innocent or guilty? What is their argument? Who are the jury – are they the defendant's peers? If not, why not? Let's re-create the scene of the crime. Now the scene before the crime etc... Or where is the market? What is the weather like? Who is selling? What are they selling? Who is making a profit today? Who is making a loss? Why?...

Why did we suggest 'image line'?

Observation is something we often take for granted, but it is essential for us as Theatre for Development people, to develop our skills so that we are able to observe in great detail, so that we can criticise in great detail, and come up with questions and ideas for change. Generalised images lead to generalised plays. and discussions which ultimately are much less useful and constructive for a community.

VIDYA comments on doing Image Work:

"Doing image work makes you feel that there are so many possibilities in life".

"You have an opportunity to create and see your inner strengths, fears and concerns"

"I can mold... I am the creator, I am the artist, I am the sculptor."

"I get the opportunity to create something important".

Sculptor and clay

Aim: Body awareness and creative imaging

Mood: Gentle

Level: Intermediate

Number of people: 2-30

Time: 20-30 minutes

Directions:

- It may be useful to demonstrate this exercise yourself using one other person before asking the group to split into pairs.

- In the pairs, one partner is the sculptor (or modeller, potter), one person is going to be like clay.

- There is no talking in this exercise, you may choose to play music after the group have practised for a while in silence.

- The person who is going to be clay will just stand, relaxed, and respond to what the sculptor does.

- The sculptors use their hands to slowly and gently shape the clay person into different shapes and positions. The sculptors experiment until they have created a still image they are happy with.

- All the sculptors in the group walk around and look at each other's work, talking about what they see in the 'sculpture garden' that the group has made.

- The sculptor and clay swap over.

- Discussion on what people saw and felt in the images. From here scenarios may be suggested for scenes and plays you might choose to develop.

Why did we suggest 'sculptor and clay'?

This exercise gives a gentle way of learning more about the body, how it moves and how it can begin to express meaning.

When the group has practised sculpting shapes with each other's bodies, you can go on to explore themes, issues and problems which are relevant to your communities and you would like to address in order to find strategies for change.

Group Image of...

Aim: To gain a greater understanding of a social theme, issue or problem, through non-moving physical images involving several bodies and sculptors, finding strategies for change, arriving at consensus

Mood: Silent concentration, thinking through the body

Level: Advanced

Number of people: 2-30

Time: 50 minutes to an hour (or more)

Directions:

- The facilitator. or group, selects a theme that the group would like to explore. To begin with this theme can be quite broad and can have many dimensions and can be seen from many perspectives so that the detail can be explored through the exercise. For example the 'group image of society', 'group image of the village', 'group image of school', 'group image of family' etc.

- In this exercise the group will work through a process to try to arrive at a consensus (collective and agreed) image, which they all recognise, and which reflects the theme they have chosen to work on. Arriving at a consensus in a group on any matter may be a difficult one, and this is part of what is learnt through the exercise.

- The image they create must be a reflection of how the issue is in reality, a *real* image, not necessarily how they would like it to be.

- One at a time participants get up and use several other people's bodies and any objects to sculpt a still image of the chosen theme. They work in silence.

- It is fine for some people to be watching and some people to be in the image.

- After the creation of each still image, the facilitator asks, do we all agree that this is a real image of the theme? The facilitator invites the group to come up. Who would like to come up and change something, add something or take something away, or sculpt an image which is completely different?...

- With one person sculpting a group image at a time, one by one they work through various versions, until an image is formed which everyone recognises and agrees is a real image and reflects the theme – this may take some time and may also involve some compromise.

- Finally a real image will be arrived at that the group is willing to accept and work with.

- Now, ask them to do the task again, but this time to construct an *ideal* image of the theme.

- When they have done this, finally ask the group to return to the real image of the chosen theme. On each sound of a clap of the facilitator's hands, the group must now make one move from the real image to the ideal image. This then is an image of *transition*. Give as many claps of the hands as it takes to get there. Ask the group to observe themselves in action noticing what change is needed to get from the real situation to the ideal.

- After the practical work the group can sit and discuss the images, and the process of transition, what they noticed, what surprised them, what they learned and how we can apply this learning to our situations.

Complete the image – the handshake

Aim: To make and read stage pictures, to use images as building blocks for theatre

Mood: Gentle to moderate energy

Level: Basic to intermediate

Number of people: 2-30 people

Time: 30-40 minutes

Directions:

- The group gets into pairs and number themselves 1 and 2.
- The pairs make a still image of 2 people shaking hands.
- There is no talking.
- Number 1 steps out of the image. Number 2 remains in exactly the same shape.
- Number 1 looks at the image of number 2 from all angles. This process of looking is sometimes forgotten as the exercise gets more complicated, but it is very important that the participants keep this element as part of the exercise and take a very good look.
- Number 1 steps back into the image, but this time in a new position (not a hand shake). They can be encouraged to make clear physical choices and to experiment with using different levels, to work in three dimensions and place themselves at different angles etc. (It is useful to always have one point of physical contact between the two bodies)
- They hold the position for a moment, noticing what the image suggests to them.
- Then number 2 steps out. Number 1 keeps the shape she has made. 2 looks at the image.
- 2 steps back in and takes up a new position.
- The cycle of images continues.
- The players should be encouraged to 'think with their bodies', using different levels, working from all angles.
- After a while pairs can watch each other, and describe what they see, what stories emerge for them, what issues. In image work there is no right or wrong answer!

Variation:

- Another form of greeting can be used to begin the exercise if this is very unfamiliar in your community. However, using some form of greeting which involves some form of physical contact can be useful to start the exercise.
- Try the exercise with music to create a different dynamic.
- Try it without physical contact, playing with distance.
- The exercise can also be practiced with 3 people. (2 in a handshake. 3 enters and adds to picture, then 1 changes, then 2 then 3 etc).

Extension of 'complete the image':

- After carrying out the exercise without words, the participants can now individually add a word, or a short sentence together with each image they make. Be careful though - usually when we introduce words, the bodies become less dynamic. Encourage the group to keep the body expressive, even when they start using words.
- After practising with still images plus words, the participants can start to bring the still images to life through continuous movement and words (rather than just still image to still image) and into short improvised scenes. Let the scenes play for some time.

Why did we suggest 'complete the image' and the extension of it?

This beautiful exercise is very simple yet can be very fruitful. Firstly it encourages people to think with their bodies. It can also be very useful for discovering the link between body, image, story, word and scene. By the end of the exercises the group will be performing a piece of theatre, and all it started with was a simple handshake!

Issues and themes which are important to the group will also be revealed in this exercise, without the facilitator dictating what the themes or issues should be.

Image of the word

Aim: To explore themes through still images, to practice bringing images to life

Mood: Varied

Level: Basic to intermediate

Number of people: 2-30

Time: 20-30 minutes

Directions:

- Collect themes and issues that the group is interested in working on, for example 'love', 'fear', 'school', 'the harvest', 'homelessness', 'domestic violence', 'growing old'... The themes might be collected through discussion, or there may be themes which have recurred from previous exercises (such as complete the image) which you may want to explore in more depth.

- Ask the group to stand separately from each other, in a circle with their backs facing into the circle.

- The facilitator will call out one of the themes.

- The participants are going to make a still picture with their bodies that expresses this theme for them.

- Count the group down from 10 to 1 ending with 'turn around and show your picture!'.

- At this point the group should all turn inside the circle to face each other and spontaneously present their individual images with their bodies.

- Ask the group to hold the image they are making at the same time as taking a look at the other images in the circle.

- The participants are invited to say what they can see in the images, they notice which shapes recur, what emotions and situations come to mind and what this says to them about the theme.

- The group turns back into the circle another word is chosen and so on...

- Once the exercise is established, different participants can call out themes.

Variation

- As above.

- This time the images are 'brought to life' in various ways. For example, the facilitator says 'play sound' – the images remain still but the participants make corresponding sounds which go with their images. Or 'play movement' – the participants bring the images to life through movement', or 'play in rhythm', the images come to life on a rhythm and so on.

- The facilitator can conduct the sounds and movements coming from the images (see 'conductor circle' in the section 'making a team').

- The facilitator can also instruct the participants to move toward their opposite image. The participants move like statues on wheels, holding their image in place but travelling forward. They make pairs with the person who seems to be in the opposite shape to theirs. These groups of images can thereby be brought together into very short quick scenes with the pairs moving and having a dialogue with each other – 'play scene'.

- The same can be done by participants holding their image and moving toward others which are similar to theirs.

images of 'fear' in conversation

Character

In almost all plays the very essence of acting is that you are performing someone who is not you. Even if you are performing your own story you will not behave on stage exactly as you do in normal life. You will be playing a theatrical representation of you. All of these are characters.

So you have to become another person, different from yourself, and believable to those who are watching.

VIDYA happiest moments...

Bhikiben: At the age of 56, I played the character of a 13 year old girl. I remembered my childhood and I forgot what age I am and only focused on what character I was performing.

There are many methods and theories of how to approach character, ranging from the very psychological: e.g. "know everything which has happened in your character's past which influences how she/he is today"- to the very external: e.g. put on a mask and learn how to play its movements.

Of course the actor needs to know both the mental and physical state of the character so we can blend those elements, and present a complete picture to our audiences.

For us, we need to represent characters who our audiences can recognise, so we need to change ourselves to have enough characteristics which they will see and know.

Here are some methods you can use:

Character approached through the body shape

We saw in **Bodies** (*above*), that by changing shape we start to react, think, feel and sound different. So you can easily start to search for the body of your character – is it open or closed? is it angular or flowing? which part of the body is in prominence? etc.

Start to move it in the space until it feels right. For more extreme characters e.g. frail, old people, this may be a big change in your body. For others it may be just adding a little tension in the jaw, or shortening your steps, raising your shoulders or something similar.

Character approached through Breathing

Every character will have a slightly different breathing pattern, long breaths or short sharp breaths, frequent held breaths, shallow breathing, irregular breathing etc.

Walk neutrally in the room thinking about your character and try to let the breathing he/she will have enter your body. In turn the breathing will affect your walk, your tension etc. and take you closer towards your character.

Character approached through Rhythm

Rather like the breathing, every character will have a different rhythm of movement. Just watch people on the street, how different are the busy, determined people from those who have all the time in the world. How different are the rhythms of children, teenagers, middle aged people and the old. Some have sharp, clipped regular rhythms, others have irregular stop-start rhythms, others have slow and heavy rhythms.

Walk neutrally in the room, thinking about your character. From your neutral rhythm allow your body (particularly the feet) to shift to a rhythm which suits your character. Notice how you feel different from your normal self once you adopt this new rhythm.

Character Hotseating

You will meet "hotseating" again as a technique in rehearsal. Here we use it when a character is already in development to deepen their knowledge of the character, and to help them on the path of discovery. It can be used after one of the body language exercises as people form characters out of body shapes, or when actors are forming character from a written text.

It is a simple technique of interviewing someone about themselves, and is important because it is a cooperative exercise with the group – not a solo discovery.

- Place a chair – the hot seat – in front of the group.
- The person developing the character sits in the hot seat.
- You may ask them to introduce themselves.
- Then anyone in the group can ask questions of them.
- Some questions may relate to areas of the character already known e.g. events which happen in the story or play.
- Most questions, however, should be to build up knowledge we cannot know from the play; about the character's background, likes and dislikes, political persuasions etc.
- The actor has to come up with answers and, surprisingly, they normally do. Some may be answers the actor has already thought about, but many decisions have to be made on the spot, possibly bringing answers from the actor's subconscious.
- If the actor cannot find an answer (this is rare) then at least

she/he knows which areas need consideration or research.

- Of course the art of questioning must be constructive. You are trying help them discover and communicate their character. So don't be over aggressive in your questioning and give them time to answer.

Character journey

This is another way of finding depth and texture in a character.

- Take a big sheet of paper and trace a "map" of all that has brought you to the character you are when the play begins. Just like any map, this journey may show high points in the character's life, low points, danger points and so on. Use pictures, text bubbles, lines, arrows, whatever you like. All details are of interest. You might surprise yourself with some of the details you find.
- Now bring your colleagues to see this "life-map" and, in character of course, tell them your story.
- Tell it in character, which means you may stress some areas and reduce the importance of others.
- Let them question you about it.
- Answer in character.

All this work is like a prolonged character improvisation to help you bring this person to life.

"That sounds fine if I am playing a normal person but what if I am playing a crow, or a god?"
Crows have stories too!
So do gods, lots of them!

Observe and Copy

Perhaps the oldest theatrical art is copying, or mimesis. We looked at this when looking at Bodies (*above*). If you know someone who is like your character, go and spend time with them, or watch them from a distance if that is more appropriate. Use your skills of observation to see how they walk, gesture, speak, react to people, direct their eyes, laugh, scowl etc.

Back in the rehearsal space try to absorb this information into your body to shape your character.

Are you getting close to the character now? You have a feeling of how you are when presenting (becoming) this character, but need to fill out the picture. Try this:

Day in The Life

This takes a little time but is well worth it. Simply imagine, and bring to action, what your character does during the whole day. Decide how your character sleeps and put yourself in that position.

Go through the process of waking, getting up, washing, dressing, eating..... one action after another, making instant decisions.

Of course you don't do the whole day in real time, but look at the key moments: how do they travel? where do they work? where do they go when work is finished? who with? etc etc.

When you get to the moment of going to sleep you will have given a lot of fine detail to the outline you were creating, and you will have done it through your body and actions, not just through internal thought.

NB. If several people are working on characters, the director/ workshop leader can guide the process by calling out key moments, eg:

- Waking Up,
- Breakfast
- Noon
- Three in the afternoon
- Seven in the evening ... etc.

What Animal are you?

Some actors respond fantastically well to this. The idea is simple; decide what animal your character resembles. This might be quite "realistic"- you think your character has the rhythm and movement of a bird (what sort of bird?), or it might be more metaphorical. In some cultures foxes are thought of as cunning, jackals are cowardly, owls are wise etc.

Having made this decision work in your rehearsal space to embody the animal as much as the human body can:

- How does it walk (where is the weight? what is the speed?)
- How does it look around? (high on a rock, from a hole, in the long grass.....?)
- How does it breathe (what rhythm?)
- How does it find food?
- How does it protect itself from predators?
- How does it care for its young?
- How does it (and where does it) settle down to sleep?

By taking all these into the body you come close to the physical dynamics of the animal you have chosen. Keep this moving in the working space.

Now on a count of 10 concentrate all those dynamics into a "normal" human body, keeping rhythms, breathing patterns, eye patterns etc but walking in a recognisable human way.

This can bring new tensions, alertness and physical vocabulary to your character, and give you ways of reacting at key moments in your play.

Feeling The Change

This is a great exercise to feel the difference between you and your character. The difference may be in body shape, voice range and quality, tension, eye-line etc. The important thing is that your character is not you, or at least not the "you" in your normal everyday state.

A simple way to play this exercise is:

- All the actors stand in a circle
- One by one the actors enter the circle
- As they enter they introduce themselves with their real names
- The director or workshop leader then counts a slow 1,2,3,4
- During that count the actor slowly changes into the character
- The character introduces him/herself with the "new" body, voice etc.
- The character returns to the circle, then relaxes
- The rest of the group comment on whether they saw (and heard) the change.
- The next actor enters.........

N.B. If one actor plays more than one character, they should change from actor to character 1 to character 2 to character 3 etc. This will really help them establish the differences between roles, and avoid any confusion from the audience.

VIDYA memorable moments...

Bhikiben was performing in her community and she had to play the role of a character who dies on stage. A woman believed that something had really happened to Bhikiben so she ran up on stage, crying and started shaking her. Through improvisation, the other characters were able to get Bhikiben to tell the woman that she is acting.

Emotion

We are always in some kind of emotional state. On stage we have to identify and re-present the emotional states necessary for our character. Because our stories will tend to be dramatic, from the more extreme parts of life, the emotions will tend to be stronger than on an ordinary day.

And strong emotions can affect us deeply, so we have to be careful when re-discovering emotions for the stage.

VIDYA memorable moments...

Bhikiben: After performing the play 'Munni', a well-known Gujarati television actress came onto the stage and performed her intervention. During the rape scene in 'Munni', she slapped the actor that was playing the character of the factory owner who was trying rape her. As an actress, she believed that the acting performed by the VIDYA member was real.

We have to be aware of the emotions but we must not allow the emotions to take control of us and, potentially, damage us. In other words we are "playing" the emotions.

There are some types of actor who try to totally re-create the emotion and others who say that you should be feeling the emotion with half of your being, but thinking of tonight's dinner with the other half – in other words keep yourself rooted in reality while playing the emotion.

Certainly we have to be aware enough to remember our words, our moves on stage etc. so the emotions cannot be allowed to take control. If we are not careful with people who have never worked with their emotions, as actors must, they can be overwhelmed by them and be very upset. So we have to work carefully, knowing what we are doing and why we are doing it.

The following is a good way for beginners to learn to play emotions without them becoming too strong to control:

Visualisation

- Walk around the room as neutrally as possible. Be aware how you feel. Try to let go of any traces of emotions which are stopping you being neutral.

- Stop in this state. Close your eyes. Try to see just blackness.

- Now start to imagine – visualise - someone in a particular emotion, for example, fear.

- Allow an image of that person to appear in the blackness of your closed eyes. The person is not very close, perhaps in the next room or along a corridor.

- The person is not you. But they are 100% in this emotion.

- Watch them in your imagination. Observe the rhythm of their movements, the tension, the gestures, the eyes.

- Keep your eyes closed and start to copy those features, until you are "acting" what you see in your head. It is your image, so you can always be in control of it.

- Open the eyes while still keeping those things in your body. You may feel a little of that emotion – that is quite normal, but as you are copying something you saw at a distance you will be able to keep the emotion under control.

- Move around the room exploring those movements and tensions and rhythms as the outward signs of the emotion.

Now repeat that exercise with other emotions:

- Love – (there are many sorts of love),
- Anger,
- Joy,
- Jealousy,
- Pride,
- Sadness, etc.

As we explore this world we need to create scenes in which an emotion will provoke a further emotion. Reaction is as important as action. Below is an exercise to help develop our skills in conveying an emotion and reacting to an emotion through a safe exercise with clear boundaries, guided by instructions from the facilitator. It is quite long (minimum 45 minutes) and intense and should only be explored by a group who have worked through some basic training first, such as the steps outlined above. The facilitator should make sure that participants stay in control of what they are doing.

Acting and reacting to emotion

- Participants divide into pairs, A and B, stand opposite each other with at least 2 metres between them, they are neutral and making eye contact with each other.
- With a large group (more than 16) split the group in two, ask some participants to watch and then swap over. They will learn a lot just by watching the others.
- A is going to play a character who is strongly experiencing the emotion of 'anger'. B is going to play a character who reacts to what A does through any emotion they feel is right. B therefore is going to play from a range of emotions. B's reaction to A's anger may be joy, it may be fear, it may be apathy, it may also be anger, it may be a mixture of these and B's emotional state may change at any point.

- It is important that the actors are clear that they are playing characters, there is some distance from themselves, although of course they will draw from their own experience.

- A is only going to play the emotion in the way the facilitator instructs them to.

- First - A must convey the emotion of anger only through their breathing. They must be careful not to convey this emotion through their eyes or body and they must not make any sound. They may only express anger through breathing.

- B reacts, in any way they feel, but only through breathing.

- Allow this to continue until the emotion is conveyed very clearly through the breath and B's reactions are strong. Someone entering the space should be able to feel a great deal of tension in the atmosphere.

- Continue from breathing, without stopping, A now conveys the emotion of anger only through eyes and breath. They must be careful not to convey anger through anything other than their breath and eyes.

- B reacts, also only through breath and eyes.

- When the emotion is convincing and is being played powerfully, you can move on.

- Now A conveys anger through breath, eyes and their body. B also reacts through these means. Neither A nor B may move around the room or speak yet. But they can experiment with different movements and gestures from where they are standing.

- When the pairs are ready to move on, A may now convey anger through breath, eyes, body positions and through moving around the space, B may react through the same means. The actors are now starting to develop a scene.

- As the pairs are working in silence ask them to start thinking in more detail about what characters they are playing, what their relationship is to each other, where they are, what they want, why A is so angry and what has happened to lead up to this point etc.

- Finally A may use breath, eyes, body shape, movement and speech. B may react. The two are now in a dramatic scene with words.

- After the scene, swap over tasks. B is going to act. A is going to react to B. Guide the pairs through the same process as they did above, this time with new characters, again with the emotion of anger.

- Check with the pairs, they may need a short break to talk and reflect on what has just happened before they go on to the next stage.

- Do the same again with a character experiencing the emotion of sadness with both players having a chance to act and react.

- Finally do the same again with a character experiencing the emotion happiness with both players acting and reacting.

- Have a discussion. How did the exercise feel, what did they discover, what surprised them, which physical technique was most helpful, which characters did they imagine they were playing, what situations were they in, what did they want, what issues came up, who had more power, are there any characters or stories we can use here in our plays in the community? etc.

When you start to create and rehearse the scenes for the plays you will perform in your communities, you can come back to these exercises and apply them to the characters the group will be playing.

As a facilitator, and later as a director of theatre, when working with actors and acting, always watch and ask yourself "Do I believe the performance I am watching and hearing? Do I believe the characters?" If not, then you need to encourage the actor to find a helpful way of making what they are doing, more convincing.

Short stories, scenes and plays

Many of the training games and exercises in previous chapters are excellent starting points for making stories, scenes and plays. Here are a few techniques which take this work even further. This chapter suggests ways to develop skills in constructing stories, improvising scenes and developing short plays.

Constructing Stories

Most theatre tells a story. The great theatre director, Peter Brook, described a theatre company as a "multi-headed story teller". You are now ready to develop stories which may form the basis of your pieces of theatre. To make a basic dramatic story you need to introduce the characters, their desires must be expressed, there will be a conflict of desires and the story will reach some point of crisis which may or may not be resolved.

In all of the following exercises, make a note of the characters, desires, locations, objects, emotions, themes and issues which emerge. They may provide you with rich material for creating a play for your communities.

Story circle
Aim: To construct a dramatic story as a group
Mood: Thoughtful and focused
Level. Intermediate to advanced
Number of people: 3 - 30
Time: 1 minute per person

Directions:

- The group sits in a circle to make a story together.

- One member of the group begins by offering a sentence. The next person takes the story forward by giving another sentence which connects to the one before. Then the next person, and so on, until the last person in the circle brings the story to an end.

- Participants should be encouraged to listen carefully to what has been said before, paying attention to who the characters are, what their desires are, where the story is located, which objects are significant in the story etc. Each player should stay within the world of the story, building on what the participants before them have offered.

- Sometimes groups can tend to make the exercise easier for themselves by offering a list or a stream of events. This will mean the story is not dramatic. In drama the story usually needs to build to some point of conflict. Encourage your group to offer clear characters who have strong desires. Let the story explore how the characters' desires are in conflict.

- Try the exercise a few times in order to have an opportunity to build the group's skills and also discover useful material.

Fortunately / Unfortunately

Aim: To practise creating a dramatic story where a series of problems are identified and overcome

Mood: Thoughtful and focused

Level: Intermediate to advanced

Number of people: 3-30

Time: 10-15 minutes

Directions:

- Prepare by trying the exercise above – 'story circle'.

- This time, the first person begins the story. The next person in the circle will continue the story but must begin the sentence with the word 'unfortunately'... The next person in the circle must continue the story, starting with the word 'fortunately', the next person 'unfortunately' and so on until the story comes to an end.

- Working with 'fortunately' 'unfortunately' will develop a sense of dramatic tension in the story. It will also guide the group to discover material which identifies problem situations for the characters and will explore how these problems are overcome and solved, which is of course the purpose of all Theatre for Development work.

- This exercise may need to be adapted to suit the language your group works in.

VIDYA playing 'Fortunately / Unfortunately':
Rekha and Bhikiben:

Unfortunately – A tree fell while I was walking on the street

Fortunately – the tree missed me

Unfortunately – the electricity line went down

Fortunately – I remembered that I have a mobile phone

Unfortunately – I heard a small child crying inside the fallen tree

Fortunately – I dialed my friend's number

Unfortunately – the child was crying and I wasn't able to help

Fortunately – I dialed a helpline

Unfortunately – I wasn't able to tell them exactly where I was

Fortunately – I talked with the child who told me the address

Unfortunately – It started raining

Fortunately – The ambulance arrived and the rescuers helped get the child out of the tree

Unfortunately – When I saw, he was bleeding extensively and had fainted...

Fortunately – The rescuers were able to send her to the hospital

Stories from objects

Aim: To construct stories with the use of objects

Mood: Thoughtful, imaginative, focused

Level: Advanced

Number of people: 3-15 (split a bigger group in two)

Time: 15-45 minutes (depending on group size)

What you will need: A bag of objects which will spark the group's imagination. These objects may belong to the group, they may have been found or bought in the area the community is based in, there may also be unusual, unfamiliar objects which awaken other possibilities. These objects must not be seen before the exercise, the bag must be re-sealable and you must not be able to see inside.

Directions:

• The group plays 'story circle' above to prepare.

· This time the participants are not restricted to just one sentence, they may offer a few sentences each.

• The participants begin their section of the story by placing a hand in the bag and without looking they produce an object. This object will inspire their storytelling. They must use the object in some way in the story.

• The next person takes an object, continues the story, building in his/her object. And so on....

• As before, the group's story must make sense. The participants must listen carefully to what has happened before.

Why did we suggest these story-making exercises?

In all of these exercises the participants will suggest stories which are quite spontaneous and have not been pre-planned. Through working in this way, character types, character desires, locations, objects, issues and themes which are relevant to your peer group's lives, and therefore relevant to your community, will come to the surface in a very spontaneous way without the need for you as a facilitator to bring an agenda. For example, if the theme of AIDS is relevant to the group, it may be expressed in these exercises. If witch doctors are significant in your community, they may appear in a story. These techniques also provide space for raising issues that you did not know were relevant to the group. The element of surprise in all of these exercises releases creativity. Creative work arises from surprises.

Be Open to **Surprises!**

After creating spontaneous stories, we suggest taking a traditional myth or folk tale from your community and bringing it to life dramatically. Here is one way of doing that:

Show and tell the story (starting with myths and fables)

Aim: To retell traditional stories from a new perspective and bring them to life dramatically

Mood: Physically active

Level: Intermediate to advanced

Number of people: 5-30

Time: 15-20 minutes

What you will need: You may want to have simple storytelling objects available such as cloth, sticks, boxes or stools strong enough to stand on or build with.

Directions:

• The group sits in a circle. The storyteller stands.

• The storyteller slowly begins to tell the story. At each point in the action participants jump up, enter the circle, and create either a still or moving image which expresses that element of the story

• Begin by using a traditional folk tale. After the exercise ask the group to identify the problems raised in the story. Now try the exercise again but telling it from the point of view of hidden characters, or characters who are not traditionally given a voice in the story.

> **VIDYA show and tell story:**
>
> **Storyteller: It was monsoon season, and the rain poured down hard...**
> *- A person gets up and plays the rain-*
> **Storyteller: ...on the busy streets of the capital city...**
> *- A person plays a child playing in a puddle, another 3 play a rickshaw, a motorbike and a car, and a police officer guiding the traffic in the busy city - .*
> **Storyteller: The king decreed...**
> *A person gets up and plays the king, another plays his robes and crown... and so on.*

Why did we suggest Show and Tell the story from myths and fables?

A local myth or fable will often provide rich imagery to inspire performance. Performing such well-known stories in the community will also be an instantly accessible way of communicating with your audience. Local traditional stories also often reveal social structures, values and stereotypes which may reinforce inequalities and prejudices in the community. Therefore telling such a story from the point of view of someone who is marginalised or oppressed is an excellent approach to raising debate in the community and challenging social problems.

Blind Men and Elephant Game (but don't tell people the name of this game before playing it!)

Aim: Team building, Improvisation, imagination, non-judgemental playing, non-verbal communication

Mood: Investigative

Level: Advanced

Number of People: 5-20

Time: 10-12 minutes

Directions:

- Send everyone outside the room except for three or four people.

- The facilitator tells the people in the room that there is a very dirty elephant in the room and they have to clean it without saying a word. They consult on how to do it and begin. They keep their eyes closed while carrying out their actions.

- Those outside the room do not know what the task is.

- The facilitator quietly tells one individual from outside the room to enter and take a ten second look at what the individuals in the room are doing, after which he/she must help those involved in the action by adding to what they are doing – both eyes closed and no talking or asking questions – he/she becomes the next blind man.

- The facilitator continues this with the remaining participants – telling them one by one to quietly take a ten second look at the people inside and then go in, take a position and help them without talking and with their eyes closed and without copying existing movements.

- When everyone has entered and found their place in the action, the facilitator stops the game. Everyone opens their eyes to see the whole room and everything happening in it.

- Everyone sits in a circle to share their experience, and describe what they thought they were doing

- The people initially "washing the elephant" should speak last, and disclose that they were washing an elephant, give the group a few seconds to think over their actions and how they helped.

• Discussion.

Why did we suggest 'the elephant' game?

We all see things differently, and have to make assumptions about what is happening.

This game gives participants the chance to realise that a situation is not always what you first perceive it to be. This game allows the participants to think with their bodies and helps in the development of the group's analytical skills. Improvisation and imagination are used to determine a person's perception. Once determined, the process of why that person thought as they did and why they did the actions they did, can be discussed. Determining a scenario in the span of a few seconds, and then taking part in that process, helps the group question why they thought what they did and if they could have seen things differently.

This game is based on.......

The Blind Men and the Elephant

A number of disciples went to the Buddha and said, "Sir, there are living here in Savatthi many wandering hermits and scholars who indulge in constant dispute, some saying that the world is infinite and eternal and others that it is finite and not eternal, some saying that the soul dies with the body and others that it lives on forever, and so forth. What, Sir, would you say concerning them?"

The Buddha answered, "Once upon a time there was a certain raja who called his servant and said, 'Good fellow, go and gather together in one place all the men of Savatthi who were born blind... and show them an elephant.' 'Very good, sire,' replied the servant, and he did as he was told. He said to the blind men assembled there, 'Here is an elephant,' and to one man he presented the head of the elephant, to another its ears, to another a tusk, to another the trunk, the foot, back, tail, and tuft of the tail, saying to each one that that was the elephant."

When the blind men had felt the elephant, the raja went to each of them and said to each, 'Well, blind man, Tell me, what sort of thing is an elephant?'"

Thereupon the men who were presented with the head answered, 'Sire, an elephant is like a pot.' And the men who had observed the ear replied, 'An elephant is like a winnowing basket.' Those who had been presented with a tusk said it was a ploughshare. Those who knew only the trunk said it was a plough; others said the body was a granary; the foot, a pillar; the back, a mortar; the tail, a pestle, the tuft of the tail, a brush."

Then they began to quarrel, shouting, 'Yes it is!' 'No, it is not!' 'An elephant is not that!' 'Yes, it's like that!' and so on, till they came to blows over the matter.

The raja was delighted with the scene. "Just so are these preachers and scholars holding various views blind and unseeing... In their ignorance they are, by nature, quarrelsome, wrangling, and disputatious, each maintaining that reality is thus and thus."

UDANA 68-69

Improvising Scenes

What is improvisation?

Improvisation is the practice of acting and reacting, of making and creating, in the moment and in response to a stimulus. This stimulus may be a word, a theme, other people, an object, an environment, a picture, a piece of music, a sound etc. Many performing artists, including dancers and musicians, often improvise. In drama improvisation usually leads to the spontaneous creation of a dramatic scene, with or without words. An improvisation can be a performance in itself.

Improvisation is a skill, one of the most important skills an actor can develop, and is crucial for theatre for development work. Improvisation, by definition, is something where you do not know what is going to happen and the only way you can really know what it is, is by doing it!

> **Savitaben:** In improvisation it is important not to go off the track of the story; try to bring it back if it diverts.

The following exercises enable your group to develop and practise their improvisation skills. So keep your notebook handy and be ready to write down ideas!

When improvising with words, it is important for performers to learn that **how** you say a word or sentence is often as important as **what** you say. Here is an exercise to develop performers' skills, expressing meaning through the voice and gesture.

'A's in an A

Aim: To find expression in sounds, words and dialogue, and to develop imitation skills.

Mood: Lively

Level: Basic

Number of people: 3-30

Time: 10-15 minutes

Directions:

- The group stands in a circle.
- One person steps forward and makes a vowel sound together with a gesture which expresses an emotion or idea. (NB. Vowels might be different in each language; English has aah, ee, oh, ai, oo.)
- The rest of the group copies the sound and gesture exactly.
- Another person steps forward with a vowel sound and gesture, expressing a different intention, the group repeats and so on. Make sure everyone has a few turns.
- Work through all the possible vowel sounds in your language, making sure you find as many variations on how you might express that sound, in volume, tone, speed, length etc.

Extension:

- Once you have worked through sounds. Choose a sentence. Find as many different possible ways of saying that sentence. For example, 'I love you' can be said in many different ways. In English, 'I love you' can be said in such a way that it actually expresses 'I hate you', or 'I want you', or even as a question 'I love you?'.
- Now try one person saying the sentence directly to another person in the room. The second person then responds to what has been said. In this way, a small verbal dialogue begins.

'A's in an A helps participants to discover sounds, words and begin to play with them. Liar's Mime is a game which encourages players to find possible actions in an improvisation. This game works especially well with children.

Liar's mime

Aim: To find actions in improvisation

Mood: Active and fun

Level: Basic

Number of people: 5-30

Time: 10-15 minutes

Directions:

- The group stands in a circle.
- One player goes into the middle and begins an action.
- A second player enters the circle and watches the first player carrying out the action. After a short time, player 2 asks what are you doing?
- Player 1 continues his action and says he is doing something quite different from what he is actually doing. He then leaves the circle
- Player 2 then begins to carry out the action player 1 said he was doing
- Player 3 enters the circle, and asks, what are you doing? And so on...

but playing
football

but riding a
bicycle

but making candles

Here is another exercise to free the participants' imaginations and get them improvising scenes together.

Box of tricks

Aim: Imaginative improvisation with objects

Mood: Varied

Level: Advanced

Number of people: 1-30 people

Time: 10 minutes

Directions:

- The group sits in a circle.
- They are asked to imagine a box of objects in the middle of the room
- One at a time they reach inside the box, draw out an imaginary object and begin to use it in an improvisation.
- They can involve another player in the improvisation with them and the object.

The next exercise is language-based and may need variation according to the language of your group.

Yes but, Yes and, Yes and let's...

Aim: To explore the effect of language through verbal improvisation

Level: Intermediate to advanced

Mood: Gentle, building to active

Number of people: 2-30

Time: 20-30 minutes

Directions:

- The players get into pairs. They are going to improvise short verbal dialogues together.
- Player 1 makes a statement.

- Player 2 responds by beginning their sentence with **"Yes but..."** Player 1 also responds always with "Yes but". The improvisation continues in this way.

- After the pairs have played 'yes but' for a while, let the players find new partners.

- This time player 1 makes a statement or suggestion. Player 2 responds with a sentence which begins *'yes and'*. From this point on, all of the sentences from each of them must begin with 'yes and'.

- Swap partners again. In this version player 1 makes a suggestion. Player 2 responds with *'yes and let's...'* and then the speaker will complete the rest of the sentence. From this point on, all of the sentences from each of them must begin with 'yes and let's...'

- Discuss the effect of these words on the improvisations, the conversations and the mood.

Why did we suggest 'Yes but, Yes and, Yes and let's'?

Generally, in all improvisation, actors should accept ideas that fellow performers present (whether in words or in actions) by always having an attitude of 'yes'. Sometimes this literally means saying 'yes' in the improvisation. This exercise enables us to explore the potential of 'yes'. We have also discovered that sentences with 'yes but' are more likely to cause debate, argument or conflict, sentences with 'yes and' create a more friendly dynamic, conversations with 'yes and let's' encourage you to get up and do something, to take action. It is really useful for performers to learn how the use of language has an effect on relationships in improvisations as well as in real life. This exercise also helps to develop the group's level of literacy and sentence construction.

VIDYA plays Yes but	VIDYA plays... Yes and	VIDYA plays...Yes and let's
Savita and Rani:	**Kalu and Vijay:**	**Sureshbhai and Mehmudaben:**
S: I heard from my friend that today there is a rickshaw strike in the whole city today.	K: The harmonium is broken.	M: I was thinking that we should go to visit the orphanage.
R: Yes but my child is waiting at school for me.	V: Yes and we can get it fixed. V: Yes and we can check the budget to see if we have enough money.	S: Yes and let's go in the afternoon. M: Yes and let's go this Saturday.
S: Yes but how will you get there, it is almost impossible isn't it?	K: Yes and if we don't have enough money we can manage without it.	S: Yes and let's perform a play for them.
R: Yes, but my husband can go and pick them up.	V: Yes and we can use the drum instead of the harmonium.	M: Yes and let's make it fun for them.
S: Yes but does he have a scooter?	K: Yes and the group can follow the beat.	S: Yes and let's find a good artist there.
R: Yes, but it is in the garage for service.	V: Yes and it will be a new experiment.	M: Yes and let's invite them to work with us.
S: Yes but he can ask his boss for the company bus.	K: Yes and we can use cymbals as well.	S: Yes and let's give them training.
R: Yes but the boss might not allow him.	V: Yes and we can use the mouth organ too.	M: Yes and let's get them to make a play and perform it.
S: Yes but he has a good reputation.		

End with a question

Aim: Verbal Improvisation skills

Level: Advanced

Mood: Potentially varied

Number of people: 2-30

Time: 10-15 minutes

Directions:

- In pairs. One player makes a statement. The second player must respond in anyway they choose, but they must end their response with a question. Player one responds to that question, and in turn ends their response with a question. And in this way the improvisation continues endlessly!

Why did we suggest 'end with a question'?

When working with words, it can sometimes be difficult to imagine how to keep the improvisation going. One helpful way of keeping a dialogue going is by asking a question. This technique can be particularly useful in interactive theatre.

The following two exercises lift improvisation practice from an exercise to the level of actual performance.

I've got something to tell you

Aim: To discover the dramatic power of entrances, exits, and the desire to tell

Level: Intermediate to advanced

Mood: Medium to high energy

Number of people: 2-30

Time: Varies according to the size of the group

What you will need: A room with a door, or a space with a curtain or screen to enter from.

Directions:

- The group is the audience, all facing a door, curtain or some kind of entrance to the space.

- One at a time the performers go behind the entrance. When they are ready they enter.

- One at a time the performers experiment with entering the space. Do they slowly curl their fingers around the curtain and draw it back? Do they look through the curtain showing only their head at first? Do they suddenly open the door and run in, look at the audience, run out again, and run back in again? Do they wander in casually? Do they walk in sharply? Do they slam the door behind them, close it gently? Do they walk in backwards? Do they fall into the space? Do they crawl in? Do they walk in breathing out through their mouth? Do they walk in breathing in sharply? Do they walk in holding their breath?... The possibilities are endless and each choice of entrance helps to tell a story.

- Do the same with exits.

- Once you have practised entrances and exits ask all the participants to think of something which their character is desperate to tell someone. The information that they want to share can be good news or bad news, it can be something they have known for a long time or something they have just discovered, the most important thing is that the character has a strong desire to tell.

- One at a time the performers enter the space to tell this news, their news will of course affect the way they enter.

- However they do not tell their news straight away. It's a kind of game, to see how long they can hold in their news and not tell anyone, but still keep the audience very interested.

- Eventually the performer will tell their news. But the aim is to see how long they can keep their audience waiting, so that the audience are as desperate to hear the news as the performers are to tell it.

- These scenarios will give you lots of ideas for plays to take to your community as well as building within the performers a sense of urgency about the theatre that they make.

Advertisements

Aim: Improvisation, devising and performing around issues

Level: Intermediate, building to advanced

Mood: Medium to high energy

Number of people: 4-30 people

Time: 30-45 minutes

Directions:

• The group gets into pairs, and label themselves A and B.

• A and B choose a product or project they would each like to promote. This could be related to the issue that your Theatre For Development peer group is addressing. For example it could be new school books for children, or condoms reducing the risk of contracting HIV, or a new support group for people wanting to end an addiction.

• A is the door-to-door sales person. B is at home. A tries to sell or promote their product or project to B.

• After the improvisation the pairs can have a small discussion on the sales technique and how the improvisation went.

• The pairs swap over. B now tries to convince A to accept what they are selling.

• They have a small discussion.

• The pairs now spend fifteen minutes working together to create an advertisement promoting the product or project. Like a television advert they can use music, a song, catch phrases, dance, rap etc.

• When the pairs have finished creating their advertisement they present it to another pair in the group, and swap over.

• Feedback on the task.

Why did we suggest 'Advertisements'?

This is a fun exercise which guides our group from free improvisation all the way through to devising and then actually performing. It is therefore very useful for groups with little experience of theatre. This exercise is also a great way for your group to become very clear about the issues they are addressing through their work.

The Vidya group often use advertisements in their performances in the community, as well as interactive plays and workshops. Advertisements are a useful form as you can incorporate song, dance, memorable catch phrases and are a quick way of getting a message across. We do not encourage using advertisements to 'preach' to your audience about what is right and wrong. However there are sometimes useful pieces of information that you may want to communicate. For example an advertisement could be used after a play addressing child sexual abuse, to inform the audience of a free telephone helpline for children.

This next exercise works well after the group has practised with easier exercises such as 'Complete the Image', 'Liar's Mime', 'Yes but, yes and, yes and let's' and 'End with a question'.

Walk the Line

Aim: To clear your head of your "internal censor" and be creative in the moment

Level: Advanced

Mood: Fun but scary

Number of people: 1-30

Time: 10-20 minutes

What you will need: an open space and a line on the floor (tape or chalk or a rope)

Directions:

- In the largest space you have, make a line on the ground. If your space is small you may work on a diagonal and have the line at right angles to it, half way across your space.
- Everyone gathers at one end of the room.
- One by one they walk towards the line and cross it.
- As you cross the line you enter a "new" space
- The new space has endless possibilities. It could be burning

hot, a sticky floor, full of flies, a tightrope, floating in space etc They can be emotional spaces, spaces in which your body changes, anything your imagination gives you.

- The only rule is that you must wait until you cross that line to discover what the new space is.
- Therefore there must be no planning before you get to the line – no thinking what you are going to do.
- When one person has crossed the line, inhabited the new space for a few moments and exited it, the next person can approach the line, and so on until everyone has tried it.
- If you find that your mind is racing with ideas and not allowing you to create in the moment of crossing the line you can try:
- Run towards the line
- Jump 10 times before starting to walk towards the line
- Sing a loud "aaaah" until you get to the line
- All these are ways to avoid you pre-planning, and allowing the instant associations to emerge.
- Try it several times until it becomes easier to allow your imagination the freedom it needs, and you can ignore that inner voice which is telling you what to do, or not to do.
- Trust yourself.
- Surprise yourself.

Variation:

You can draw two lines, parallel and a few metres apart. Walk to the first one as above, cross it, be in a different space until you get to the second line, cross it and be in yet another space. You will be so involved in being in your first discovered space, you certainly won't have time to pre-think the next space!

Remember:

Only you will know if you are pre-planning or if you are allowing your spontaneity to work, so be honest with yourself.

Why did we suggest 'The Line'?

A lot of people never allow themselves to be spontaneously creative because of the "inner censor" who tries to limit them to what is safe, acceptable, clever etc. To escape that judge is very important because so many ideas will start to flow, and your ability to act/react in the moment will be strengthened.

Developing Plays

Many Theatre For Development groups may never have seen a play. Once the group members have awakened their imaginations through storytelling, and have done plenty of improvising, you can move on to exercises which give the participants an understanding of what a play is.

So, what is a play?

A play is a story which has at least one character who communicates with actions, and often with words, to an audience. The characters in the play have a conflict of desires. They usually want something, or don't want something, which contradicts something someone else wants.   The conflict is usually built up through one or more scenes and often reaches a climax point. The play is located in one or more settings, into which the characters enter and exit. Often by the end of the play the characters' lives have changed in some way, which may arouse thought (and often emotion) in the audience when performed. Plays are usually written into a script.

The following exercises help to practically demonstrate what a simple play may consist of, and they may also help to generate material for the group to develop.

Two Revelations

Aim: A structured improvisation to develop a short play

Level: Intermediate

Mood: Varied

Number of people: 2-30

Time: 30-45 minutes

Directions:

- The group gets into pairs. They are going to improvise a scene together, through guidance from the facilitator who will give them a clear structure.

- Before they begin, the pairs have 10 minutes to decide 4 things in detail:

  1. Who are they going to play? For example what age are they, which gender, what class and cultural background do they have etc.

  2. What relationship do they have? The relationship between the two characters needs to be one that is significant and important to them both, they need to care about the relationship. For example are they family, old friends, partners, close work colleagues...?

  3. Where are they going to meet? For example are they meeting in a house? If so, whose house is it? Which room are they in? If it is in the street, what time of day is it, what is the weather like?...

  4. Who is at the meeting place first? One person is at the meeting place, the other is going to join.

- The pairs have decided these four things together. However, they must decide the next piece of information alone, without talking to each other. It is crucial that the pairs do not discuss this next point. Individually, the performers are each going to decide on a piece of news they are going to reveal to their partner during the course of the improvisation. This is why it is important that the relationship is significant to them. If I tell my local shop keeper that I am going to have a baby he may congratulate me but it will mean nothing to him. If I tell my husband that I am going to have a baby but we both know he has been sterilised and it cannot belong to him – a huge drama will ensue! And drama is what we are looking to create!

- After each performer has decided on their news, remind the group that it is very important that they do not reveal their news until the facilitator says they can.

- The facilitator will now guide the group through the improvisation in the pairs. Everyone can perform at the same time, no one will be watching them at this stage.

- Ask the pairs to create the space they agreed upon through using any objects which are available (e.g. stools, cloths, cushions, boxes, sticks etc).

- Ask the player who was going to be at the meeting place first to enter and take their place, and begin whatever action they are involved in.

- After a while ask the second player to enter the scene and begin to improvise. The pairs do not reveal their news until they are instructed to by the facilitator.

- After a few minutes of improvising, the facilitator calls out "reveal your first piece of news". Then one of the players reveals their news.

- There is a reaction to the news.

- Then the facilitator calls "second piece of news"

- There is further reaction.

- Finally the facilitator calls 'one person leaves". One of the performers exits the scene.

- After the improvisation, ask the group to sit in a circle and share who they were, where they were, and what happened.

- If pairs want to show their scenes they can, but do not have to do so.

Variation:

- Play as above. The only difference is that instead of inventing and then revealing a piece of news, the two pieces of news will arrive by letter (delivered by the facilitator), and neither player will know what is in the letter before the improvisation.

Why did we suggest Two Revelations?

For participants who have very little experience of drama, 'Two Revelations' offers a structure which is typical of many plays:

- There is a defined space.
- Characters enter that space.
- The characters have, or develop, a significant relationship.
- Something is revealed in the play or something happens to the characters which will change their relationship and their lives forever.
- Characters exit the space.

The themes which arise from playing 'Two Revelations' will also often reveal the issues that are relevant to that group. For example if HIV is disclosed in many of the scenes, you can be sure HIV is a relevant issue to explore further. The exercise will potentially give you rich material from which to build a play.

The exercise offers participants the opportunity to gain confidence and improvise a short play over a longer period of time without the pressure of being watched.

Playmaking sequence

Aim: To increase the participants' understanding of the various elements which go into creating a stage play

Mood: Concentrated, studious

Level: Advanced

Number of people: 8-30

Time: 30-45 minutes

What you will need: Paper and pens/pencils

Directions:

- The group gets into pairs, in a large circle.
- Each pair has a piece of paper and a pen. One person is going to write down the ideas.

- The pairs think of five actions (verbs) which are going to happen in this play, involving two characters and one place.
- The pairs write down the five simple actions (verbs), two characters and the place on a piece of paper in very clear handwriting. They must make sure there is plenty of space before and between the words and the sentences. They do not need to put a full stop at the end of the sentences. For example:

Two characters, one place, five actions:

1. Ahmed   walks   into   the   reception   of   the government   building

2. Mrs   Jain   turns   the   page   of   her   newspaper

3. Ahmed   turns   off   the   fan

4. Mrs   Jain   stands   up

5. Ahmed   walks   out

- The pairs each pass their piece of paper to the pair on their left, and take the paper from the pair on their right.
- The pairs read the new piece of paper. They must now add descriptive words (adverbs) into two or three sentences to describe the pace the actions are carried out in. For example:

Two characters, one place, five actions, pace:

1. Ahmed   walks   into   the   reception   of   the government   building

2. <u>Very   slowly</u>   Mrs   Jain   turns   the   page of   her   newspaper

3. Ahmed   turns   off   the   fan.

4. Mrs   Jain   <u>suddenly</u>   stands   up

5. Ahmed   walks   out

- The pairs each pass the piece of paper to the pair on their left, and take a new piece of paper from the pair on their right.
- The pairs read the new piece of paper. They must now add <u>adjectives or adverbs</u> into two or three of the sentences to describe the emotions in which the actions are carried out . For example:

Two characters, one place, five actions, pace, emotions:

1. Ahmed   walks   <u>fearfully</u>   into   the   reception of   the   government   building

2. Very   slowly   Mrs   Jain   <u>sadly</u>   turns   the page   of   her   newspaper

3. Ahmed   <u>angrily</u>   turns   off   the   fan

4. Mrs   Jain   suddenly   stands   up   <u>afraid</u>

5. Ahmed   walks   out ,   <u>happy</u>

· Again each pair passes the piece of paper to the pair on their left, and take a new piece of paper from the pair on their right.

The pairs read the new piece of paper. They must now add <u>words</u> into two or three of the sentences to describe what the costumes and setting of this short play look like. For example

> **Two characters, one place, five actions, pace, emotions, costumes and setting:**
>
> 1.   Ahmed   walks   fearfully   into   the   reception of   the   government   building   <u>wearing</u>   <u>ragged</u> <u>brown</u>   <u>shorts</u>
>
> 2.   Very   slowly   Mrs   Jain   sadly   turns   the   page of   her   <u>gigantic</u>   newspaper
>
> 3.   Ahmed   angrily   turns   off   the   <u>tiny</u>   <u>modern</u> <u>pink</u>   <u>desk</u>   fan
>
> 4.   Mrs   Jain   suddenly   stands   up   in   <u>her</u>   <u>designer</u> <u>suit</u>   afraid
>
> 5.   Ahmed   walks   out,   happy,   <u>through</u>   <u>the</u>   <u>revolving</u> <u>door</u>

- Again the pairs pass the piece of paper to the pair on their left, and take a new piece of paper from the pair on their right.
- The pairs read the new piece of paper. They must now act out the play they have read incorporating costume and set as much as they are able to do (they or may not be the pair who wrote the first version of the play). They should rehearse the scene a few times, improving it each time. Finally each pair presents their short play to each other. The group feed back what they noticed about how the plays emerged from the original ideas.

Variation:
- Words can be added at the first stage. Or the players can improvise dialogue at the last stage.

Why did we suggest this 'Playmaking' sequence?

This exercise gives participants a good idea of the different elements, roles and their functions, which go into creating a play. First of all there will be the idea for the play, which will indicate the characters, their wants, dialogue, their actions, the location etc. In commercial theatre these ideas will often come from the **playwright**, in Theatre for Development and Community Theatre the play often comes from the group. Then in Theatre For Development a member or members of the group will decide how this play should be performed (for example the pace, the emotions etc), in commercial theatre this role is often taken by a **director**. Then the group will decide what the setting and costume should look like. In commercial theatre this role is often taken by the **designer**. Finally the **actors** will bring their interpretation to the characters, and they will rehearse and then perform the play to the audience who will watch it, interpret it, be affected by it.

Through this exercise the group will experience that creating a play, whether in commercial theatre or theatre for development, is always a **collaborative process**. The ownership for this process is not with one person, but many people, including the audience. This fact is especially important for the group to recognise before they go on to make plays which are inspired by their own personal experience. Often it can be hard for individuals to realise that, although the story may have been their idea or from their experience, the nature of theatre means other people will contribute to it and develop it, so that the play, when it is eventually performed, may look quite different from how you first imagined it would. Theatre making is a series of surprises.

Enjoy Them

Closing exercises

This type of work can raise the body temperature, heighten emotions, and require a great deal of personal investment and energy from the participants as well as giving them many things to think about. Therefore it is often useful to offer the group a way of cooling down, gathering their thoughts, affirming who they are, what they have achieved and preparing them to go back into everyday life outside. The following exercises offer a way of closing the session. The exercises may also provide the facilitator an opportunity to find out how the group are, what they want and what could be improved for next time.

Pass the pulse

Aim: A sense of unity and calm, fun

Mood: Gentle, focused

Level: Basic

Number of people: 3-30 people

Time: 5 minutes

Directions:

- The group stands or sits in a circle holding hands.
- The facilitator begins by gently squeezing the hand of the person next to them.
- This person then sends this pulse on by squeezing the hand of the person next to them.
- The pulse can go in any direction.

- Work at it until the pulse is running easily around the circle and not being blocked or delayed anywhere.
- Gradually build up so that there is more than one pulse going around the room

Relaxation

Aim: To relax!

Mood: Gentle, focused

Level: Basic

Number of people: 1-30 people

Time: 10 minutes

Directions:

- The group lie down on their backs, each in their own space. Their arms are by their sides and their legs stretched out straight or, for people who require more lower back support, with the soles of their feet on the ground and knees up.
- The facilitator guides the group and talks them through an experience which will make them feel comfortable and relaxed. This may depend on where you are in the world but here is one we like:
- Imagine you are lying on a beach in a comfortable temperature.
- Feel your body give its weight to the sand.
- Listen to the gentle sound of the waves.
- The tide is coming in. Feel the water gently touching your feet and lifting the weight.
- Feel the water moving up your calves, gently lifting them.
- Feel the water moving up over your knees to your thighs, lifting them.
- And so on, body part by body part until the water is right up your body to the back of your head and is lifting your weight. You have given all your weight and your tensions to the (imaginary) water.

Gifts

Aim: Affirmation

Mood: Gentle, focused

Level: Basic

Number of people: 1-30 people

Time: 10 minutes

Directions:

- The group sit in a circle.
- They are asked to imagine a huge pile of beautifully wrapped colourful gifts of many different shapes and sizes which is in the middle of the circle. In the pile there is an individual gift for each participant which has their name written on it. The gift contains what they need in order to be the Theatre For Development practitioner they want to be.
- Some relaxing music is played.
- One at a time members of the group are invited to go into the middle and find the gift with their name written on it.
- They take the gift and return to their place and begin to unwrap it and discover what is inside. They do not need to tell anyone else what their gift is.
- Once everyone has the gifts they need, the group is told there are more gifts. One at a time they are invited to find a gift for someone else and hand it to them.

Freeing the birds

Aim: A closing ritual to bring our thoughts to the world outside

Mood: Gentle, thoughtful

Level: Basic

Number of people: 1-30 people

Time: 10 minutes

Directions:

- The group stands in a circle.
- The facilitator mimes having a flapping bird in the hands.

- These imaginary birds are passed around the circle one at a time until everyone has their own bird flapping in their hands.
- The facilitator says that these birds are all of the skills they have gained during the training.
- The group imagines what the birds represent for them personally.
- After some time to reflect, the group is invited to move together towards a window or door and on the count of 3, the 'birds' are set free.

Why did we suggest 'Freeing the Birds'?

This exercise is a practical symbol of how the group will be using their skills in the community, and reminds them that everything we have learned, we shall take outside and share.

Repeat a warm up exercise

You may also choose to simply repeat one of the exercises you may have used in a warm-up as a way of closing the session. Exercises we have mentioned in previous chapters which are particularly useful for closing include 'Counting 1-10' which helps to focus the group mind, 'Hug tag' which is a safe way of expressing affection and support through a game and 'Group yes' which allows the group to decide how they would like to close. Singing songs together is also a very life-affirming way of closing the session.

Talking time

Lastly, simply giving the group an opportunity to speak one at a time in an uninterrupted way, can be a very useful way of allowing people time to wind down and reflect, it will also enable the facilitator to gain some feedback. You might ask the group to share -

- Something they liked about the session
- Something they found difficult

- Something they would like for next time
- A question they would like to ask

Some groups are very skilled at listening to each other, but for most of us it is a skill we need to practise. It can be useful to have a "talking stick". Whoever is holding the stick has the right to speak. No one may interrupt the participant who has the talking stick. Participants should be encouraged to speak but not to go on for longer than 5 minutes. Participants should also be encouraged to begin with 'I'. This may help people to speak honestly about what they felt, to take ownership for their own feelings, and not to blame anyone else for how they felt. Speaking from 'I' also helps us to avoid conflict.

TRAINING SESSION 3

Aim :   Beginners' drama training for a new Theatre
             For Development peer group
Number : 15
Time :   3 hours (with a break)

Preparation:

Name game

Newspaper game

Sounds and hands

Exploration:
Image of the word

Improvisation Circle

Discussion

Break
Creation:
Devising short scenes arising from discussion ideas

- Presentation:
Present the scenes and offer feedback

Conclusion:
Name Game

TRAINING SESSION 4
Aim: Intermediate drama – those with some experience
Number:2 +
Time: 2 hours

Preparation:
Voice and body exercises

Duels

Sounds in pairs

Exploration:
Complete the image – words and improvisation

Discussion

Creation:
Devising

Presentation:
Present their scenes

Conclusion:
Pass the pulse

Training for Forum Theatre

Forum Theatre is one of the key tools we use in Theatre for Development and we shall be discussing it in detail later, but we do need some training in Forum Theatre before we create the plays and think how they will be used in our communities.

What is Forum Theatre?

A forum is a place for debate. Forum Theatre is a theatrical debate where the audience finds solutions to problems and oppressions affecting their lives through interactive performance. Augusto Boal introduced the term 'Forum Theatre' and he has done a huge amount to develop and write about this crucial technique. Many of the games and exercises in this section are based on his work, and we recommend reading his books and books about his work (see bibliography at the back of this book).

This kind of work is also known by other names in other parts of the world – 'intervention theatre' is another general term for it. All such plays have the following basic features:

- A play is presented to an audience.

- The play is one which focuses on a central character who is oppressed (or made powerless) by other characters and situations in the play. Power is used against them to stop them from getting what they want or to make them do something they do not want to do. Therefore there is conflict between the central character's desires and those of people (and institutions) more powerful than them.

- The problem that the central character is experiencing is one that is not unique to them, but is recognisable in the wider community.

- The audience must be able to identify with the problem faced by the central character.

- The central character tries hard to deal with the problem in the play, and to fight his / her oppression.

- However, the central character fails to get what they want by the end of the play.

- The central character may reach some kind of crisis point, or tragic ending, as a consequence of the situation.

- After the play there is a short discussion with the audience, identifying what the problem was in the play and how things might have been different. This discussion is led by a facilitator. Boal calls this role the 'joker', who is like a 'joker' in a pack of cards. It has nothing to do with telling jokes!

- The facilitator explains the 'rules' of the Forum Theatre game for what comes next.

- The play is then presented a second time.

- During this presentation any audience member who feels they could do something differently to change the outcome of the play can shout 'stop!' or indicate they want to stop the play, at any time. They are invited by the facilitator to come onto the stage, replace the central character and do whatever they want to change the outcome of the play.

- This moment is called an 'intervention'. Its aim is to make the situation better for the oppressed central character by finding how they can become empowered.

- The other characters in the play react as their characters would react. They do not attempt to make the situation easy for the intervening audience member, they attempt to give real reactions to real problems.

- The audience members who intervene are not stuck within the scenes of the play. They may feel that the character needs to go somewhere we have not been to in the play, or meet someone we have not seen. Therefore new scenes may be improvised on stage.

- As many audience members as possible can come up, one by one, at any point in the play to try and find ways of solving the problem, and breaking the oppression.

- The audience can try whatever they want in order to break the oppression. The only 'rules' are that if they want to try violence they must not make actual physical contact with anyone, only mime it. Secondly they cannot make magical (or hugely improbable) solutions. They may only do what a human being could do.

- Following each 'intervention' the facilitator invites comments from the audience, and they discuss the intervention, whether or not there was progress and what the consequences of the action might be. The audience is invited to share ideas and information with each other.

- At the end of the Forum Theatre session the audience may have found solutions to the problem and a way to break the oppression. What is likely is that the audience will have seen and discussed various alternatives to the oppression and various possibilities to fight it, as well as having had an opportunity to share information.

N.B. The audience member who comes to intervene in the action and rehearse an alternative outcome is sometimes known by the hybrid name "spectactor" a fusion of spectator and actor. We find this a rather awkward word in English and prefer not to use it, however you may come across it.

We have also found that the terms 'oppressor' and 'oppressed' are difficult in some societies. Using words about 'power' or 'powerlessness' may be preferred.

The following exercises are training tools for Forum Theatre. They can be used in the order they have been written down here. In general they increase in depth and difficulty.

Pushing against each other

Aim: To physically warm up and to explore the dynamic between actor and intervening audience member during a Forum Theatre intervention

Mood: High energy

Level: Basic

Number of people: 2-30

Time: 10 mins

Directions:

- The group gets into pairs.
- The pairs place their hands on each other's hands.
- They push against each other using as much force as possible.
- When a player realises their opposition is not as strong as they are, they use less force. If the opposition pushes harder, they use more force.
- Do the same thing back to back, and bottom to bottom.
- Discuss what happens in this exercise and how it works in the same way as Forum Theatre (see 'why did we suggest' this below)..

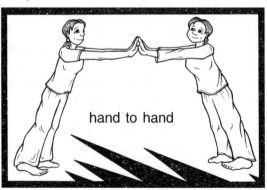

hand to hand

back to back

bottom to bottom

Why did we suggest 'pushing against each other'?

This game represents exactly what happens between an actor and audience member in a Forum Theatre session. The idea is for the actor playing an oppressor to push their will against the will of the audience member (who plays the oppressed), to make the task challenging for the audience, to encourage the audience member to try hard to fight the oppression, yet not to totally overwhelm them either.

One of the aims of Forum Theatre generally is to understand

how power and oppression work, in order to challenge them. One of the key factors which stops individuals challenging an oppressive situation they are experiencing is fear. The next game entitled 'Fear and Protector' offers a good warm-up introduction to exploring the emotion of fear. Despite its title, it is actually also a really fun **dynamic** game which gets people mixing and moving around the room, and it is a good **warm-up** at the start of a training session or workshop.

Fear and protector

Aim: To explore fear and protection as a group

Mood: Exhilaration induced by fear!

Level: Basic

Number of people: 5-30

Time: 10-15 mins

What you will need: A space free of objects

Directions:

- Ask the group members to walk around the room in various directions, not following anyone but taking their own path. The group should keep moving throughout the exercise.

- Whilst they are moving, ask the players to each think of someone in the room but not show that they have chosen them.

- Tell the group the person they have just chosen is going to represent something that they fear. Their task therefore is to try to keep away from the thing that they fear, to try to keep as much distance between themselves and the fear.

- Let this continue for a while. The dynamic in the room will start to change.

- Ask the group members to keep this person as representing the thing they fear, but to now also choose a second person in the room and not show that they have chosen them.

- The second person that they have chosen will now represent the thing that can protect them from their fear. So the aim of the game is now for the participants to try to keep the 'protector' between them and their 'fear'.

- Tension can be added to the game by asking the group to move faster, or counting them down from 10 to 1, saying that by the time you get down to 1 their fear will be at its most extreme. This is a good place to stop the game.
- At the end of the game ask the group to freeze and look at the stage picture they have made.
- They can now point to the people who represented their fear and their protector.
- Ask the group to make observations, for example how did their breathing change, how did their bodies change, what shapes did the group make, how did the game and the roles they played feel etc.

Forum Theatre is, in part, an exploration of power. An individual or an institution in a Forum Theatre play is using its power to oppress our central character. Therefore a crucial part of training for this kind of work is to look at power. The next exercise 'Hypnosis' is a very useful starting point for discussing power. It is also an excellent exercise for concentration, group connection, and physical expression.

Hypnosis

Aim: To explore movement and power

Mood: Intense, focused, movement-based, potentially playful

Level: Basic, intermediate or advanced (the participants define the level)

Number of people: 2-30

Time: 15-20 minutes

Directions:

- Ask the group to get into pairs and to decide who is A and who is B.
- A will place their hand about one hand's distance away from B's face. The bottom of A's hand will be approximately in

line with B's chin, the top of their hand in line with the top of B's forehead.

- Wherever A moves the hand, B will follow (as if they were hypnotised!). Therefore all A's movement must be humanly possible for B to follow.

- The 'A's begin by moving their hands quite slowly, they can then build up until they are gradually moving around the room and moving their hands to different levels and in different directions, in order that both partners begin to explore expressive movement and the limits and potential of their bodies.

- The exercise is carried out without any speech.

- The participants should not stop moving until the end of the exercise.

- Once the pairs have got really expressive ask them to swap so that B becomes the leader and A the follower.

playing 'Hypnosis'

playing 'Hypnosis'2

Variations:

- When this first version of the game is established, let it continue but start to move the participants around. For example the player who is leading, can now lead two people, one on each hand. The leader may be leading two but also is led herself by someone else. Two players can both lead and follow each other at the same time. You can mix the group so much that they are all connected to each other in some way!

- Music may be played during the exercise. But make sure the music is varied and changes pace, otherwise participants will tend to get stuck in the same rhythm and pace.

- If the group, or some group members, are blind or partially sighted, perfume or sweet smelling oils can be placed on the palm of the hand and the participants may follow through their sense of smell.

- Discussion is very important after this exercise. Ask the group to share how they felt, which role they preferred, which parts were pleasurable, what was challenging, what was unpleasant, how did it feel, what did it remind them of, what surprised them etc.

The next exercise is an investigation of power through objects, images and bodies. It encourages participants to analyse how power looks in the world and how we can begin to stage it.

Game of Power

Aim: To recognise and explore power, through placing objects and people

Mood: Thoughtful, practical and active debate

Level: Intermediate to advanced

Number of people: 5-30

Time: 30-60 minutes or more

What you will need: 6 chairs or seats, a table and an empty bottle if you have one available.

Directions:

- Ask the participants, one person working at a time, to arrange the chairs, table and bottle in a way that makes one of the chairs more powerful than all of the other objects. They can arrange the objects in any way that they wish.

- After several people have arranged the objects ask the group to choose one arrangement, one image, which they agree makes one chair more powerful than any other object.

- One at a time participants are asked to come up and place themselves in the arrangement by making a still image with their bodies. Their aim is to make themselves more powerful than any of the objects, but without moving them.

- Each person must try to make themselves more powerful than anyone else in the image. The group watching decides whether each new person looks more powerful or not and in this way the group discusses how power looks in the world and on stage. If the person is more powerful they stay in that position and the next person tries. If they are judged not the most powerful they leave the image and try again later.

Example of playing the game of power

After you have looked in depth at the concept of power through some of these exercises, you may be ready to look at what happens when power is used against a person to stop them from expressing their desire or to make them do something against their will – oppression. It is crucial to start to understand what oppression is, so that we can start to question it and find strategies to fight it, through techniques such as Forum Theatre. The next exercise is quite a deep exploration of what oppression means to us and should only be undertaken when a good level of dialogue and trust has been attained in the group.

Image of Oppression

Aim: To explore oppression

Mood: A deep meditation on oppression through images; reflective, thoughtful, challenging

Level: Advanced

Number of people: 5-30

Time: 45-60 minutes or more

Directions:

NB: This exercise involves sculpting so make sure you have done some sculpting Image work before undertaking this exercise.

• Explain what is going to happen in the exercise. This will help to establish safe boundaries for people and will help people decide how deeply they want to explore the work.

- Ask the group to get into smaller groups of about 5 people.

- One at a time, each person in each small group will sculpt an image of oppression, or what oppression means to them. They will use the bodies of the other 4 members of the small group to sculpt the image, lastly they will also place themselves into the picture. Each 'sculptor' can also use objects in the room to help construct the picture if they wish to.

- It is important to communicate to the participants that they can create any image they like. The image can be realistic, symbolic, abstract... There is no right or wrong. It will simply be a picture with the title 'oppression' using 5 people. The sculptors will put themselves into the picture but they do not need to 'play' themselves at all.

- Like the sculpting exercise (*above*) Image of Oppression should be practised without words.

- Each sculptor should work quite quickly.

- After a few minutes, another member of the small group will sculpt their image of oppression, until each member has made a picture. The small groups should then practise remembering and presenting each still image, like showing a series of photographs. They should be able to make each image without help from the sculptor who first made the image.

- After each small group has made its image and has practised reconstructing the images, the groups will present their series of images to the whole workshop group.

- Participants will be invited to look at the images and to talk about what they see in the images, in two ways.

- Firstly they will be asked to describe what they see from an **'objective'** point of view. This means just describing the facts, not how they feel about the pictures, as if they were giving evidence in a court. For example "in this picture I see four people standing and one person lying down. Two have physical contact, there is no eye contact." Objective descriptions will happen for some time.

- Then the group will be asked to describe what they see from a **'subjective'** point of view i.e. what they feel the images are saying. For example the four people standing are angry with the person lying down etc. This discussion from both 'objective' and 'subjective' points of view is a very important theatre and group training tool in itself, and is crucial for being able to deconstruct images and understand them better, as well as being able to distinguish fact from feeling, a very useful skill in resolving group conflict.

- It is very important that group members do not ask questions about the images. The exercise does not involve any interrogation of the person who made the image. Indeed once the images are made, they can remain quite anonymous. The exercise is about what we see and how we learn from what we see. Yet by listening to the observations and reflections other group members make about the images, each person might come to a better understanding of their own oppression, in order to overcome it.

- One by one each of the groups presents their images and the wider group observes what they see objectively, and reflects on what they see subjectively.

- Once all the groups have presented and the images have been talked about, it is often fruitful to have a wider discussion to summarise what we have learned about oppression through the exercise. It is very important to identify what many of the pictures had in common. There are often recurring images. Identifying the shapes and pictures that recur time and again will help in the understanding of what oppression is, and will feed into staging your plays. Indeed some of the images could form the basis of an entire play.

So, in training to create Forum Theatre, it is important to explore the concept of power and oppression creatively and how these ideas might be expressed in theatrical images. Forum Theatre, however, is also a technique which requires excellent improvisation skills. A Forum Theatre play will hopefully provoke audience members to want to get up and challenge the oppression. In the second playing of a Forum Theatre play the actors never know what is going to happen. They will need to think instantly and improvise. Here is an example of an improvisation exercise that will help to build the participants' skills, before you go on to make your Forum Theatre play, and can be used to refresh their acting skills generally at any time. This exercise can follow on very well from 'complete the image'

Improvisation Circle

Aim: Develop improvisation skills

Mood: Depends on participants

Level: Advanced

Number of people: 3-30

Time: 15-45 mins

Directions:

- Stand in a circle

- The first player to start the exercise goes into the middle of the circle and makes an image with their body. The players all look at the image for a short time.

- A second player enters the circle and begins to react to that image. The first player brings their still picture to life in response to what the second player is offering. Both players should be encouraged to use movement and speech. In this way a scene is created.

- When the scene has reached a high point, the leader calls 'freeze' or 'stop'. The two players hold whatever physical position they are in at that moment.

- The first player who entered the circle steps away leaving the second player in 'half' an image. Just like in the 'complete the image' exercise (*above*) new ideas will arise. The players again look at the image for a brief time.

- Then a third player enters the circle and in response to the image which player 2 is in, starts to improvise a new scene. Player 2 responds accordingly.
- This continues until all players have experienced stepping into the circle to improvise.

Variations:

- Gradually add more people to the improvisation
- Add objects to the improvisation
- Add furniture to the improvisation
- Suggest characters to go into the circle
- Suggest levels of power or status for the characters

Extension for Forum Theatre practice:

In Forum Theatre an audience member may intervene with the desire to solve the problem by going to a location which is not featured in the play. Actors will have to improvise a location very quickly. We can never know all the places an audience member may want to create. However certain scenarios often arise in Forum and it is good to practise creating locations in seconds. After you have practised general improvisation skills with Improvisation Circle, try suggesting locations for the actors to make as quickly as possible, with clear characters in them. For example:

- The police station
- The court room
- The advice centre
- The hospital
- Newspaper Offices
- A best friend's house
- A religious place
- A school and so on...

In Forum Theatre audience members will intervene to improvise with the actors to challenge the oppression they see portrayed on the stage. In a sense Forum Theatre is an advanced improvisation game the aim of which is to take power from the oppressor and put it in the hands of the oppressed. The following is a fun improvisation game, which explores how to negotiate taking power, and can be used for the actors to practise dealing with an audience member who is effectively trying to take power.

The Seat of Power

Aim: Improvisation skills, negotiating taking power

Mood: Fun, upbeat, challenging

Level: Advanced

Number of people: 3-30

Time: 15-45 mins

What you will need: A chair

Directions:

- A chair is placed 'on stage'. All the participants face the chair.

- It is explained to the participants that this chair is a seat of power, and it is one that you would really like to sit on. In order to get their imaginations going, ask the participants to suggest what this chair might be, for example a throne, a toilet, the seat of a luxury car, a chair at the head of a great decision-making table, a comfortable arm chair in a family home... and who might be sitting on the seat of power?...

- A player volunteers to sit in the chair and they remain there for a short time. They are playing someone with power. The other players watch him develop a character sitting in that chair.

- A second player gets up and improvises with the first player, they try to find a way (with or without words) of trying to get the character the first player has created, to get up from the chair.

- Only if the seated player is convinced that they would get up, do they give up their chair. If the second player does not succeed, one by one more players come to try to convince the first. Only when the player in the chair is convinced that their character would get up, do they give up the seat of power.

- The game continues until many different people have had an opportunity to sit in the seat of power.
- The key lesson for the actor is for the person in the seat of power to learn to give honest realistic responses, and to give way if they are convinced by the intervention.

The seat of power is also a very interesting game to explore in training to be a Forum Theatre facilitator, and for learning techniques in encouraging the audience to get out of their seats and on to the stage!

NB: Improvisation is an acting technique of its own and is not only useful for Forum Theatre.

Here are some tips for ways to keep improvisations going:
- If you get stuck – ask a question during the improvisation.
- Listen to what the player/s who are improvising with you are saying, watch what they are doing.
- React to, accept and respond to what is being offered to you in the improvisation.
- Moving your body in a gesture, for example, may open up new possibilities.
- Don't try too hard to be clever, funny or original – relax.

The following exercise is an excellent way of learning the basic structure and rules of Forum Theatre and tor exploring oppression, and how to break it.

Projected Image (a forum model) – Dancers & Marchers

Aim: Learning how the Forum Theatre game works, fighting oppression, discovering possibilities for change

Mood: Dynamic performance

Level: Advanced

Number of people: 5-30

Time: 30-45 minutes

Directions:

- 5 people from the group volunteer to be in a short moving image or scene of oppression, which is:

- Four people march in rhythm and in step together, marching back and forth across the space several times.

- A fifth person dances at the side (with music if you have it).

- Each time the marchers travel across the space they move closer and closer to the dancer, s/he has less and less space until the marchers surround the dancer so that she has no more space to dance.

- Finally the dancer sadly joins the marchers, moving with them.

- The rest of the group watch the moving image or scene.

- The group is invited to 'project' their own interpretations onto the image. What do they see? What does the picture mean to them? Have they ever felt like the dancer feels?

- There is no right or wrong. For each participant the image may mean different things to them.

- The image is played again. This time any participant can say "stop", come and replace the dancer, and try to find a way of making the situation better for them.

- After each intervention into the scene, participants are asked for their responses.

Dancer and marchers

Forum Theatre, like all theatre, may be rehearsed over a number of days or weeks. However, some groups will have little time to work together. In that case here is an exercise that enables you to make a quick instant Forum Theatre play.

Making an instant Forum play

Number of people: 5-30
Mood: Challenging, creative, performance task-based
Level: Advanced
Time: 45 minutes to 1 hour
Directions:

In groups of 5 decide the following:

- An oppression (e.g. burning social issue with a power element) that you would like to address in a play.
- Who is the central character.
- What the central character wants.
- Who the oppressors are.
- What the oppressors want.
- Where the play takes place.

The exercise then involves creating an instant play by making images in small groups and bringing them to life in different ways. For each stage of the exercise they have 10 seconds in which to carry out the instruction. Count the group down over 10 seconds:

- The group make a still image of the central character experiencing the early stages of oppression – image 1 (created over 10 seconds).

- The group make a still image of the central character at a point of conflict with her oppressors – image 2.

- The group make a still image of the central character at a point of crisis – image 3.

- The group returns to image 1. They breathe in the pattern that feels right for them arising from the image they are in.

- They do the same for image 2.

- Then the same for image 3.

- The group returns to image 1. This time they bring the image to life by both breathing and moving in slow motion.

- They do the same for image 2.

- Then the same for image 3.

- Back to image 1. The group bring the image to life by breathing, moving and also making a sound.

- They do the same for image 2.

- Then do the same for image 3.

- Back to image 1. The group bring the image to life this time by breathing, moving and speaking words to each other arising from the image and the characters they are playing.

- They do the same for image 2.

- Then do the same for image 3.

- The last time they return to image 1 and play the scene through all of the images in movement, with words, improvising through the images, without stopping, until they reach their end point.

Now the small groups each have a basic play. Ask them to talk about what they have created. They may need to make adjustments to the story and make sure they have the following elements:

- the issue you are dealing with needs to be clear and relevant to the audience.

- the story needs to be clear.

- all the characters' desires must be strong and clear and believable.

- the central character needs to be in a situation where power is being used against them to stop them getting what they want, or making them do something they do not want to do, in a way that is unfair and harmful to their well being.

- the central character is someone who tries to fight that power but eventually fails.

- the oppressive characters need to be convincing.

- there may also be a potential ally, or witness, to what is happening to the central character, someone who could help if they were convinced.

- as in all drama the play needs to have conflict.

- the central character needs to arrive at a point of crisis.

The groups can now spend 10-15 minutes re-rehearsing the short play, working from the images and improvisation as a basis and developing the play in light of the discussion.

After re-rehearsal, the small groups present their plays to each other, and they can practise Forum Theatre interventions and facilitating the event.

Training the Forum Theatre Facilitator

The role of the Forum Theatre facilitator is one of the most challenging in Theatre For Development work and should not be underestimated. A facilitator in Forum Theatre needs to have all the skills of a good leader and peer group member (see abovo). Here are some recommendations on how to facilitate a Forum Theatre event and some ideas towards practising the skill.

The facilitator's role

Before the play the facilitator...

- Observes the audience as they are entering the space and begins informal conversations with them where possible. This will give you an idea of who is present. This is crucial as a Forum Theatre play is aimed at people who are experiencing, or who may experience, the situation that the central character is dealing with. If a different kind of audience arrives, you may need to adjust what you do. (See *Performing* below)

- Introduces themselves and the actors. They must communicate clearly and confidently. The facilitator describes how the event will run and prepares them for a **different** kind of theatre where the audience will be active, and therefore they will need a 'warm up'.

- Warms up the audience to be active participants through physical and vocal games or songs. It is often useful to play games with the audience which are simple for them to participate in.

- Asks them to watch the show extra carefully, and to observe the central character in particular. This is the character who is the least powerful in the play, she / he is the one who needs our help. It may be useful to introduce the actor playing the central character at this point. The facilitator asks the audience to watch where the central character goes, who she / he meets, what she / he wants and how she / he deals with the problems she / he will encounter.

- Asks the audience to think 'what could I do differently if I were the central character'

- Tells the audience that later they will have a chance to change things and make things better for the central character.

- Asks if the audience is ready to watch.

- Asks if the actors are ready to perform.

- **"Then let's begin"**............. (*starts the play*)

During the Play the facilitator...

- Both watches the play and observes the audience. The reactions of the audience may give a good indicator of what they may respond to in the play and whether they relate to it.

After the first run of the play ...

This is one of the most crucial moments in the whole Forum Theatre event. How the facilitator works with the audience in this moment will influence how ready, prepared and willing the audience is to intervene and change the action. So immediately after the play the facilitator...

- Gets on stage again.
- Asks the audience questions, invites responses, listens to the responses of the audience, builds on each question, challenges the audience about what they have said and summarises their responses. This is not a time where the facilitator 'makes speeches'. The aim is to start a dialogue. The quality and clarity of these questions is very important. The facilitator might ask questions such as :
  - "Was the story clear?" – this can often be useful especially with a new play.
  - "Are you happy with that ending?"
  - "Did it have to end like that?"
  - "What could have been a more positive ending for the central character?"
  - "What did the central character want?"
  - What was stopping the central character getting what they wanted?"
  - "What could they have done differently so that they have a happier time and get what they want?"
- Sometimes the audience might be reluctant to speak out at first. To begin with you can invite responses through voting. For example:

- "Raise your hand if you felt there was anything the central character could have done differently to make life better".

- "Raise your hand if you think there is nothing they could have done differently". Be persistent in getting a response, for example:

- "Raise your hand if you haven't raised your hand yet!". Once people have gestured, the facilitator knows the people are thinking. From here they may ask:

- "So at what point in the play do you things could be improved for the central character?"

- "What was the real problem in that story?"

- It is often useful to give the audience an opportunity to talk to each other in the audience. So the facilitator can say – "talk to the person next to you – discuss what happened, come up with 3 moments in the play where something could have been different". It is important in this discussion that the audience does not talk too much about what could be done differently, just to identify that something could be different and the moments in the play where things could be different is enough. If the audience talk too much about alternative actions, they are less likely to get up and do them – and action is what we want.

- It is sometimes useful to ask the actors on stage to listen to the audience's ideas about the moments in the play where things could have been different. This helps to break down the barriers between actors and audience. If they have spoken to the actor informally before the Forum, they are more likely to get up and face them on stage. But keep these discussions very brief!

- After some brief discussion, the facilitator explains what is going to happen next. Their explanation may be something like this:

  - "Great, so let's see if we can change that ending and improve the situation for the central character (and for us too). We are going to perform the play for you again. This time at any point where you feel things could be different for the central character you raise your hand and shout **stop**! Then we will stop the play, and if you want to, you can come up here, take the central character's place and do whatever you want to do to make the situation different. You can say anything you want, go to any place you want and do anything you want. You are not stuck within the world of the play. If you think things could be different by going somewhere that we have not seen in the play or talking to someone we have not seen yet then we can create that scene for you. Only you can change things, only you can show us how things could be different. The play will end in **exactly** the same way **unless** you change things".

- It is important that the facilitator is very careful about the language that they use. Notice that we are emphasising the term "different". Forum Theatre is about finding as many possibilities for change as we can. All the game requires is that we do something different from the original play. We avoid saying "come up and do something better" or "was this intervention better or worse?". These kind of statements invite moral judgements. And this is not the purpose of Forum Theatre. Equally, the facilitator is not there to judge, teach, manipulate, preach to, dictate to or instruct the audience. **The facilitator is impartial.**

- There are only 3 rules (sometimes it is best to give these rules as you go along in the Forum, you may also choose to explain them now):

1. No Magic – you can do anything, as long as it is humanly possible, and likely (eg winning the Lottery is not a probable event, it is more like magic).

2. No touching on stage – if you want to you can mime violence but you may not hurt the actors!

3. You only replace the oppressed character – she / he is the one we are trying to help.

   And then....

- (*to the audience*) Are you all ready to watch and try to change the story?
- Before we begin let's practise shouting "**stop!**" So at any point where you feel you could do something differently and make a change, you shout "**stop!**" What do you shout?... (audience should reply "**Stop!**" – repeat this until it is easy for them)
- Are you ready?
- (*to the actors*) Are the actors ready?
  Then let's start.......... (*re-starts the play*)

> **Savitaben:** Forum Theatre is about giving people an opportunity to express their views and come out of their oppression.

During the Forum – the 2nd run of the play

The facilitator...

- Watches the audience from a highly visible position, showing they are ready for anyone to shout stop. Often at the beginning of the second run of the play the audience can become fascinated by watching the action again. So the facilitator can talk to them whilst they are watching the play "Just remember, shout stop", "Nothing changes unless you make a change", "you saw what happened the first time, don't let it happen like that again"... etc. The facilitator can also help by stopping the play and asking the audience again "could anything be different for the central character here", "who would like to come and show something different? etc".
- Eventually if the play is strong enough an audience member will shout "**stop!**"
- The facilitator stops the play on stage.
- Prompts the audience to give a big round of applause for the audience member
- Welcomes the audience member on stage and asks their name.
- Facilitates the replacement of the actor by the newcomer.

The actor might hand the audience member a prop or piece of costume to "give" them the role.

- Asks "where do you want to start your idea from?"
- Gets everyone in position and starts the action.
- OR, if the audience member wants to offer a change by going to a different location, the facilitator instructs the actors to set up the new scene.
- Starts the action and watches the intervention and the remaining audience.
- Supports the intervention by moving people if they cannot be seen or heard by the audience.
- Makes sure the intervention does not go on too long, yet also makes sure the audience member has had enough opportunity to do what they want to do.
- Stops the intervention with sensitivity.
- Asks the audience member "did you achieve what you wanted?" and listens to how they feel about it.
- Thanks the audience member for doing something different and making a change, then sends the audience member back to the audience (more applause).
- Asks the audience "what did they do differently?". Again it is important that responses are handled sensitively, so as not to destroy anyone's confidence, yet also start a really useful debate in the audience. "Did this intervention make any progress for the central character?" "How was progress made?" "What more could be done? Who would like to come and try something different?" "You may have been in this situation, or you may be in this situation one day, now is your chance to practise how you might do things differently so that we don't have that horrible ending again".
- If no one wants to come at this exact point, return to the point of intervention. Continue working through the play till the end, inviting and taking as many different interventions as possible, getting responses from the audience, having a debate, sharing possible solutions, and sharing any information which may be useful to know when dealing with a problem situation such as the one in the play.

> **Kaloobhai:** When I am stuck in a Forum Theatre intervention I always try to look to other characters, I ask them questions, I invite new people to come into the scene, I listen to what the characters are saying and respond.

After the Forum

The facilitator...

- Thanks the audience for their willingness to enter into the challenge of finding an alternative outcome to the play.
- Summarises the main points raised by the audience
- Asks them to continue thinking about these problems so they can deal with them in real life.
- Gives them any information they may need about sources of information or help (or tells them where they can get such information, or asks actors to come on and give such information).
- Introduces any final element e.g. a closing song.
- The facilitator may conclude on a positive note by inviting suggestions from the audience for an ideal but achievable image of the central character's life if the right change were made. The actors show this image.

As with acting, the most important way of training to be a Forum Theatre facilitator is practice, practice and more practice! The training never really ends...

A Suggested Intensive Forum Theatre Training Course:

In an ideal situation you and your group would train in Forum Theatre over at least two weeks or more. However many groups will not have the resources to spend a longer time training. Following is a suggested intensive two-day training course outline, based on some of the exercises above:

Forum Theatre Training Day One
Aim: To explore power, oppression & Forum Theatre structure
Preparation:
Introductions and aims

Name game

Exploration:
Fear and Protector

Hypnosis

Discussion on power

Short break
The Game of Power
- Meal break -
Person to person

Sculpting

Creation:
Image of Oppression and discussion

- Short break -
Presentation:
Forum practice with projected image, focusing on the role of
the facilitator in Forum.

Conclusion:
Make a call and response warm-up song to end the day.

Forum Theatre Training Day two
Aims: To develop Forum Theatre improvisation and facilitation skills, create a Forum play and practise skills

Preparation:
Questions arising from day one

Aims of day two

Pushing against each other

Improvisation circle (including actors practising creating quick alternative locations in Forum Theatre)
- short break -
The seat of power (focusing on the role of the Forum actor)
- Meal break -

Creation:
Make an instant Forum play

Rehearse the Forum play
- short break-
Presentation:
Present the Forum plays (make adjustments to the plays in accordance with what is needed in a Forum play)

Forum theatre practice (with facilitators practising on different scenes)

Conclusion:
Discussion.   Call and response song

Making Plays – Devising Plays

Now you have experienced training in team building, theatre skills, improvisation and preparation for forum theatre, you are ready to create plays for performance.

All of the work so far will have given you rich material for play-making, you can even use the games and exercises as a starting point. And while you are making plays there is always the sense that you are training. In theatre training never ends!

In general we recommend creating your own plays rather than using existing ones. The personal stories which come from inside your group, or inside your communities will have an immediate emotional connection with your audience. They will recognise the stories and characters as something which might have happened to them or someone they know. Your stories are likely to be their stories too. Your characters will be people they know.

Of course the plays will be around issues which are important to you and your audience, issues which you may have known from the start of your work, or which you have discovered through research or contact with your communities. Keep the issues fairly simple at first. If you create a play about literacy and domestic violence and alcohol and HIV/AIDS and health care, the audience might lose focus. It is better to create a number of short plays where each issue can be highlighted.

By doing this we allow the audiences to focus on the main issue and start to consider how things might be different, how the change might occur.

So it is a good idea to have a BIG Question within the play:

"Why are girls being raped?"

"Why are there not enough homes for everyone?"

"Why is there so much violence in the community?"
etc.

And all your plays should provoke the question

"How could it be different?"

We suggest keeping the plays to less than 20 minutes. This is especially important for intervention (forum) plays where the audience interventions can easily take another hour. And if you need time to gather your audience – with songs or music - and time to talk to your audience – through the facilitator or through group members in the audience, you do not want the whole event to take too long. There is nothing worse than your audience having to leave the performance space (to eat or to sleep, or to work) just when the debate is becoming important.

Some of us have made this mistake, so keep it to the right length.

Using Existing Plays

Although we suggest always creating your own plays, there are some exceptions. You may find there is a well known play which you could adapt to your issues, or you may find a play from another Theatre for Development group is right for you.

Don't be afraid to adapt existing work, to place it in your community, change the place names, character names etc to make it recognisable to your audience. With some plays you might need to ask permission to use existing works.

Using a playwright. Why not use a playwright?

The decision to use a playwright depends on you. If you do, however, ensure that they work with the ideas from the group and do not impose their ideas upon you.

Playwrights who are not from the community with which you work will probably have a different perception of community development and do not understand the grassroots reality. Playwrights often base their ideas on external research such as magazine articles, NGO reports etc. In addition, they may have their own stereotype ideas about reality and be insensitive to personal issues.

At Vidya we used a playwright for the very first plays but decided against it since the peer-group was better able to narrate the issues they were dealing with.

The playwright was given material from the group and went away to write it into a play. When the play was ready a scene in which a slum girl writes poetry about her wishes was missing because, the playwright claimed, "Slum people don't write poetry"!

That was the end of using a playwright.

The Straight Play –
Why and How, the role-model,
the success story, the aspiration,
the story of the possible....

Play synopsis – the story

VIDYA NA SAPNA – Vidya's dream:

A play focusing on the importance of the Girl-Child and her dreams.

Vidya is the protagonist of this play. She is the youngest of three daughters to a widowed alcoholic father. Vidya's father and grandmother verbally abuse her. Her elder sisters work in junk yards while Vidya is refused an education and is married to an alcoholic man by her father and grandmother. Vidya's husband abuses her and earns no income for the household. Vidya later becomes pregnant herself and decides that she wants a daughter instead of a son. Her dream is that her daughter will have a different life to herself.

The role of Theatre for Development is to engage audiences in all possible ways to reflect on their circumstances and to encourage them to find realistic ways of changing their circumstances.

While intervention plays (forum etc.) are extremely useful tools there are some areas and outcomes they cannot cover. For this we can create plays which have a different structure and which do not involve active intervention, although they may provoke a lot of debate.

We shall call these "straight" plays, only because they are closer to normally accepted forms of theatre. They can be a very useful counterbalance to the intervention plays and introduce ideas which are not possible in forum

Whereas intervention plays need a negative outcome, in order to construct a dialogue about alternatives, the straight play can take a different route or a different perspective.

Here are some examples of our "straight plays":

"What if?" Plays

This can be less negative in its story-line, indeed it can have a very positive outcome. It can be based on the principle of "What if?". For example,

- **What if** you did educate your girl child to read, what advantages could that bring to your family, to stop you being cheated, to generate more income? etc..

- **What if** the community came together to prevent the industrial waste-pipe being built right next to the village? You could show the struggle, show the devices used to overcome opposition, show the setbacks and finally show the better future.

With this structure you are pointing out all the positive benefits of action, not the negative results of inaction.

Role Model Plays

A "Role-model" play is an achievement play. It could be the story of someone who overcame adversity and achieved something memorable, someone who did not allow social conditions to keep them down. So many societies have real life examples of this that it is strengthening to a community to be reminded of them. If not, then take the archetype and create a story of, for example, the girl who studied, worked at night to get money for books, slowly worked her way up in spite of male opposition and became the head teacher? head surgeon/ local mayor/ scientist / prime minister – make your own goals!

Oppressor's Perspective Plays

This can have a strong narrative dramatic element, even a negative one, but from a different perspective to the forum play which tells a story with the focus on the oppressed. By creating a play about an oppressor with all the intricacies of that person's life you can make people in the audience recognise their own behaviour (for example a wife beater, a malicious mother-in-law etc.) and that all-important moment of recognition can be the catalyst for change.

BUT REMEMBER: Straight plays should not be morality plays (the good always win – they don't!), they should not have unlikely or "magic" moments. They also stay firmly in reality.

So how do we devise them?

An imaginative mixture of research, discussion and mapping, trying out action, and shaping/structuring is required. Here is one model of how to do it:

1. You decide on your theme. "We want to show what will happen if…….."

2. With a huge sheet of paper note down any stories you know (personal or from others) of the beginning situations of the story with all the obstacles.

3. On the same paper (perhaps on the other side or in a different colour) note the positive outcomes you want to show may be possible.

4. Use story-telling techniques (see above) to develop your narrative.

5. Using the Image skills you learned (*see above*) make strong stage pictures for key moments in the story, e.g. the beginning situation, the first major obstacle, the first success, the big set-back, overcoming the problem, the opposing forces, the final image. Do this several times, always discussing which images work, if you need more or different images, who the characters are in the pictures etc. At this stage you can be changing who plays which character, because everyone will bring something different to a picture. Remember that just telling an easy "success" story is quite uninteresting, and not very useful for us. There must be difficulties so we can examine how to overcome them.

6. As you start to agree on some major pictures, bring each one to life for a few seconds – see which actions, tensions, words etc emerge. Play the same game and only allow one character to speak each time. They can speak as they would in the situation or they can speak their inner thoughts, to better understand the characters.

7. Now you are probably in a state where you can decide on the characters you really need to allow the story to develop. Use all the character-building skills you learned before (see above) to give the characters physical and vocal reality. When you are ready you can "hot-seat" them.

> **"Hot-seating"**
>
> *put a character on stage and get everyone to ask them questions about themselves and particularly about the situations and other characters in the play. This can add depth and interest to a character.*

8   More story telling. You have the outline story, key moments, the characters and some images. Try a story-telling circle to tell your story. Then try individuals telling the story in a given, short time (1 minute?). These exercises can add details and colour but also keep you to the essential points of the story.

9. It might be worth going back to a large sheet of paper again. Find a way of sketching the shape of the play – as a map – as a graph, or find your own method. On this paper start to define the scenes you need – the key meetings, the key discoveries etc.

10. One by one improvise these scenes. Start slowly, for example from an image you make, and decide only what you need to establish in this scene. Let different people play the characters. Allow everyone to comment on whether the emotions are right, the relationship between people is right etc. After every attempt try to remember moments and words or phrases which were effective. Write them down.

11. When you have worked through each scene (and you may have invented some new ones along the way), you will have a ROUGH WORKING SCRIPT of the play.

12. **Well Done!**   With this you can try to read through the entire play and then read it with some movements – just to see what you have created.

13. Now you have to shape the material. For example it is not a good idea to have all the action, or all the obstacles in the first 25% of the play and then just have a nice long happy ending. There are many theories on dramatic structure but your audience will certainly appreciate:

   • An introductory phase where characters and situations are revealed.

   • A fairly early (after 20% of the play) obstacle/drama which needs to be overcome.

   • A period when things are progressing well with smaller dramatic tensions but perhaps we can see danger approaching and …

   • after about 80% of the play, a major dramatic incident which threatens disaster but, in this play, is overcome (or not if that's how you want your play to end)

- THINK ABOUT STRUCTURE AND SUSPENSE – THESE KEEP YOUR AUDIENCE WITH YOU.

- Your rough working script is getting improvement through this structuring and now you will bring it to life through rehearsing. In this type of theatre the script is not absolute – it can be changed as you find better ways of communicating to your audiences what you want them to see, feel and think about.

- Even when you are performing – you are still devising. After every performance you can probably spot the moments which still need some re-working.

- The audience's reactions and comments after the performances are vital. Let them be part of your devising.

- Always be ready to change.

What is a play? What does it look like?
Try this exercise to get going -
Story Boarding

Number of people: Any number

What you will need: Large sheets of paper and colourful pens

Directions:

- Draw sketches of the crucial moment of each scene on large pieces of paper
- Next to the image write any basic text used in the scene
- Soon you will build up a working document - the beginning of a play script
- Keep refining it as you try ideas in practice **(NB this is how film scripts are put together!)**

Image Scene 1	Text ideas scene 1

Image Scene 2	Text ideas scene 2

Image Scene 3	Text ideas scene 3

Image Scene 4	Text ideas scene 4

Interactive Plays

We highly recommend using interaction between the audience and the performers in Theatre For Development performances. Theatre For Development is the theatre of dialogue. The community is encouraged to gain a greater understanding of issues and to debate them through theatre. Yet Theatre For Development is also the theatre of action. In Theatre For Development the community is encouraged to take action to change problem situations. The performance itself is the perfect place to enter into dialogue with the audience and get them activated.

There are many ways of using interaction in a performance. One of the most effective ways we have found is Forum Theatre.

Forum Plays

As we have seen, Forum Theatre is an interactive theatre technique where a play dealing with a specific issue is presented to an audience who have direct experience of that issue.

The play focuses on a central character who is negatively affected by that issue, power is being used against them by people (and possibly institutions) to stop them getting what they want, or to make them do something they do not want to do – they are 'oppressed'. The play ends either in a negative state for the central character, or at a point where they are at a crossroads and do not know what to do next.

After the audience members have seen the play once, they are invited by a facilitator to watch the play again. During the second performance at any point where an audience member feels they could do something different to alter the outcome of the play, and improve the situation for the central character, they shout 'stop!' – and are invited to come on stage, play the central character (the actor steps out of the scene) and try out what they want to do. The other actors react as their characters would realistically react, changing only according to whether the audience member's idea would affect them. Members of the audience come up, one at a time, to try to change the outcome of the play, for the better. Each intervention is discussed briefly by the audience to evaluate what has happened.

So Forum Theatre is a kind of theatre debate, a theatre game, an empowerment exercise, in which the aim is to take the power, to fight the oppression, and come up with as many different possibilities for change as the audience can imagine.

Sureshbhai: We performed a play about women's role in governance where the national flag is raised in a ceremony. In India a woman in Government has the right to raise the flag. However in our play only the female protagonist's grandfather or her husband were allowed to raise the flag and they stopped the woman from doing it. The men said "no woman had raised the flag here in over fifty years!" This happens in real life. During the Forum a woman who is in government came on stage to intervene. Her body was shaking with rage. She said "this is my right!". She raised the flag and received huge applause.

So how do we make a Forum Theatre play?

To make Forum Theatre you create a strong play which moves and challenges the audience, much like any other play. So all you have learned from the devising and straight plays sections (above) will be a great help to you.

However, because Forum presents a play with a powerful problem that needs to be solved, and because the audience need to be strongly motivated to shout 'stop!', it often needs a very clear structure built into it.

In order to devise a Forum Theatre play, work through the games, image work, and improvisation techniques we have already suggested in the Training for Forum section in this book to create a story structure, and ultimately a play, which has the following elements:

- A clear and well researched issue which is going to be presented through the specific circumstances of a story, yet reflects a wider general social concern.

- This issue should be one that the peer group have direct personal experience and knowledge of, and which is relevant to the community.

- A central character – the oppressed, or disempowered, person. This character is someone who is severely affected by this issue, someone who tries hard to get what they want but does not succeed, or is made to do something they do not want to do. The character needs to be someone the audience will directly relate to and identify with, and they need to be someone who has strengths and weaknesses like anybody else.

- Oppressors – other characters close to the central character. The oppressors use their power to block the central character's desires. The oppressors do not need to be all on one level of power, they could range from someone mildly unhelpful in a family to someone extremely brutal at the top of a big institution. The oppressors are people, like any other person, although in this circumstance they are people who have desires in conflict with our central character, and they are in a position of power over the central character.

- It is often useful in Forum to have an ally, or a witness, someone who could potentially help the oppressed if they were approached in the appropriate way.

- The play must be a story which shows the central character's desires, their situation and the people around them. It must show the central character trying to get what they want, or trying to resist what they do not want, at several different points in the action. These points in the action are potential **intervention points** and must be increasingly powerful moments where the oppressed tries and fails. They need to be points which are dramatic enough to motivate the audience to want to say "stop – I could do something differently!"

- The action points, where the central character tries and fails, should build up in importance to a key moment of conflict which has serious consequences and ultimately leads to a significant crisis for the character.

- The crisis point is the point at which the play will come to its end, and the audience will be invited to see the play again and, the second time, take part.

- The play must not present a problem which is impossible to solve, nor must it be a situation with an easy solution: it must be complex, and immediately recognisable and relevant to the audience.

- Forum can be performed in any theatrical style you choose, as long as the audience is able to intervene and take part.

- For our work we have found that three to five scenes are often a good number for a short Forum Theatre play – although more scenes are possible.

It is often effective to have the beginning and end scenes slightly shorter with the middle scene(s) being slightly longer. Most audience members tend to intervene in the middle of the play rather than the beginning or end. In the beginning they are getting used to the idea they should intervene, the middle is usually where you will have most conflict, and it is here that you need more detail. During the second performance you may not get to the end scene because this is where you see the central character at their lowest point.

Intervention and change usually need to happen sooner rather than later to solve problems!

Dipteeben: Forum Theatre can sometimes be unhelpful if it only ends in a negative way. Especially when performing to children who quickly take on bad role models and copy examples of bad behaviour. Instead you can present a positive picture at the end of a Forum Theatre session with suggestions from the audience.

Mehmudaben: I once watched a Forum Theatre play where I was not allowed to express my views. I felt manipulated. Forum Theatre can sometimes be used to present stereotypes of cultural groups. It can be used to increase tension between groups in conflict, and to raise prejudices, it can be manipulated by political agendas. We must be careful of this.

Rekhaben: Forum Theatre goes badly if the audience only intervene to be violent. The facilitator needs to focus the Forum on finding many different solutions to the issue, and keep an eye on the audience.

Example Forum Theatre play structure:

Scene-1   Introduce central character, their desires, the oppressor(s) and the oppression (3 minutes).

Scene-2   Introduce potential ally witnessing a further stage of the oppression (4 minutes).

Scene-3   Show a big point of conflict between central character and oppressor(s), the central character does not win (7 minutes).

Scene-4   Show the negative consequences for the central character arising from the conflict, with the central character still battling with the problem (4 minutes).

Scene-5   Show the central character at their lowest point, in despair and crisis (2 minutes).

OR

Scene-1   Introduce the central character, their desires, the oppressor(s) and the oppression (4 minutes).

Scene-2   Show a big point of conflict between central character and oppressor(s), where the central character does not win (8 minutes).

Scene-3   Show the central character at a point of serious crisis arising from the conflict. (3 minutes).

Example Forum Theatre play shape:

Forum Theatre plays often have the following shape.

the slight peaks on the diagram might be very important intervention points

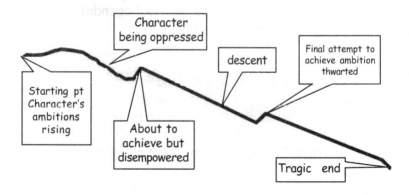

Character being oppressed

descent

Final attempt to achieve ambition thwarted

Starting pt Character's ambitions rising

About to achieve but disempowered

Tragic end

Forum Play Synopsis

"ASHA":

A play on the importance of education and the consequences of superstitious beliefs and traditional practices such as dowry.

Asha is the oppressed protagonist. She is oppressed by her parents, then by her mother in-law and husband. She wanted to pursue an education but was refused by her parents and married to a foul man. The mother-in-law did not take dowry from Asha's parents because no one wanted to marry her son. She in turn gave money to Asha's family.

Five years into the marriage, Asha's mother in-law and husband continually harass Asha because they have no children. The family blames Asha and takes her to a witch doctor (another oppressor). After continued harassment, Asha speaks up and her mother-in-law and husband overpower her and burn her alive. They cover up the murder, saying there was an accident in the kitchen.

VIDYA happiest moments...

In the slum Prajapathi ni Chali, a woman who had a sari covering her entire face came up onto the stage to perform her intervention for the play 'Asha'. In the scene where the husband and mother in-law pour kerosene on Asha, the woman took a long scarf that was one of the props and tied-up the husband and mother in law!

A girl name Geetanjali came up on stage to perform an intervention in the play "Asha" in a scene when Asha is being overpowered by her husband and mother in-law. She told the oppressors that you cannot burn me and said Asha should fight back and take the culprits to the police station.
She was only seven years old!

More interactive performance techniques.

As well as (or instead of) using Forum Theatre you could also invite your audience to:

- Join in a call and response song.
- Question the characters (see 'hotseating' in the character section above).
- Form a queue to make interventions rather than shouting 'stop!'.
- Discuss possible interventions with the performers themselves before trying them out on stage.
- Invite the actors into the audience and start a scene with them there.

Although these techniques can be useful and fun ways of engaging your audience, the power of Forum Theatre lies in ACTION. Social and personal change is usually brought about through action rather than just verbal talking. This is why we encourage the audience to come up on stage and do what they could do differently, and practise an action which they may indeed then take in real life.

How to write your playscript.

You may write your script during devising, you may finalise it during rehearsal or perhaps you will not write it until after the first performance. Some people never write their scripts which exist almost like an oral tradition. But we do recommend you write it down as an important part of your documentation, or if you want to revive a performance later.

There are a few ways of writing down a script. The following is a guide for you:

- Character names on the left
- Spoken text in the centre and right
- Stage directions, musical cues etc in italics/brackets – centred.

For example:

Inside a police station, it is dirty,
with broken furniture and one cell, in which is a young man.

Abdul: How long do I have to stay here? It's not fair. I should be in college.

Policeman: Shut Up! I've told you we are waiting for your parents to call back.

Abdul walks to the bars of his cell and shakes them

Abdul (shouting): I told you I didn't do it. Don't you listen?

Policeman: Save it for the judge.

Abdul: Judge? What are you talking about?

The phone rings. The superintendent enters to answer it.
She is in a bad mood.

Superintendent: Yes, hello,... what? I have no idea. Just a moment.

(to the policeman)

Do we have an Abdul Rahman here?

Using material from traditional forms and stories

If you have your own forms – Use Them!

Just as it is a great idea to look at local theatre forms to inspire your training to become performers (see above) so it is really useful to draw from local theatre forms to create your plays.

Why?

Because if you use a local form, which local people know and respond to, then it is an easy and available medium for communication. If they are used to seeing masked characters, why not use masked characters to explore your issue. If they are used to shadow puppets, rod puppets, rhythmic speech or plays which use animals to reflect human patterns, these will be easily acceptable to your audience.

There are so many different forms of theatre around the world that we can't list them here. Just look around and use what you have.

BUT A WARNING.... We are looking for the best ways of communication so don't try to revive an old form of local theatre because you think it should be resurrected. It won't be a known medium to your audience. Sometimes we have to accept that our audiences may never have seen any theatre at all but they are very aware of soap-operas or commercial movies. Even if we don't particularly like these forms we may have to use them (and improve them of course) to convey our message.

> **Vidya performances often start with songs using popular melodies from Bollywood movies. Everyone knows the tune, but the words have been changed to introduce the issues. They have also experimented with rhythmic speech patterns which derive from local folk theatre, but are also used a lot in t.v. adverts! They resonate with everyone.**

Of course some theatre forms may be sacred and you may feel it is not right to use their material, but most forms are part of a live culture and are in a constant state of change. And many forms which are now classical were once invented from a fusion of existing styles. You can be part of that tradition.

You will find your own best examples but here are a few we have found:

- In Sri Lanka there is a folk theatre form which uses a story-teller to start and stop the action of the other actors. He/She can "freeze" the action and then invite the audience to comment on what they see. Much older than "forum" theatre but very much in the same direction.

- In West Africa there are story telling traditions which tell "Dilemma Stories" They tell the story but towards the end they invite the audience to decide how it should end (which man should the king marry to his daughter?, who should inherit the fortune? etc. etc.). Lively discussions and debates can follow!

- In parts of Zambia there are very strong mask and drum traditions. The masks are deemed to have considerable authority. Plays about HIV/AIDS sometimes use these masks to gather the people from a marketplace, or a village, to come to an "important" play.

- In the Middle East there is the tradition of the Hakawati who is a storyteller who may enter into a dialogue with the audience and discuss problems in a way similar to that of the Forum Theatre facilitator.

Drawing from Traditional Stories

This is also a very rich area for your plays as people in your community will almost certainly know a lot of traditional stories, folk-tales or even religious stories. If they know the characters the play will seem less distant to them.

Again there are so many of these stories that it is for you to think about those which your audiences will know.

But how do you treat this material? Here are two ways:

1. Look for a Prejudice and Change it.

Like it or not, many traditional stories pass down, in their delightful narratives, some very reactionary thinking which serves to resist change by keeping society exactly as it is. There are so many stories where the woman is never asked her opinion, where the outsider is always evil, where someone of a different colour/ country is a troublemaker to be rejected, where the beautiful wife is locked away, where twins are unlucky, where a widow is not to be trusted, where the sick-man is to be chased away and so on.

If you can find one of these stories which is associated with your theme, try to tell the story from another person's viewpoint, especially from the oppressed person's. Try changing the ending to give it an alternative outcome. Here is just one example. There is a Dilemma Story where, at the end, the story-teller asks who the king should choose for his daughter.

Turn it Around!

Ask the daughter, not just who she wants, but what she thinks of the whole process. Empower her by telling it in her words.

2. Have a known character take a fresh look at a dilemma.

Are there characters in the folk or myth of your area that everyone will know? For example Mulla Nasrudin is known in many Muslim countries. Create a play in which he visits the dilemma in your community and comments on it.

In the Vidya project a suggestion was made to create a play in which the god Shiva, who in one form is half-man, half-woman, visits a community to ask why one half of the people who worship him (the women) are so badly treated. Why are they insulting half of him?

Think about it in your own context. Find a character and apply the same devising processes we have given above to bring something very local to a new and relevant life.

A few answers to regular questions:

Q1. How many characters should our plays have?

A1. You are trying to make your story very clear so don't have more than you really need. If you have more company members they can take other tasks e.g. 2nd facilitator, information team, introductory songs etc

Q2. How many scenes should we create?

A2. Again it should be the right number to keep the play clear and focused. Too many scenes might make it difficult to follow. We have suggested 3 or 5 for the Forum plays but sometimes a series of several short clear scenes can be used to show a state of oppression or success.

Q3. Is there a limit to the timescale of the piece?

A3. This varies. Jumps of 20 years between scenes might make forum difficult but could be totally acceptable in folk plays or in positive "role model" plays to show how doing something now might have an effect in the future.

Plays without words

The use of non-verbal straight plays and forum plays to get people speaking - by *not* speaking.

After a few years of using words in plays the Vidya company evolved some fascinating short plays around urgent social issues but without words. These arose from improvisation and discussion in their daily training.

Here is their account:

Performing in communities in India differs greatly from many other countries because in the slum community you have to deal with people busy working, massive noise from traffic, wandering children and animals. In such an atmosphere, and with audiences of 1,500 it can be difficult to get your words heard.

Non verbal plays began as an experiment and we found that by using our body language, strong facial expression, rhythmic actions and vocal sounds (nonsense speech), we were able to evoke unspoken emotion in our plays and have the audience pay more attention.

Non-verbal plays are simple in structure. They allow the audience to pay great attention by using their eyes to understand the character's emotion and story. We start with entertaining activities to grab their attention. Then the non-verbal play is performed. The actions may be underscored by rhythm (e.g. on a drum), or by using "nonsense speech". By keeping the play word-free, you are allowing people to connect to the expressions and the feelings of the characters and identify with them. This is a different method because it allows each individual spectator to fill in the words they would use – it gives them the chance to make their own text.

Interestingly, in non-verbal forum plays the interventions from the audience have almost always been verbal. This leads to the fascinating possibility of the audience speaking during interactions but the actors "answering" them non-verbally. The facilitator, of course, does have to use language.

If you work in a similar situation or perhaps in a multi-lingual community, perhaps you can evolve similar plays.

SYNOPSIS OF A NON VERBAL FORUM PLAY:

about the importance of education and literacy.

- A family receives a very important letter, but no one in the family knows how to read or write.
- The husband approaches several people in his community to aid him but everyone is too busy to read the letter.
- Finally, the husband approaches the owner of the community store, who is a miser and a very cunning person, to read him the very important letter.
- The sly owner promises to do so only after the husband carries all the heavy supplies from one end of the store to the other and cleans the entire store.
- Accidentally, while working, the husband drops one of the heavy sacks of grains which spill over on the floor.
- He quickly tries to pick everything up.
- However, the store owner, angry with the husband that his sack was dropped, kicks him.
- He then rips up the letter and throws it into the husband's face.
- The husband looks at the torn pieces of paper and starts weeping.

Music and songs

Songs play an important role in not only entertaining and engaging the audience, but in emphasising the message. Songs can be included in the play, or performed before and after the play. Or both!

Kaloobhai: When I sing I feel emotional. I once composed a song with Sureshbhai about a boy who becomes disabled. When I sang it, it really touched me and the audience. They even wanted to learn our song. Singing also helps me to relax, to forget my stress and worries.

Vidya has written more than 40 songs for its performances, and uses 10 minutes of songs before performances to attract the audience.

The role of music and song:

- In popular folk theatres music and songs are frequently used to engage the audience, before, during and after the performance.

- Music and song can provide an entertainment element to a more serious event.

- Songs can motivate audience to give a sense of positivity at the end of performances.

- Good songs are memorable. Audiences may learn or recognise words when they have seen a number of performances. And of course they may join in.

- Songs can introduce the themes of the project.

- If you use patriotic / famous / popular tunes the audience will recognise and be drawn to them. Create your own lyrics which are relevant to your theme and this becomes an excellent vehicle for them.

Vidya uses Indian folk and film songs, which are widely known. Changes are made to the words to project the issue, using the same tune and rhythm. When Vidya returns to many communities, their changed songs are often sung to them by the children in the community.

Creating your own Songs:

1. Songs before the play is performed:

- These benefit from being recognisable, catchy, fun, popular, classic tunes to gather crowds before the play. Use your own created poetry and lyrics to fit these tunes.

- Use these songs as a way to introduce the issues in the play and of your organisation.

2. Is the song going to be included in the body of the play? If yes, you should consider the following:

- Relate the song to the issue at that point in the play

- Which character/characters will sing the song?
- Is the song used to create a mood, to take the story forward or to explore a character in more depth?

Some groups are natural singers but others have problems finding real power when singing as a group. Even if they can sing well socially, they often falter when in front of an audience.

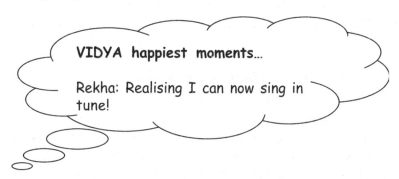

VIDYA happiest moments...

Rekha: Realising I can now sing in tune!

All the work on Finding a Voice (*above*) is your starting point but here are some further exercises especially for singing on stage:

Before singing, do some relaxation exercises to release the tension in your body.

Now, practise the following breathing and vocal exercises.

Exercise for Breathing and Tone:

1. Stand upright with your shoulders down and relaxed. It is important to have proper posture when singing.
2. Breathe into your abdomen, not into your chest and shoulders.
3. Take a deep breath and as you inhale, allow your stomach to expand as much as it can, (almost as if you are pregnant).
4. Hold for a second. Your stomach should feel tight.
5. Remember to relax the rest of your body during this exercise.
6. Release the air, making a "hissing" sound. See how long you can make the sound last in one breath.

7. Now breathe into your abdomen to a count of 4.
8. Exhale, with the "hiss" to a count of 4.
9. Breathe into your abdomen to a count of 4.
10. Exhale to a count of 8.
11. Breathe into your abdomen to a count of 4.
12. Exhale to a count of 10, 12, 14, and 16.
13. When you have found your control try the same on an open tone —"aaah".

Mouth and Vocal Warm up Exercise:

1. Breathe into your abdomen.
2. When exhaling, sing "ah-ah-ah-ah-ah" then "ay-ay-ay-ay-ay", then "ee-ee-ee-ee-ee", then "oh-oh-oh-oh-oh" and then "ooh-ooh-ooh-ooh-ooh" with the mouth wide open and relaxed. This exercise will help warm-up your vocal chords. It also helps getting used to making different shapes with your mouth.
3. Try it individually and then as a group. Try to find the same tone for the whole group. The group should have one voice.

Notes on singing in tune:

The key element in singing in tune as a group is
Listening;
listening to the starting note and listening to each other
It's about singing what you hear and not what you <u>think</u> you hear. This sometimes takes a lot of practice and here are some ideas to help you:

- In vocal exercises like the one listed above begin very quietly and stand very close together as a group.
- Use an instrument or a strong singer to give the group a starting note.
- As you begin to sing, listen carefully to the starting note and try to match your voice to it. It is useful to repeat the note often.

- Within a group listen to the people next to you and try to match your voices to each other as well as to the starting note.
- When you have achieved what sounds like one voice, try another note.
- Slowly build up to different combinations of notes.
- Do this daily when you are working together.
- Sometimes the problems in singing in tune occur when people are singing flat (under the note) or sharp (above the note). Singing flat is more common than singing sharp. To avoid these problems try the following:
- As above, using an instrument or a strong singer to give you a note is a good idea.
- Play or sing a note and have each participant copy it. Really listen to what they are singing. Does it sound like the note being played or is it flat or sharp?
- If it is flat, ask the participant to sing the note again, trying to place it in the front of their face, as though you are letting it out through your forehead, cheeks and nose.
- Ask them to imagine there is a bee buzzing in that area and that is what is making the note.
- If they are having problems, or they are scared of reaching the note, (some people are) ask them to utilise their abdominal muscles by giving them a slight internal push every time they get to a difficult note in a song.
- If the note is sharp (which is less likely) ask the participant to think lower as though the note is coming from the ground or their feet.
- Make sure they are not straining when singing and ask them to utilise their abdominal muscles so that the voice is not just coming from the throat.
- Break down the relevant song into notes and short phrases, and utilise these exercises accordingly.

Adwoa-Shanti Dickson
Voice Coach & Pan Associate Artist

One of Vidya's issue-based popular songs:

In Hindi

Fulo ka taro ka
Sab ka kehna hai
Ek hazaro mai meri
Gudiya hai

Sari ummar hame
Padhna likhna hai

Padhke likh ke
Tuj ko ek doctor
Ban na hai

Doctor ban ke sab
Ka illaj karna hai...

Translation:

Flowers and stars all say my little girl is one in a thousand.
All your life, you have to read and write.
By learning, you have to become a doctor.
By being a doctor, you have to cure everyone.

This song continues onto other professions such as teacher, lawyer, nurse, etc. Through this popular Hindi song tune from the 70s, VIDYA changed the words to promote education to girl-children. Copies available from Vidya.

STEP 20

Design

Theatre for Development does not usually take place in the kinds of theatres where a lot of intricate scenery is used. Neither does it normally have the amounts of money to generate very beautiful sets and curtains. In fact it is a theatre which normally relies on the power of the imagination to bring to mind the scenes and places for the plays.

However we can use very simple devices to help us suggest moods, places and ideas to our audiences. And, if most of your performances are outdoors, it may be very useful to have something visual to give a focus to the audience, or a frame for the play.

What is most important is to use what you have around you, whether that is materials or talent. Most importantly, use your imagination.

*   Is there someone in your group who can draw? Could their line drawings be enlarged on cloths to hang around the space?
*   Is there someone who is good at handicrafts? Could they make simple masks from paper or other easy-to-find materials?
*   Using 150 cm long wooden sticks or bamboo can make instant pictures on stage to complement your physical imagery.
*   Rope, string, fishing nets or other available items can similarly

be used to suggest shapes or even to show emotional states (someone hemmed in by a rope can be seen as imprisoned in his/her situation).

- Working after the tsunami in Sri Lanka our participants used materials from the debris of their homes to create a space, which carried a deep and resonant message.

- It is normally not necessary to be too realistic, so exaggerated props, e.g. from papier-maché, can be excellent at bringing the importance to a gun, a letter, a knife or other key object.

- For forum plays it is a good idea to have a box of props which might be used – a telephone, a clock, a stick, a pair of spectacles, whatever you think might be needed.

And don't forget that **costumes** are also part of design and are a wonderful way of instantly changing the mood. Four people suddenly putting on police-caps instantly suggest a host of associations to your audience; a doctor's coat is immediately recognisable. So it is a very useful idea to have a costume box in rehearsal and on stage for the changes demanded by your audience's interventions.

Rehearsals

Eventually you will have a play which has been created through your devising process. Maybe you have written it as a text, maybe it is in your minds but unwritten.

Now we enter a process of finding the best way of presenting that material to our audience. It is a process of looking at all the possible ways of playing a scene, of showing a character, of arranging characters on stage, to maximise the effect of our work.

In French the word for rehearsal is "repetition" and that describes it exactly: repeating, repeating, repeating, until we are confident that the performed play will communicate precisely what we want. And repeating it until all the actors know exactly what they are doing, and know it so well that natural nervousness in front of an audience cannot break their concentration.

A lot of people who don't have theatre experience will find this process a little strange. "Why should I do it again? We have made the play, let's perform it now!"

But rehearsal is necessary to fine-tune your ideas. And it needs a different discipline to the devising process. Here are some guidelines to help you decide how you want to rehearse:

- **How long should we rehearse a play?** This will be very variable from company to company and may depend on your financial situation. For a 20 minute play – straight or forum – we recommend a minimum of four weeks of full time work, or its equivalent, spread out over a longer period. However long you take, it will never be quite enough and there will always be a rush to the first performance.

- **Decisions** One of your first tasks will be to take some important decisions (you might want to look again at decision-making processes above). These will include:

  - **Casting** – who will play each character? This may not be the same person or people as in the devising process. There may be some conflict or rivalries in this time. Although traditional theatre decides casting in an autocratic way, we recommend full consultation with the group so that there is agreement and not resentment.

  - **Other tasks** - Who will take responsibility for other factors which are needed to make a performance: costumes, technical requirements, properties, music rehearsals?

So what exactly do we do in rehearsals?

Outsiders find it strange that so much time is spent in rehearsal and often ask "what do you do all day?"

Well the time can be used in many ways, but here are suggestions we have found useful:

- Start by reminding yourselves of the whole play. If it is a text you may want to read it aloud (we call this a read-through). You may want to re-tell the story in your own words. This will show if you have all got the same impression of what the play is about.

- You may want to discuss the issues in the play, even if you were part of the team which devised the piece. This discussion may focus on what you think will be the most important points to stress to the audience. You may discuss the structure of the play with regard to where the rhythms change, where it can be calm, where it will be faster or more dramatic. You may discuss each character and what their roles represent in the greater story.

- Now you are ready to work through the play scene by scene.

- In each scene you will be looking at how the story unfolds **in space.** This includes where the entrances and exits are, how the characters are grouped to show the dynamics between them (think of all the Image Theatre we looked at earlier). How can you best allow the audience to see what is important in the scene?

- In each scene you can ask "What does this character want in this scene?" or "What does this character fear in this scene?"

- You may have several possible ways of playing a scene. Rehearsals are a way of trying out these ideas to find the best one. (The German word for rehearsal – *probe* – means a test or a trying out.)

- There may be several ways of speaking your words; soft and menacing/loud and angry/ hesitatingly/thoughtfully etc. Rehearsals are a way of trying out these ideas to find the best one.

- Slowly the scenes take a shape and you move onto the next one until all the scenes have been worked through.

- Now you can put the scenes together to re-visit the whole story in the play. Does it make sense? Have some scenes become too long? / too important / too slow? Now is the time to consider and correct.

All the time in rehearsal we should be asking if the story is clear, if the story is real, if the story and the characters are believable. And

"is it interesting?"

Here are some rehearsal techniques to help you achieve these goals.

Stop and Tell

At any moment in a rehearsal the director / rehearsal-leader can call **"FREEZE!"** Everybody stops in that position and, when touched on the shoulder, speaks their thoughts at that moment. (Remember doing this in Image-Making)

Silent Scenes

Play the scene as you have rehearsed it, but without any words. Does it still make sense? Does your body language tell the story. Can you improve the physicality of your scene?

Gobbledegook Scenes

Play the scene as you have rehearsed it using only Gobbledegook (Nonsense Talk). As you don't have the meaning of the words you will be obliged to express yourself more clearly physically and, of course, through the sounds you make. This should give added depth of expression to your voices which can be kept when you bring back the text.

Character Journeys

Let each character have the stage space to move around and tell the story of their character from beginning to end of the play, concentrating on the changes in their character – the journey through the play. It is important for the actor to realise that they are (probably) different at the end of the play from how they were at the beginning. They can stand still and tell the journey or move around as if re-visiting the scenes. Don't let it last too long. Five minutes should be enough to get the essential character journey.

Hotseating

This could follow Character Journeys. Hotseating is a technique where the character (not the actor!) takes a seat facing the audience (probably the other actors) and answers any questions from them about the character. These could be about the character's past life, reasons for actions within the play, feelings about other characters, hopes for the future etc.

The character has to answer without hesitating. If this technique is practised when rehearsals are well under way, the actor should know enough about the character to answer. Often unexpected questions bring unprepared answers, which come from the subconscious and reveal interesting facets of the character which the actor has been considering.

Animals

What kind of animal is your character? There may be animal stories in your culture which are metaphors for human behaviour. Play that in reverse for a moment. Decide the nearest animal to each character in a scene. Let the actors start to walk and find voices of that animal. Then play the scene in this style. Watch how the physicality and the tensions (perhaps even the proximities between actors) become clearer. Sometimes moments from this exercise are so impressive that you could keep them in the final version of the play: a snarl, a sniffing of the air, an arching of the back etc.

Swapping Roles

This is particularly useful if you are finding a scene difficult, or just a moment in a scene.

Quite simply you exchange roles to see how someone else would play that moment or that scene.

> **Example:** The scene is of a mother saying farewell to her son when he goes to join the freedom fighters.
> Scene is played by Actor A - mother, Actor B son
> Then let another actor (C) take part.
> Now the scene is played by Actor B – Mother, Actor C son
> Then actor D takes part

Scene is played by Actor C - Mother, Actor D son............
and so on until several actors have shown several
possibilities of playing the scene.

All the above techniques will help you gain much more depth to
your performance. When you feel it is obtaining a coherent form
you may wish to "test" your work-so-far through...

Group Feedback Rehearsals

These can be as frequent as you like. The idea is for any of
those people not directly involved in the acting to watch
rehearsals of scenes or the whole play. In a peer-group these
will be people very close to your subject.

Ask for their feedback on the clarity of the narrative, on the
credibility of the characters and the situations, on the "interest-
value" of the performance. Listen and respect their opinions.
They are your peers and the audience's peers. They are a way
of getting to know if your theatre will engage people.

Sureshbhai: I felt shy in rehearsals when we
had to act as husbands and wives, and when we
had to kiss. But now I know that acting and real
life are different, even though the audience must
believe it's real.

Open Rehearsals

These are rehearsals in front of invited people to gain feedback
from them. Ideally the invited guests are from the same
community you will be performing to. Explain to them that this is
still work-in-progress and you would like them to give their
opinions, that they are a valuable part of the process. Then

perform the play, or scenes from it, as well as you can, and then listen to them. Ask if the play was credible, possible and clear. Ask if they recognise the situations as close to their experience. Ask if they have experiences or stories like those they have seen. Ask if they enjoyed it.

Listen carefully, not just to the praise but to the criticism and to their own ideas – they may feed real possibilities into your performance.

Hopefully your production is progressing well through the hard work of rehearsals. But you may still need to polish the work, make it more engaging, more "present" and more "in the blood" for the actors.

These techniques may help:

High speed rehearsals

These are fun, but really challenging. How fast can you perform the play without losing the story, the characters and the emotions? As long as every word, gesture, movement is there you can go as fast as your body and your mind will take you.

Entrance and exit rehearsals

These help keep the pace and the punctuation of the play at optimum level. You only rehearse the moments of entry and exit of any character. Make sure each entrance and each exit is clear. What are you showing the audience with each new character, each decision to leave the stage? Don't let entrances and exits be just drifting on and off. They are key moments to keep the story moving and changing.

Forum Play Rehearsals

As well as all the above rehearsal techniques, forum plays need to rehearse for possible scenes which may be suggested by the audience members during interventions. It is very important to project what interventions might come, even though you can never imagine all the things an audience will suggest.

This can be done first from within the acting group, imagining where interventions might come and how they might develop (new scenes, new characters, new arguments etc). Act out these possibilities. Then you can ask other company members or invited guests to be the forum audience and intervene with their ideas.

All audiences are different and will give you different impulses but it is great to have some experience of how you will have to improvise before you face the community audiences.

As you come close to your first performance you will need to practise using everything that will be there for the real performances so you can have.....

Technical rehearsals

These are for you to work with any sound or lighting equipment that you will need. If you are using microphones, get used to them now. If there is recorded music, rehearse getting the exact timing of the cue for it. The same with any lighting you are using. If you are moving furniture or props between scenes, rehearse doing it until it is smooth and does not interrupt the flow of the performance.

Dress rehearsals

Finally all costumes and properties and technical requirements are ready. The aim of a Dress Rehearsal is to give a complete run-through of the play as it will be for the first performance. It might be a good idea to do it exactly the same time of day you will perform, and you may want some people to watch it so you get used to the idea of playing to an audience. It may seem a little dry, as it is not yet the real thing, but give it all your energy so that you are in control of your work.

The Rehearsal Room

In some companies there may be a natural progression from devising to rehearsing. But, as you have just seen, rehearsals normally need more detailed focus and attention than the initial creative excitement of devising so you may consider setting some rules with the group to make this easier. For example:

In the rehearsal space:

- Keep an atmosphere of concentration on the rehearsal.
- No casual talking which may distract the work, go outside if you are not involved in the rehearsal and need to talk.
- No eating or drinking in the rehearsal space.
- Allow time for people to discover how to perform a scene – don't keep suggesting things to them. This is particularly important in very emotional scenes; domestic violence, rape, murder etc
- Give time and space for anyone who has "lived" the experiences being shown in the play to come to terms with seeing the action again. Take care of them.
- Allow space for experiences of other group members to help the scene.
- The whole group does not need to be in rehearsal the whole time. Some companies like to have everyone there, but you might find an advantage in just having those who are necessary for a particular scene. This can give added concentration without feeling judged by the others.

In the midst of this rehearsal process is **the director**. Who is she or he? What is the director's role in Theatre for Development?

The Director

The name sounds as if it is someone who "directs" people what to do and where to go, like a creative traffic policeman. That is certainly true in some kinds of theatre but it implies that the performers have no choices, that all the power is taken away from them.

In our work we need the director to be someone who will help the whole company discover the best way of bringing their work to their audience. However there is a very special role for the director which is to be the...............

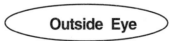

Outside Eye

who sees the play as the audience will see it. Because however much the actors are involved <u>in</u> the play they cannot be <u>outside</u> it to see it as a whole.

So we could say that the director's first job is to ask:

- Is the story clear and well told?
- Can I see it all clearly (are the stage images and movements visible and understandable?)
- Can I understand it? Or are there moments of confusion where we don't know what to look at, or who is doing what?
- Can I hear it (are the voices loud enough and the words clear enough)?
- Does it have a good pace with the key moments well pointed out?
- Is it engaging, interesting, dynamic, moving theatre?

Of course to achieve that will probably be a lot of work with the actors, slowly helping them to get the best results. To do this the director:

- Should instil confidence in the actors that they can achieve their goals (not fear that they are getting it wrong or are incompetent!).
- Should encourage and criticise constructively – concentrating on people's strengths.
- Should know how far the actors can go but not push them too far – especially in very emotional scenes which might be personally difficult for them.

- Should encourage the actors to discover how they can develop a scene rather than demonstrate it to them (then they will just be copying the director, not finding their own way of doing it).
- Should be clear and honest with the actors. If she/he doesn't know how to develop a scene, tell them, let a discussion solve the problem – directors are not gods - they don't know everything!
- Should ask questions to the actors and to the others in the room if appropriate.
- Should keep the whole picture in view when actors are concentrating on their detail.
- Should time the rehearsal process with the first performance in mind – make sure all scenes and actors get the right amount of time in rehearsal.
- Should motivate the team and encourage them when energy is low or they might be losing confidence.

So who is this director?

Although they need a different approach to work when directing, it is quite possible that members of the company who normally act might be very good directors.

You do not need to always have the same director. That might put too much power in one person, and might risk the plays always being similar.

Members of the group might want to try directing some scenes during workshops. If the group feels they have the right qualities, let them become a director.

You want to be a director ? Try it !

In general we feel that there is little point in having an outside director. Although they may be very skilful at arranging scenes they will not have the knowledge of the community and all its issues to guarantee the credibility of the production.

Vidya Performance Timetable – An ideal week

Day 1: Promotion and information dissemination in the community

- To get as many people in the community to watch your play the next day

- If the play to be performed is targeted towards women, for example, then encourage as many women as possible to attend the performance.

Day 2: Performance day

Arrival, arrange stage, perform, with discussions and debates afterwards

Day 3: Going round in small groups gathering reactions to the performances:

- To find out the impact of the performance

- To gather feedback on the performance

- To discover the issues that the community members are facing and learn their stories

- To collect stories and experiences which relate to the play's issues, then going back to the rehearsal room and improvising around these stories

- Create short plays (8-10 minutes) based on stories from the community

Day 4: Going back to the community and performing these short plays in smaller, more intimate (street) settings:

- To get people who hadn't intervened on stage to participate in the short plays where they are more comfortable (e.g. In their own courtyards with smaller groups)

- Further discussions with community members.

Day 5: Getting feedback from the whole week, and writing a report based on the week's work.

This can be through splitting into small units and chatting with people; buying tea for people at the tea-stall and gaining their confidence to talk; meetings of groups of mothers / fathers / children etc. A workshop with people might also give you their reactions.

- How do people feel about the issue now? (this may be 5th or 6th visit to this community)

- Evaluate the performance and its subsequent impact?

- Discuss with the company members what interrelated issues were discovered through the performance and workshops. Are these possible themes for future plays?

Performance

You have the plays and the songs, you have rehearsed the forum interventions and how to lead the discussions. Now you are ready to get out there and meet your audience.

So what more do you need? What do you have to think of as you prepare for, and set out for, the event?

> **Do you need police permission, or municipal permission?**
> **Have you done your publicity?**
> **Are there people/volunteers waiting for you there?**

If you are able, in your area, to have an indoor performing space, then the atmosphere of performance is much more controllable. If you are outside you may attract spontaneous passers-by who stay and become very involved.

> **Savitaben:** I remember performing with VIDYA when I was heavily pregnant and I had to play a crow. I felt shy in front of all those people with my big bump!

The following is about dealing with outdoor spaces and of course there are many different types of these.

- **Visibility.** You have to be seen. That's obvious but if you just perform on ground level and people gather round, it limits the number who can really view your performance. And if you then have scenes with one or more actors sitting on the ground, visibility is restricted perhaps to the first and second rows of people. Some groups may have a mobile stage, others can construct a platform stage. If not, look for somewhere with slightly higher ground, or on top of a low structure. Or find a place where the audience can look down on the action such having them sit on a hill-side or slope. After all your work you must be seen by the maximum number of people. Make sure there is space for people with disabilities.

- **Where's the sun?** If it is in the eyes of the audience they cannot see the action. If it is in the eyes of the performers they cannot see the audience. It can also be extremely hot!

- **What times of day** are most people free? Your research should have told you when you can get all (or most) members of the community watching.

- **Make the performance accessible**, draw the people in. Use the singing and music to attract them. This may take 10-15 minutes before the performance.

- **Use of voice / microphones** – generators and power. Even the best voices cannot reach an outdoor performance of thousands with background noise. Where will you get your power supply? Have you got a long extension cable?

- **Make the best of an outdoor environment.** Try to use whatever is present when you position yourselves. Are there trees or buildings for shade, or a wall which will be a backdrop. Where can people sit to watch your performance? On the ground, on rooftops, on steps? Avoid any busy roads or lanes which may bring traffic close to your performance. Think about the layout of your space.

During a village performance in North Gujarat, the electricity went out. The villagers, who are mainly farmers, used their farm torches to light up the stage so that Vidya could continue performing.

- **How will you encourage excluded or marginalised members of a community** to stay and watch and to enter the dialogue? Some may be uncomfortable because they feel threatened by the theme (are they the liquor supplier – the pimp etc?) or ashamed by it. You can't force them but if you have done some door-to-door publicity the day before (see timetable, above), remind them it is the community's problem which they have raised. Perhaps they have an interesting view. Tell them that all views are welcome.

  - **For example** if your play is about a woman experiencing domestic violence and most of the audience are men, you might want to find out where are the women in the community. You may decide to go and meet with the women and find out why they did not attend. Perhaps your research was not correct about when and where is the best time and place to perform. Or perhaps the women have been prevented from attending. You may decide to run a workshop with the women instead. Or have a discussion with the men. The issue of gender balance can be a common one in Theatre For Development work. You could decide to have women-only and men-only performances. Or have the women at the front and the men behind, or on separate sides. Each cultural location is different and these are things you can explore with the peer group. What is essential though, is that whatever the play is, the audience who intervene must be in a similar position to the central oppressed character. You can discern this by being an observant facilitator and entering into dialogue with the audience as they arrive.

- **Members of your group can encourage the audience** to enter the debate whilst sitting alongside them. However your members should **never** start a Forum Theatre intervention.

- **Dealing with stone throwers and conflict!** Stop the show, be quiet – don't try to retaliate – if it continues start to pack. This is likely to motivate the community to ask you to stay and perform. A dialogue between them and those committing the violence can start. This dialogue is as much part of what we do as the plays themselves.

> In eight years, Vidya has performed to almost two million people and has conducted several thousand workshops throughout urban and rural Gujarat and across India.

VIDYA EXPERIENCE

Challenges with forum interventions - possible effects

the empowerment process begins when an audience member says "stop" and comes to the stage to intervene. The process of absorbing this change into everyday life starts after the performance and in the workshops that take place the next day.

In our experience, the community will usually support and encourage those who intervene in forum plays. However sometimes we find that interventions can cause a problem within someone's family or the community. The individual who made the intervention may be viewed differently. They may be shunned or taunted for voicing his/her opinion in the open.

We always encourage and reassure that person and ask him/her what support structure he/she needs. We also work with other groups in the community who deal with issues such as those raised in the play. This helps individuals and the community to accept the vision for change.

Monitoring the effects and keeping in touch with audience/ community is therefore an extremely important part of our work.

Vidya worst case scenarios –

Be Prepared:

- **Community tension**
  - Always remember to have and maintain a good relationship with the members of the community so that, if there is tension, they will tell you if you should perform or should come back another time.
- **Person dying in the community**
  - When you go on Day 1 to promote your event and find out that there was a death in the community, then postpone your performance if wished.
  - If the death occurs the day of your performance, pay your respects and then leave.
- **Wedding in the community**
  - Postpone your performance, many of the community members will be busy with the wedding and will be using the community's space.
- **Festivities going on in the community, etc.**
  - The community space will be in use so talk to the community as to when a better time would be for you to perform.

Check the community's timetable first then adjust yours accordingly.

It is very important to maintain a good relationship with the community – if you adjust to the community's needs then they will accommodate yours!

Post-performance

VIDYA happiest moments...

During one performance, a gang of youths started throwing rocks at us. People in the crowd stopped them and ensured our safety. A few years later, one of youths that threw the rocks, joined our youth workshop because he realised his mistake and saw the difference that VIDYA makes in the community. He also apologised for his mistake.

The performance is over. You are all tired, hopefully happy that you have communicated ideas for the dialogue. What next? There is always follow-up work to do, to maximise the effect of your performance. We at Vidya have found...

- Immediately after the performance the audience needs information. An Information team might sing, calling out the relevant material for your performance and related issues. You may have printed flyers with information to give out.

- Of course the forum interventions (above) are already feedback but we also need to gather other kinds of feedback so that we can monitor success –
    - responses to the performance
    - impressions from actors going into the audience
    - results of discussions with audience – stay half an hour and talk to your audience

- Go back to base and log all your information, discuss the feedback. What can you learn from it?

- Counselling can begin immediately after the performance. Try to access existing expertise in the community e.g. advocates for health care, psychiatric help, legal assistance etc.

- Similarly you can begin introducing available resources e.g. NGO's who have micro-finance schemes, books for schoolchildren etc. Often people don't know what is available in their communities. Let them know.

- On the next day you can create short plays from your audience reactions (see timetable) after a walkabout in the community.

- Talk to the community about setting up a volunteer Information cell, updated by you, to provide continuity between visits. Once a month the volunteers can keep people informed of any developments in health care provision, micro-financing, consumer courts etc.

VIDYA difficult moments...

Mehmudaben: When the feedback after a performance of 'Asha' focused on alcoholism and gambling, a bootlegger in the community stopped our leader Manishaben and threatened her. We all went to her side and explained that we work on issues related to the girl-child and alcoholism and abuse affect her. But I still remember how afraid I was.

- And then, if the dialogue can be expanded through practical work, we can invite members of the community to one of our community workshops.

.........community workshops

(STEP 24)

We go into a community, we perform our plays, we encourage feedback through interventions or post-performance discussions. These can be very positive experiences for all involved but they are also, by their nature, very public, open experiences, sometimes in front of hundreds or even thousands of people. Try as we might, the people who intervene or speak up in a discussion will be those with most confidence or with the strongest ideas.

So there is a more private way to engage people, to give smaller groups the time and space to use creative means to reflect on the issues in their communities and see them more clearly.

This is what we call a "workshop".

Normally, of course, a workshop is a place where objects are designed and made (e.g. a metal workshop, a carpentry workshop), where different materials are turned into a new product with the knowledge and skills of the people working there.

A theatre workshop also uses many different materials (our bodies, our voices, our songs, our games) and we design new things with our knowledge and our experience.

A theatre workshop is a meeting of people to explore issues and ideas through play, through telling stories, through acting out actual or imagined experiences in order to develop our ideas, and further our dialogue. It can be planned to take a few hours, a day or a week.

A theatre workshop is more than just a discussion because there is a chance to be very active – making a song about a theme or acting out a situation or relationship. But there is also time for discussion when we reflect on what we have just done, what ideas are generated, what problems or solutions we can see.

A workshop should be enjoyable and liberating because we can gain strength from working in a group to realise the things we have in common, and how we can help each other explore our lives, our hopes and our fears.

A workshop is a safe space, perhaps a closed room, or perhaps just a fairly private area where we do not bother about the outside world, we do not judge how good each person is, and we are not preparing to present to an audience (although sometimes a workshop produces excellent material which you may choose to refine into a performance).

A workshop normally has a leader or leaders who introduce the topics, the games or exercises, and lead the discussions and reflections forwards.

A workshop can be open to anyone in the community or you may decide to have a workshop for a specific target group, for example only for women, for HIV-affected men, for children. In fact children's workshops are an excellent way to include young people in playing out issues in their lives, things that concern them about now or about their futures. And of course they may tell us more through a workshop than we will ever discover through research.

A workshop can be after a performance. In this case it is an ideal opportunity to reflect on what has been seen, how it applies to individual lives, even to try and recreate scenes from the play and give them alternative outcomes.

A workshop can also be before a performance. This will help introduce issues and ideas which the participants will later see on stage. Through the workshop the theatre event is demystified, the idea of intervention can be introduced and people have already started to think about how it applies to their community.

VIDYA difficult moments...

In 2004, after a successful children's workshop in a community, that community's leader tried to negotiate how many children he would provide VIDYA for the next workshop and how much he would charge VIDYA for the children. VIDYA decided to go straight to the kids and their parents instead of working with the leader of that community.

Why a Workshop?

If you were not able to take part in the interventions or discussions around a play, or if you have a desire to go further with the issues because they affect you, then a workshop is an ideal place for you.

For the members of the theatre group, they may wish to find out more about a community. A workshop is ideal to gather new ideas for future plays, as you hear concerns and personal stories from the participants.

A workshop can give members of a community a way of discussing issues through enactment, discussion, re-enactment. If they do this enough they may develop material into a performance they can perform or they may be able to continue "workshopping" without you.

A workshop can be a great place to spot future leaders for theatre work in the community, volunteers to help expand your work, or potential members for your peer group.

Running a workshop needs listening and leading and is excellent for developing the leadership skills of the peer group. As it is a peer group the leaders become role models for members of the community who see "people like them" developing an exciting and rewarding event.

REMEMBER: If you are going to be a workshop leader you will need to train yourself to do this. The performance training above is a good start but you will need to read the following section in great detail and try out your workshop-leading skills on your fellow peer group members to know how you can best introduce ideas, games and discussions. Listen to their comments and criticisms to fine-tune your skills.

NB. Make sure your workshop is at a time when people can attend. Ask potential participants for the best time. For example an early evening workshop may get very few women because they are busy preparing the evening meal.

How we run a workshop

Before running a workshop we recommend you **make a plan**. A workshop plan is just like a map which shows your starting point and where you want to get to. A map may show an ideal route, but when you are actually travelling, you may discover that there is a route which suits you more. So make a workshop plan, but be prepared to change your plan if that is what is needed.

Remember a workshop is an interactive creative experience not a formal class where you will deliver a message. It is an **active dialogue** between yourself and the participants, the participants and each other, the participants and themselves! It is not a monologue which you are going to give. Therefore, as workshop facilitator, it is important that you listen, and respond to what the group needs during the workshop, to ensure that they get the most out of their time with you. If this means abandoning the plan – then do it!

Kaloobhai: The community needs to feel that we are one of them. We sit down with them, we are not above them, they know we are equal to them.

Sureshbhai: In the community there might be people that do not want us to work there. So I try to talk to them, explain our work and convince them. Sometimes I might form a small group of two or three people and get them to talk to the community. But if a community still does not want us, we try to find out why we are not wanted. We can change our plans. But sometimes it is right to walk away. We do not force our work on anyone.

In order to make any plan and run a workshop, take some time to ask yourself the following questions. The answers to these questions will effect what kind of workshop you are going to design and deliver – they are part of your essential **research**.

Dipteeben: When I am doing research the most important thing I have to do is speak to the leader as well as the community themselves, we try to get them involved and find out as much detail as we can about the people.

VIDYA happiest moments...

Sureshbhai: During a women's empowerment workshop, our oldest participant, Vejima, was 90 years old. She said that she felt that her life had begun as of that day because she had now realised what she has done and how she can add value to her existence. She now sees her life differently from how she has lived it in her last 90 years. Although you saw life's experience on her face through her wrinkles and skin, she just experienced a new birth through our workshop.

Questions for the workshop leader

Who am I?

How old am I? What gender am I? Where do I live? What class am I? What languages do I speak? Am I from the same background as the group I am leading a workshop for? What life experiences have affected me? What prejudices do I have? What skills can I bring to this workshop?...etc

It is important as a workshop facilitator that you really look at yourself and decide how your identity may affect the choices you make. Although the workshop is not about you, or for you, you are still a person in the workshop space, a person with a degree of power, so it is important to think about who you are. This will have an effect on the workshop you are going to run, and how the group may relate to you. For example you may be female, this may be significant to how you plan the workshop if you are working in an all-male prison. Your first language may be English, the group you are working with may have a different mother tongue etc.

Ideally, we recommend that at least two facilitators run any workshop. This will mean that at least one person is always able to keep an objective eye on how the workshop is going. As a facilitator you will have someone to consult and negotiate with before and during the workshop and you will be more able to evaluate the work afterwards. If an accident happens in a workshop or a participant is experiencing a problem, at least one facilitator will be able to stay with the group whilst the other attends to the participant who is experiencing a difficulty. We suggest that you run workshops in no more than groups of 30.

Who are we?

Who is taking part in the workshop? What is the gender balance? Where are they from? Do the participants know each other? Do they all speak the same language? How many people will be there? How many people do I want to work with? What skills do the participants have? What are their experiences? What issues affect the group? What fears and hopes do they have? Have they made theatre before? What are their hobbies, interests and ambitions?...etc

Who the group-members are will affect the kind of workshop you are going to plan. So find out some details about the group beforehand. For example you may discover that three participants in the workshop are blind, so you might start to think about how you are going to make the work inclusive, adapt exercises beforehand to ensure they can participate fully. You may have a workshop with a large group of girls and one boy. Therefore you may need to have sensitivity towards the feeling of 'being different' in a group – this might even be a fun subject to explore. You may have a group of people who do not understand each other's languages, therefore you may plan a workshop which is less verbal. You may have a workshop where certain members of the group have been sexually abused, therefore you might be sensitive about whether or not you use exercises around touch,. You may discover the group enjoy a certain hobby, you might take this a starting point to work from etc.

In some cases it may not be possible to find out much about the group beforehand. If so, you may need to find out some of this information at the start of the workshop. You might use a game or an exercise at the beginning of the workshop to find out this information – and you'll need to put this into your plan (e.g. see "groups and shapes", "anyone who"... above). If you do not have much information about the group, you will need to make a plan which is very flexible, which will be **accessible** to lots of different kinds of people.   Your workshop plan may emerge according to who the group are and how many there are.

Where are we?

Where is the workshop going to take place? Is it outside / inside? What temperature will the room be? What kind of floor surface will we be working on? Is it a private space / public space? Does the space have doors, windows? Is the space quiet / noisy? Does the space have associations which may affect the group? Can we hang things on the walls? If the space is inside, is it lockable and, if so, who has keys? Do we have to leave the space at a certain time? Does the space have objects in it, if so are they hazardous? Is there a raised area or stage in the space? Are there rules attached to the use of the space? Is there running water, electricity?... etc

The answers to all of the above questions will have an effect on the kind of workshop you plan for and run. As a workshop facilitator, it is fine to say what is the minimum you require from a space. For example you may require:

A safe, clean, space, fairly neutral or with positive associations, which will be largely free from outside interruptions for however many hours you want to work. If this kind of space is not readily available to a community, you may decide to try to find another space, or adapt and work with what you have. What is most important is that you do not compromise on **safety.**

Theatre is an art form in which the use of space is fundamental. The space you are working in will affect the group and your work. So, what kind of effect do you want and what kind of space do you need? For example if you want to do lots of work which involves lying or moving on the floor, the surface may need to be clean and even. If you are working in a hot environment, you may want to find some shade. If the space has certain associations, for example if you are working in a school room used for maths or a religious space, you may want to transform the area to give it a fresh identity.

It is always a good idea to visit the space you will be using before the workshop starts, so that you can plan with the space in mind.

What do we want?

What do we want from this workshop? Why are we having this workshop? What are the aims of the workshop? Who decided these aims? Do the workshop participants want the same thing as the facilitators? What are our expectations? What do the funders or NGO partners want?

It is important that the aims for the workshop are clear and specific, then you will be able to select the games, exercises and tasks which help you to achieve these aims. If you have decided the aims before the workshop, then make sure that the group accepts these aims. If not, you may need to adapt the aims. No one should be forced to do something they do not want to do.

Equally it is important that whoever is sponsoring, funding or supporting your project is in agreement with your aims. For example you may aim to plan a workshop for a group of young people who do not want to attend school, to explore how to improve the school environment. However, the participants may believe they have been put in the workshop as a punishment and their aim is to resist the workshop. Unless you agree the shared aims at the start, there may be problems! You may be working with a group of girls who have a dream of staging a theatre production based on a ready made popular film script. However, an NGO may have asked you to run a workshop with a group which addresses child marriage. You may therefore decide to negotiate with the group a fresh aim, for example you might take a popular film script storyline and create new scenes based on the group's experiences.

How are we going to work?

What style of workshop are we going to have? Will this be a non-verbal workshop, a physical workshop, a storytelling workshop, a music workshop...? Which language are we going to work in? What rules are we going to have in our work? How long are we going to work for? How much time do we have? What kind of work do the participants enjoy doing?

Once you have considered who you are, who the group is, where you are going to work and what your aims are, you can start to decide how you will approach the task according to all you have discovered, and the skills which you have. In whichever way you choose to work, make sure your workshop is:

Creative

Challenging

Interactive

Participatory

Inclusive

Accessible

Informed and

Fun!

A note on time: We recommend the minimum time for a workshop be about one hour (if you are working with children this might be slightly less). The maximum for any single workshop session should be no more than three hours at a time. You may decide to work for a whole day, a whole week or at regular slots over a longer period of time. However you choose to work, run your workshop sessions for up to three hours at a time and try to ensure each session has a sense of completion within itself. After three hours maximum, most people usually like to have a break!

Before we go on to look at how to plan a workshop, consider one more question:

What next?

What will happen after your work is over? Will there be any follow-up work? Can the group you are working with sustain itself without your involvement? How can you leave the group with the skills to continue the work themselves? Will an NGO be working with your group afterwards? Is there funding to continue the work? Are there projects which will continue working on the issues?...etc.

One could say that the value of your workshop is not in what happens during it, but what the group goes on to do afterwards. Before you even begin to plan your workshop, it is very important to try to establish what will happen to your group after your work has been completed. For example if you run a very enjoyable workshop every evening for a week with a group of child labourers about using drama to improve their literacy, and after the workshop they still have no school to go to and life continues as it did before, then your workshop may have only awoken aspirations that will not be fulfilled, possibly leaving the group quite depressed. However if you run the same workshop in partnership with an organisation which provides information and organises scholarships to school, or perhaps as well as running your workshops you run a course which trains literate adult volunteers to use drama to improve literacy, your workshop may have real long term value. It is always a good idea to have members of the community training to do what you do, to ensure the work is **sustainable**.

So you have carried out the research, and you have considered the above questions in detail, you now have all the information you need to be able to start planning your workshop. Below is a suggested basic shape for any workshop whether it be for a one hour, three hour or one day session.

Planning A Workshop

Aims

As mentioned above in the 'what do we want?' section, the workshop will need clear aims. Every game, exercise, task or technique you put into your workshop plan should, in some way, help to achieve the aims. State or negotiate the aims, at the beginning of the workshop.

Pre-workshop

Before the workshop has even begun – the workshop has begun!

Get to the workshop space early, preferably before all the participants if possible. As soon as you arrive in the space in which you are going to work, prepare it for the workshop. If you arrive before the participants you will be able to greet them informally, find out a bit about them if you have not worked with them before, and assess the mood and atmosphere of the group. These few moments before the workshop begins will give you a good indicator of issues that are relevant to the group.

Stages of a Workshop

Stage 1: Preparation

Each workshop, no matter how many times you have worked with a group, should start with some kind of preparation to work, also known as a **warm-up**. Depending on how much time you have allocated, this may be one or two games or tasks to prepare the group physically, vocally, mentally and in terms of their team work.

Stage 2: Exploration

Once you have prepared the group, making sure that their bodies, voices, minds and team spirit are ready for work, you can go on to fulfil your workshop aims through games which will release their imagination and creative expression. You may use exercises (such as image work, storytelling and improvisation) which will refine their performance skills and give them the theatrical language to explore the chosen themes in more detail.

Stage 3: Creation

So, the participants are prepared, they have explored the theme of the workshop and have been equipped with some theatre skills, the next stage of the workshop will be to give the participants some time to apply what they have learned by carrying out a creative task on their own, usually in small groups. As a workshop facilitator, it is always good to have time in your workshop where you are not 'leading' the participants, and they are working in independent groups, carrying out an instruction. This small group work will improve the group's independent creativity, artistic style, empowerment, teamwork and problem solving skills.

Stage 4: Presentation

Once the group has carried out their tasks, we suggest you give time for the participants to present what they have created, and get feedback from group members and facilitators. It is important when giving feedback that you bear in mind, that there are no distinct 'right' and 'wrong' ways of creating, but certainly you can suggest what might strengthen the piece, how it could be different and where the weaknesses lie. In a new group they may not choose to present their work through performance, they may want to talk about how they got on.

Stage 5: Conclusion

Towards the end of the workshop it is important that you allow time to bring the workshop to a close. This may involve summing up what has been achieved, how far the aims have been reached, where the work will go next, getting feedback from the participants on how they felt the workshop went and what are their desires for the future.

This crucial time at the end of the workshop will allow participants to process any issues which have been raised by the work, ask questions or gain support. This time should enable the participants to be able to leave the space, whether for a break before the next session, or whether it is the end of your time with them, to walk out into the world more empowered and more ready for what they will face next. The conclusion does not have to be merely through discussion, although discussion is valuable. You may also want to facilitate a relaxation exercise, an empowerment song, a favourite game, a group support exercise etc.

Shaping Workshops

When you are planning the workshop think carefully how each stage of the work links to the next and an order for the games and exercises. A workshop should be an experience which flows easily from one element to the next and grows in levels of difficulty and challenge.

As with performing, your skills as a Theatre for Development workshop leader will get better and better through practice and listening to feedback.

Part Three
Making an Organisation
Some practicalities:

Set yourself up

The legal status of your group may seem the least important thing as you engage with your local issues, and start the exciting journey of using theatre to discuss new possibilities.

So why should you set yourself up as anything more than a group of friends or colleagues?

The two most important answers to this would be "funding" and "stability".

Many funding bodies will only give funds to a group with some legal identity, because such a body will have rules and regulations about how money is spent and accounted for. This gives your funders the assurance that their money will be used in a transparent and responsible way.

The long-term stability of your group is also strengthened if you have organisational documents which state clearly what you do, how you are organised, how you take decisions, and who has responsibilities. As people leave the group and others join, there is a structure to maintain the ideals and identity of the work. Of course this can be changed but only by the democratic processes in your constitution, or similar document.

The Vidya group exists in a State where there is a huge numerical imbalance between women and men – The sex ratio is (according to UNICEF) 912 women to every 1000 men. Vidya is considering writing into its constitution that the company will be led by a woman until the numerical equality is restored in the State.

Each country will have rather different laws and options on how you can set yourself up as an organisation. So inform yourselves, or talk to a friendly lawyer or an NGO.

Based on the type of work you are doing, you have to decide if you will establish yourself as a company, charity, trust, society, cooperative or an NGO or whatever is available in your country.

Find out the proper authorities to approach, fill out the forms and then probably you will have to wait some time. There may be some cost involved. We have found it is worth it.

Take a look at funding sources to determine what sort of organisation receives the funding you require.

VIDYA EXPERIENCE:

When you are at work in the community, you do not think of the legality or the identity of an organisation, but when considering the future of the organisation, you must know and understand the laws as they apply to your organisation and its objectives/aims. For Vidya, we had to consider how to set up a trust.

It was difficult to obtain the correct information on what laws and rules applied but we found the right people to ask and to research the laws for us.

Vidya Education and Charitable Trust was established as an independent trust in 2003 to continue working on issues relating to girl-children and the empowerment of women through theatre, workshops and audience interaction.

There were several options to form an independent identity; a society, trust, or a private limited non-profit company. Under the Bombay Public Trust Act 1950 /section 25, a trust can exist independently of the state, be self-governed by a board of trustees, produce benefits for others and is 'non-profit' making. We felt the trust identity best suited us because we established Vidya for the purpose of education to benefit the members of an uncertain and fluctuating class. Also, because a trust is irrevocable, our work can continue for ever. We already had our aims and objectives and we then decided on our director, advisor members, and board of trustees and passed our first resolution to form a Trust certified by Charity Commissioner in August 2003 as Vidya Educational and Charitable Trust. We created our Trust Deed as our official trust document and continue to have yearly meetings on the direction Vidya is taking and have the necessary resolutions passed by the Trustees. While setting up the trust, we also asked ourselves how we could apply for funds and how Trust law would impact us. Even without a large fund, Vidya was set up because we believe that the work that was started did not finish in the three years of the initial project and there was a need for the work to continue and for the peer members to continue it.

Organisational structure

There are many structures that can be used to make your organisation more stable, and thus aid its existence, the sharing of responsibilities, and its ease of planning, handling money etc.

Most organisations are in some way "hierarchical" with a single leader (perhaps called a director) who is at the "head" of the organisation. Depending on the size of an organisation there may be any number of other layers of responsibility. Hierarchies are open to some abuse, but can also be a good way of sharing power as long as everyone in the organisation has an audible voice in the running of things.

In this format the typical Theatre for Development company might have:

- An artistic leader/director
- An administrator
- The peer group members, some of whom may have particular responsibilities (driver, costume care, publicity etc)
- And there may be trainees or volunteers who help with any of the above tasks.

This structure can put a lot of pressure on the artistic leader to keep everything together, so it is important that the administrator takes as much responsibility as possible for all financial, legal and organisational matters.

Moreover by having regular and frequent meetings with the whole group any problems or resentments can be dealt with and any ideas or wishes from the members can help share the burden. Such levels of group decision-making can be adjusted to each group. Perhaps at the beginning of the group's life the director may be the only person with experience and will have to make most of the decisions alone, but the aim should be to empower everyone to be part of the decision-making process and be a spokesperson for the company.

In many cases Theatre for Development companies are started by more experienced people, perhaps better educated, perhaps not even from the target group from which the peer members come.

The long-term goal is to pass all organisation to members of that community, so we strongly recommend, from the very beginning, starting a process whereby peer group members train to be leaders. This can be a gradual process whereby different members take on leadership of rehearsals, finances, organising timetables etc.

Other models could include:

- A Company with Revolving Leaders – every month (or six months) a new person takes the director's role.
- A Company with no overall director but group, cooperative decision making for everything.
- A Company with no artistic leader but several leaders in specific areas (directing, acting , logistics etc)
- A Company of peer members who want to retain control from within their community but who "buy-in" expertise for book-keeping, fund-raising etc.

Inevitably the way in which you structure your company will have an effect on your pay structures. This can be a delicate issue and you may want to consider such questions as:

- If we do equal amounts of work should everyone receive

exactly the same pay, regardless of experience and qualifications?

- Should we pay people according to their need, e.g. a mother with 4 children will need more than a young person living in their parents' house?
- Do those who have more experience (and/or qualifications) deserve more pay?
- Should we pay according to the amount of work done (larger roles, or more workshop leading deserve more pay than those with smaller roles etc)?

In so many groups the members do not have a full knowledge of the finances of the company, and so cannot measure their requests for pay, or pay-rises, against what is available. We strongly recommend openness in these matters.

Management board & other allies

Most legal or not-for-profit organisations will require you to have some kind of board of directors or trustees. If you are a cooperative you may be able to be your own management board, but sometimes you will be required to have a group of people who are not employed by you and are not allowed to receive any money for their services. Their role will be to advise you and to ensure that you are fulfilling your legal and financial requirements.

If all this sounds rather formal we can also tell you that such bodies can be really useful. If you choose a group of people who are genuinely interested in your work and have experience beyond that of the group (in legal matters, fund-raising, publicity, or human rights) they can be useful allies.

Here are a few ideas about such bodies:

- Use your Board of Directors as an outside & transparent control of your activities, by appointing a chair, a treasurer, a secretary to take minutes of all meetings. You may also want to have staff representation on the board and possibly community representation.

- Use steering groups for specific projects. If you are working in a specialist area e.g. HIV/AIDS you might want some doctors, NGO workers, people with HIV/AIDS on this temporary committee.

- Children's councils – can be constituted, and members voted by children in your communities. They will give you honest feedback of how conditions are, how they would like things to change and what they would like you to do about it.

- Community councils. These are wonderful ways of getting feedback from the communities where you are working, getting volunteers to help you with the work, identifying new issues, planning useful activities and much more. It also shows you are genuinely interested in people in your target communities. Meet regularly, and enjoy the contact.

Administration

Every group needs a level of administration, whether carried out by one specific person or shared by a cooperative of people. Here is a (non-exhaustive) list of the tasks that will need to be done:

- Management of Finances
- Maintaining Legal Requirements of the Project
- Gathering material to prepare Reports to Donors for Monitoring of the Project
- WRITING FUNDING PROPOSALS
- Facilitating audit
- Logistical organisation for performances: Distributing leaflets/ arranging venue/procuring necessary Local Authority permissions/dates/timetables
- Maintaining liaison with Press and Local Authorities/Public Relations
- Disseminating information to maintain constructive links with NGOs
- Maintaining office supplies
- Maintaining office working relationships
- Representing Theatre Company at Fund-raising Event/ Donors meetings
- Maintaining liaison with NGO Bureaus
- Maintaining inventories of Props and Costumes
- Updating website

and we are sure you will keep adding to this list!

Funding

There are some people who love the challenge of looking for funding. Most of us probably are quite nervous about it or actively dislike it. But the reality is that almost everyone who starts work from this book will need funding at some time.

So you will have to decide exactly what you need and what it is for. Remember it is rare for someone to give you a lump of money and say "Do what you like with it". Most givers want their money to be used for very specific purposes. This means you need to work out a budget for how you will spend that money.

So make a budget.

This could include any of the following (NB some may not apply to your situation):

Costs	Amounts	Totals
1.Salaries or fees		
Artists' fees		
Administrator's fee		
Technician's fee		
Other fees (driver? Researcher?)		
		Sub-total
2. Production costs		
Costumes		

Properties		
Sound equipment		
		Sub-total
3.Transport		
Fares for performers		
Hire of vehicle		
Fuel		
Motor insurance +Maintenance		
		Sub-total
4.Space		
Costs of rehearsal space		
Hire of performance venue		
		Sub-total
5. Administration		
Office space costs		
Telephone/internet		
Stationery		
Postage		
Electricity		
Insurance		Sub-total
6. Publicity		
Cost of printing flyers/posters		
Newspaper advertising		
		Sub-total
7. Documentation		
Costs of photography		
Video costs		
		Sub-total
8. Contingency (this money is your safety net just in case you over- spend or unforeseen costs arise)		
		Sub-total

GRAND-TOTAL

Then you need to research the types of funding available to you and which ones you are prepared to apply for.

You may consider some money is unethical for the area in which you work, e.g. some will not take money from tobacco companies when working on health issues, or from alcohol companies if there is an alcohol problem in the area. Others find that government money from an oppressive regime may not be acceptable, or may be seen as suspicious by their target group.

Normally funding can be divided into these areas:

- **Statutory funding** – that which comes from local, regional or national government, perhaps through a ministry. Sometimes through the profits of a National Lottery.

- **Charitable funding** – that which comes from established charities, trusts or foundations, sometimes set up by a rich individual or by a large corporation. These may be in your country or, sometimes, from another country.

- **NGO/INGO funding.** This is often in the form of a fee to carry out work which furthers their goals e.g. an HIV/AIDS charity may fund you to do plays which open the discussion around this issue.

- **Commercial & Corporate funding.** This can either be through direct sponsorship or a donation from a company through its Corporate Social Responsibility programme. Sponsorship normally requires you to carry the company's logo prominently at sponsored performances.

You may find that you need to be registered as a company or as a charity or educational trust to obtain such funds.

In some countries you may need to have existed for a certain amount of time before you can apply to some sources, and be able to show accounts for that period. So don't delay in registering and keeping accounts, however small they are at the beginning.

To be a successful fundraiser you must be passionate about your work and imaginative in your thinking. It may mean endless phone calls and letters. It may mean knocking on people's doors to get to talk to them and persuade them that your work is worth funding.

Before you write, or talk to them, take some time to research what the organisation wants to fund, so that you can stress those elements in what you say.

Then you can structure your appeal following these lines:

- **The Need** – what need are you meeting through your work
- **The Solution** – how do you meet that need through your work. Describe the work, and mention the time span of your project
- **Why You?** – describe how you are the best organisation to do this work
- **The Result** – how will the situation change through your work. What are the outcomes?
- **Consequences of the Work not Happening.** What will happen if you don't get the money and don't do the work.
- **The Cost.**   Include your budget to support this.

Good Luck!

> **VIDYA worst moments...**
> Kaloobhai: When I initially joined VIDYA, I didn't know what a bank was or how to save money and did not know what to do with the wages that VIDYA gave me. I had to rely on others for advice and trusted the wrong person to keep my money for me.

Partnerships – negotiating commissions

Networking with other organisations is crucial to the long term sustainability of your organisation, skills development of your group, exchange of information/ideas/resources and gaining the awareness of the other forms of social work being done on interlinked issues in communities

REMEMBER: There is limited funding and you are not building any physical infrastructure for which there may be a lot of money. You are a support service to the community and have to make efficient and effective use of the small funds available to make a big impact.

Networks can be formed to share and exchange information, ideas, future plans and resources.

When you collaborate with other organisations:

- Research the organisation carefully through their office, website, meetings, word of mouth, in the community if they have done work there and through other organisations, etc.
- What are their ideologies, objectives, ethics, size, mission, vision, people working in the organisation?
- What is their organisational structure (are people able to talk directly to the person making the decisions)?

- Is there transparency in the organisation, etc.?

What to consider when collaborating, before and during the project:

- Is the joint project worth it? Does the funding offered match the effort you are making and when you will get the money? You would be wise to ask for (for example) 30% to develop the script. 50% before the first performance, 20% on completion of performances.
- Do your organisation's objectives, values, structure, style of work, fit the other organisations and the individuals involved in the proposed project?
- Is the organisation interested in following up and monitoring the results of your work and building on what you have started for them?
- Can the people from your side work with the people from the other organisation? Is there a solid understanding of the project and its outcome? Make sure there are meetings where the goals are shared.
- Are you compromising your ethics at any point in the project?
- Will your group be satisfied with the work involved in the project and its outcomes?
- Is there openness in discussions, especially during feedback on the partnership at the end of the project?
- How does this partnership help sustain you financially?
- What will your organisation gain creatively from the partnership?
- Are you achieving your main objective in the project? Continue evaluating this throughout the project.

- What level of partnership are you willing to go to regarding the other organisation's objectives or issues?

Discuss the budget with your group and the particulars of the collaborative project. Help them see the long-term benefits of the project. Ensure there is transparency regarding the project. Your members should know the budget and particulars involved. You also have to be sure to convince them of the benefits of the project and how this helps them and the organisation.

Vidya experience.

Vidya worked with Medhavi, an NGO which works on sanitation and hygiene. How does this issue relate to the girl-child? Vidya conducted 500 workshops in the coastal areas of Gujarat – through these workshops, people became aware of the importance of clean sanitation and hygiene, and how improvement of facilities helped with girl child's health, and did not force them to go long distances where they might be endangered. This also made Vidya aware of the various government and NGO programmes that are available in the most interior parts of Gujarat. Everything is a learning process and it helps in the growth of the group and the organisation.

Vidya Experience.

One of Vidya's very first projects was with a well known, established Indian NGO working on environmental issues. Vidya would receive Rs.1500 per performance – the objective of the performance was to encourage people to maintain the water pump that was installed by the NGO within their community. Through the performance, each community member decided to contribute Rs.10/year to the pump's maintenance fund that would be handled by their community of 5000 members. Vidya's one performance persuaded the community to save Rs.500,000.

Although the fee to Vidya was low compared to the outcome, Vidya established a relationship with a well known NGO and gained experience working in a different community (a dock yard on the Western coast of Gujarat). The drawback was that Vidya would have to cut back on premiums that the Vidya members would receive. Through the discussion, Vidya's members understood that we must start from somewhere and the collaboration project fee was a minor setback but there were also long-term benefits of having the experience of working with this particular NGO and on this project.

Documentation and archiving

This seems obvious but so many groups become absorbed in their work and forget to keep a record of it.

Use a camera and video-camera if you can. Sound is often difficult to hear through a video camera so consider recording the sound separately. It is very useful for you to look back and remind yourself of past work. More important it is vital when you need to present your work, e.g. to funders or at a conference of other groups, or if you need to make a brochure, a promotional video or publicity.

Any documentation is good but it is worth making the extra effort or paying a little extra money to get very good quality and well framed images.

After five years you will be amazed to look back at what you have done.

NB. Don't forget to document the audiences too!

Monitoring and Evaluation

How do we prove it's working, how do we know who has been affected by the work?

Monitoring and evaluation enable us to measure the effect of the work we are doing as an essential part of our Theatre for Development work. It is very important to decide how you will monitor and evaluate your project before you start. Make sure the practicalities and costs of monitoring and evaluation are in your project budget from the very beginning and decide who is going to be responsible for these areas. Monitoring usually happens during your project and towards the end. Evaluation usually happens when the project has finished.

Monitoring

Monitoring is collecting and keeping a record of information about who is attending your project and how it is affecting them. This information will provide you with the evidence you may need to justify your work to funders and others. This information will also enable you to assess how far the project is achieving your aims and objectives and to make changes to the project if you need to, and plan for the future. For example you may discover through monitoring that very few girl child workers are attending the project. If one of your aims is to reach girl child workers, monitoring will have provided you with the evidence you need to support changing the time or place that you are working with the girl children. You may discover that no disabled people are attending your project, although 10% of the community you are working with are disabled. This evidence will help you to uncover why your project is not being accessed, so that you can make changes In this example, it might be something as simple as providing a wheelchair ramp. Monitoring can also include documenting your project and will help you to archive your work. The monitoring information you gather will be in two strands - quantitative and qualitative.

Quantitative information provides **objective** details about the project which you can measure in numbers, for example:

How many people attended?

How old were they?

Where were they from?

How many men / women attended?

What were their social, ethnic, religious, cultural and economic backgrounds?

How many people with disabilities attended?

Qualitative information provides **subjective** details of the quality of the project, for example:

How do the participants feel the project is going?

How far are we achieving the aims of the project?

What are participants attitudes to the issues we are dealing with – before during and after the project?

What change has taken place in individuals' lives and the life of the community?

How could the project be improved?

VIDYA memorable moments...
Daksha had dropped out of school at the age of 8 and worked with her mother doing domestic work at different homes. VIDYA motivated her to return to school at the age of 15 and worked with her and her 8 year old classmates so they could understand and work together. Seeing her going back and continuing her education was a really memorable moment.

How do we monitor?

Try to monitor in as many different ways as possible. Participants and audience members often respond in many different kinds of ways. A multiple and diverse approach to monitoring will help you or your evaluator make a value judgement on your project based on rich and varied evidence and will also make the final evaluation report much more useful and interesting to read.

You might monitor through -

- Questionnaires
- Voting on an issue during a workshop or Forum Theatre play
- Observing the community (e.g. counting how many are in attendance, observing change in behaviour, writing down a description of the interventions in the forum theatre session)
- Interviews – voice and video recorded
- Group consultations
- Discussions
- Case studies
- Anecdotal evidence
- Using image theatre

Vijaybhai: I know VIDYA's work is making a difference because during a workshop about women's role in local governance none of the women spoke up. But in the forum theatre performance, when I was on stage, hundreds of women spoke up, got up and became involved in the debate.

Where possible use these methods before, during and after your Theatre for Development work.

Remember what did not work is often more useful to note than what did work!

Don't forget, in a peer group the effect of the work on the lives of the peer group themselves is a very important part of the project and it is from this group that you will probably be able to attain the most detailed response.

Evaluation

Evaluation usually takes place when the project is finished. Evaluation involves making a judgement on the value of the project. Evaluation is therefore extremely important. Just doing Theatre for Development work is not enough. We must measure the effect of our work, to be sure that the work is having a positive effect, in accordance with our aims. We can often feel that the work is going well. But we may be called upon to prove the usefulness of our work by our communities, funders, NGO's, local government, the police, even our own families.

To make a judgement on the value of the project, whoever is doing the evaluation (the evaluator) will need information on the aims and objectives of the project, monitoring information on how the project progressed (see monitoring above) and information on the results of the project. The evaluator can be from within your organisation but we also recommend you have an external evaluator to enable a more impartial, unbiased judgement to emerge.

How do we evaluate?

Evaluation involves taking the results of all of the information gathered through your monitoring during the course of the project, and making an informed value judgement on the project based on your original aims and objectives. It is therefore very important that your aims and objectives are clear from the start.

Sometimes we do not know the value of the project straight away. So consider having evaluations at different stages, for example one week after a performance and workshop, three months later etc.

Limitations and Possibilities

Although we work hard at monitoring and evaluation, we also accept that the effect of Theatre For Development work can be difficult to measure, yet we need to measure the effect of the work in order to be able to improve it in the future and guard against problems. It is important therefore that Theatre For Development workers have an overall awareness of the strengths, weaknesses, opportunities and threats encountered in this work, so that we can realise its potential and plan strategically.

This is known as a SWOT (Strengths, Weaknesses, Opportunities and Threats) analysis.

We highly recommend using SWOT analysis as part of your own process of realising the past limitations and future possibilities of your work.

Following the template which follows, try to be as honest as possible:

STRENGTHS: write all the things that are special, strategic, effective about your work

WEAKNESSES: write about the points which are not effective, or which have not fulfilled their potential

OPPORTUNITIES: where might your work lead? What new areas could be developed in the future.

THREATS: What, or who, might stop you achieving your goals.

Try carrying out a SWOT analysis specific to your project .....

(Past) **Strengths of your project**	(Past) **Weaknesses of your project**

(Future) **Opportunities**	(Future) **Threats**

For more detail see Kees Epskamp's Theatre for Development: An Introduction to to Context, Applications and Training, (London and New York: Zed Books), 2006, pp 62-63

Publicity

Publicity is the art of letting people know about you and your work.

There is no point in doing fantastic work and then nobody knows about it.

Of course publicity can costs an enormous amount of money, but there are plenty of ways of getting the knowledge of your work to the people you want to know.

So first:

IDENTIFY YOUR TARGET GROUP – who do you want to know about your work?

Think about where they are, what they see, what they look at, who they talk to. This gives you a geographical focus for your publicity.

What kind of publicity can you use:

- **Word of Mouth**. Do you have key people in this area (you probably do if this is a real peer group). They might be family members of your group, volunteers, community teachers, health workers or NGO workers. These people can deliver the most valuable publicity in the world – word of mouth. Make sure they have the information and ask them to "pass it on".

- **Your name or logo**. Where can you get your name seen? Be imaginative. Can you print it on bags? Can you afford T-shirts with your name. Can you give them to people who help you? Can you paint it on your vehicle? Hang it at the side of your stage? Outside your working space, office etc. Get your name known!

- **Flyers and posters**. These are great short-term publicity tools for a particular event. You can post them, hand them out in the street, stick them on trees or walls (check if it is legal). But remember they are only short term, quickly covered up or thrown away.

- **Media.** This may not be so important for your target group but is excellent to get the word out to the decision makers, funders etc. Often local newspapers will publish a press release almost exactly as you send it, so practise writing good short press releases. A photograph adds enormously to your profile. TV and radio are equally useful. Try to make friends with people in these media and keep them informed of all your news.

- **Photographs, videos, CDs.** When you go to make a presentation about your work, perhaps at a school or local community meeting, it is very valuable to give people a fuller idea of what you do, by using these. They are equally important to send to potential funders to show them our work in action. This is why you need documentation.

- **Newsletter.** If you have friends of your work within or beyond the community, a simple printed page of your news with photos, will keep them up to date with your activities and maintain your relationship. Over time this may progress to be a small brochure every six or twelve months or, if you have the technology, become an "e-newsletter" – but make sure your target group can access it.

Advocacy – spreading the word

You develop your work. You know it is good. The community is developing. You could just stay in that position but don't you think more people should know about the work, more people should be doing it?

If you believe in this work you will want such work to be more effective in more places. This does not necessarily mean that you have to grow into a much bigger organisation. Maybe you will just be seeding ideas in other people's minds and hearts.

So:
- Don't stay insular and isolated
- You need to let other people know what you are doing
  - so that collaborations can take place
  - so that you are known as a centre of experience and ex pertise
  - and therefore you can train trainers and seed other work
  - so the funders hear about you

What can we do practically?:

- Go and talk about your work
- Go to community meetings
- Go to meetings of other NGOs

- Send information about yourselves to the municipality or area authorities
- Go and talk about your work in schools and colleges
- Make sure your name is on the lists of organisations who can deliver good work and good results

Part Four
KEEPING GOING

How do we keep going?

You have created your performances, you have brought them into your communities, you have opened up dialogues and discussions and you have, we firmly believe, started the process of change.

You have set yourselves up as a legal body with well regulated finances, you are letting people know about your work, fundraising for it and archiving it.

Does it just go on like this? Or...........

KEEP ON 1

Generating ideas

After a few years there is a danger that the work can go stale. Don't get complacent. Self congratulation can be very dangerous. Often when you are performing for a community (who may not have had access to a very high standard of theatre work) you can 'get away' with continually presenting a 'low' standard of theatre work. Don't let this happen. Keep on developing your skills, keep on improving your art-form. How do we keep generating new ideas to increase our skills and start new plays and routes to change?

Here are a few examples :

- Invite guest facilitators to come in and lead new creative training workshops with you.
- Invite guest directors to come and direct plays with you, giving you a fresh eye on your work.
- Invite guest speakers to come and share their experience of the issues your project is dealing with.
- Arrange cultural trips for the group to the theatre, cinema, music events, festivals etc to give them fresh creative input.
- Arrange to go away on a creative retreat together.
- Go to a forest, a beach, a mountain – any location which helps to give the group a fresh perspective, be inspired, have discussion, write new songs, new poems...
- As students do at some Universities, have a 'reading week' where group members have tasks - to read new stories, poems, newspapers or to listen to new music or watch videos. After the week come back together and share new ideas for your plays.

NB. We advised against guest directors earlier in the book, but when the group is mature and not easily manipulated it can be a refreshing change, and bring new perspectives.

KEEP ON 2

Group dynamics

One crucial aspect of sustaining your work is noticing the changes within the peer group, adapting to those changes and dealing with challenges and conflicts as they arise. Bruce Tuckman (www.businessballs.com) considers that most groups go through five stages in their life. He has given them the catchy names -

- *Forming* - where the group begins to establish itself.
- *Storming* - when the polite barriers between people have come down and the group starts to deal with challenges and when conflicts may begin to arise.
- *Norming* - when the group learns to deal with difficulties and conflicts and gets into a good rhythm of working together efficiently.
- *Performing* - where the group is working well together to achieve their shared aim (this does not necessarily mean acting on stage, but in the case of a Theatre For Development group it may mean this).
- *Mourning* - where the group ends their work together and there is a period of loss.

Often just talking together at the very start of your project about these stages will help the group to understand and accept the life that the group is going to go through. If the group realise that they will go through a 'storming' stage, and that this may be difficult, it may be easier to cope with when it arises. They may be reassured that getting to this stage is an important part of their journey on the road to norming (working together well) and performing when they will achieve their aim. The mourning period can come as a shock to some if they are not ready for it. Like all life, at some stage it will end, and a new one will begin.

However, some groups find it difficult to get past the 'storming' stage. They get stuck in perpetual conflict. Here are some ideas of how to get unstuck:

Group agreement - try going back to the group agreement you made at the start of the project, talk about what aspects of the agreement have been neglected, or where new agreements need to be made. If your group did not make an agreement, try making one.

Team work - much of the team building and creative work we have offered in this book is very good for exploring and resolving conflict and power struggles. We would encourage you to use this work not only to make theatre but to keep your group communicating in a healthy way. Here are reminders of useful exercises to help:

Revisit the chapter on team building, try playing these games and exercises again and talking about what you learn from them:

- Stuck-in-the-mud
- Ball connection
- Do Nothing game
- Rhythm of the group
- Perspectives
- Group yes

Image theatre – this can be an excellent tool for analysing situations. If the group is experiencing difficulties try sculpting an 'Image of the Group'. Here is how:

- One at a time participants use other people's bodies and any objects to sculpt an image of the group. They work in silence, without speaking.
- They work through various images until an image of the group is formed which everyone recognises and agrees with.
- The group may not be able to agree yet on an image of the group. You may have to return to this exercise a few times. Even if they do not arrive at a final image, just the process of trying will enable the group to see themselves from various perspectives and gain a greater understanding of themselves as a group, the first stage in changing it.

- When an image of the group is arrived at, ask them to do the same again, but this time to construct an ideal image of the group.
- Finally ask the group to return to the real image of the group. On each sound of a clap of the facilitator's hands, the group must now make one move from the real image to the ideal image. This then is an image of transition. Give as many claps of the hands as it takes to get there. Ask the group to observe themselves in action. Noticing what change is needed to get from the real to the ideal.

Improvisation

Speaking from 'I' is an excellent tool for exploring how language can create or perpetuate conflict.

- Ask the group to get into pairs and label themselves A and B.
- Ask A to spend a few moments thinking of an unresolved problem or conflict they have had in the past with someone *outside* the group, which left them feeling upset.
- B is going to play the person with whom A had a problem. A is going to speak to B about the problem in the following ways: They are going to remain seated, they are going to identify the problem, express their feelings and make a request for change. They do this by beginning their sentences as follows:
- **"When......."** Here A is going to identify the problem. They will complete the sentence by stating clearly and briefly what happened to upset them. As much as possible A should avoid blaming the person, they must state the basic facts of what happened without laying responsibility.
- **"I felt......."**   Here A is going to express their feelings. They will complete the sentence by stating clearly and briefly their feelings when the problem arose.

- **"I would like."** Here A is going to make a request for change. They will complete the sentence by stating clearly and briefly what they would like from the person without making unreasonable demands or threats.

> **SAVITA:**
> **When...** *I walked into the room on Tuesday afternoon and you laughed.*
> **I felt...** *embarrassed and sad.*
> **I would like...** *an apology.*

- In this way, sitting down, speaking clearly about the facts, taking responsibility for your own feelings, not laying blame and expressing your desires is a way of speaking which will enable you to address, communicate, express your feelings and deal with the problem in a way which will hopefully reduce the risk of sparking more conflict.

- After the improvisation A says how they felt, B reflects on how they felt.

- Now try the improvisation again but this time A is going to speak standing up, they are going to speak for a long time extensively about the problem, they will raise their voice, they will lay blame, they will give the responsibility for their feelings onto the other person and they will make unreasonable demands and threats – a complete contrast!

> **SAVITA (STANDING AND SHOUTING):**
> *I can't believe you of all people could do that to me, don't try to pretend you can't remember because you know exactly what you did, laughing at me the other day like some kind of stupid monkey, you made me feel like a complete and utter fool, a total idiot in front of everybody and I'm telling you now and I mean it, if you don't stand up in front of all of them and beg my forgiveness you are going to regret it!*

- Ask the pairs to compare what happened. How was this different from the first improvisation? What difference did the words have? What difference did it make standing up? What reaction did B have? What might happen next?
- Now ask B to think of a problem situation with someone outside the group and do the exercise again.
- After both A and B have had an opportunity to improvise, ask the group to consider a problem they may have with someone in the group. Encourage them, if it is appropriate, to find a quiet time to sit down and talk with the person about the problem using 'when...' 'felt...' and 'I would like...'

**Keep the drama
ON THE STAGE!**

Improvisation – role reversal

- Ask the group to get into pairs and label themselves A and B and sit down.
- A thinks of a problem or conflict they are experiencing with someone inside the group. They then tell B all about how they are feeling, being careful to begin their sentences with 'I feel'. They should not go into the detail of the problem, only how they are feeling. B listens carefully but does not speak or react.
- After five to ten minutes of speaking the pairs will improvise. B now plays A. A now plays the person who they are experiencing a problem with.
- B speaks to A about how they are feeling. B then asks A questions. These questions are designed to help A to speak from the perspective of the person they are having a problem with, in order to gain a greater understanding of the situation.
- After the improvisation the pairs discuss what they learned.
- Swap over.

Forum Theatre can also be a very useful tool for dealing with problems, especially if the problem in the group is bullying.

VIDYA difficult moments...

Dipti: When Hitesh and I started liking each other, it was difficult for the group to understand and accept. They weren't sure that we were going to get married and were worried about how our relationship would impact on the work.

Here are a few more tips for sustaining a healthy team...

- Don't forget, the leader is also part of the team, and members could be experiencing a problem with them.

- In Vidya, the leader is rotated so that everyone gets an opportunity to lead the group and experience different leadership styles. You can have a different leader for a month, a week or a day...

- Ask a facilitator to come in from outside the group to look at group dynamics and conflict resolution.

- Keep all your decision-making processes, structures, finances etc. completely transparent so that there is a good level of trust in the group.

- Keep your communication channels flowing. Make sure you have time in each session for people to talk and to listen. Use a talking stick – whoever is holding the stick is the one to talk and they may not be interrupted. Make sure you hear from everyone.

Be good to yourselves. Theatre For Development work can be very intense. Make sure you have plenty of breaks, changes of location, fun days out, meals together etc.

KEEP ON 3

Survival – sustainability

Many excellent projects are born out of a sense of purpose, commitment and vision. They work hard, they produce very good and very effective theatre and start to make a mark in their community. But then, when the money runs out, or the first set of ideas run out, the project cannot continue.

How can we keep a project alive, expanding and fulfilling its potential?

We have spoken of how to keep the ideas fresh and alive but the question of money and funding will always return.

True sustainability is when you have the resources within your group to generate the money you need to continue. Even if you have started your project with a big grant or linked to a larger host organisation (as Vidya did), ultimate independence comes when you are in control of your operations, including generating funds.

There are many ways of doing this and the ideas below are to whet your appetite. You need to find what is right for you.

- The peer group members could train themselves, or get training, in fund-raising, so that they can go out and obtain the money for the future.
- We know of two groups, in Kenya and in Mozambique, which bake bread and sell it to fund their activities.
- Vidya discovered, through their work, that in the Ahmedabad slums there were many women who were good at needlework, sewing and embroidery. They worked with them

to produce quality items which could be sold in shops, boutiques and even exported. This gives those women a living and generates enough surplus to support one of the actors. This area of work is known as **Vidya Dhara.**

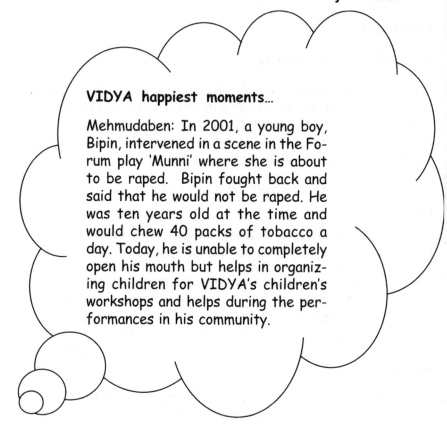

VIDYA happiest moments...

Mehmudaben: In 2001, a young boy, Bipin, intervened in a scene in the Forum play 'Munni' where she is about to be raped. Bipin fought back and said that he would not be raped. He was ten years old at the time and would chew 40 packs of tobacco a day. Today, he is unable to completely open his mouth but helps in organizing children for VIDYA's children's workshops and helps during the performances in his community.

- A fundraising drive from the Friends of Vidya gathered enough money to buy an auto-rickshaw (a *touk-touk*). This is rented to a driver who supports his family from the fares, and the rental supports one actor and her family.
- Recycling products can also raise money, even making bags from waste materials can generate income.

- Can you make a CD or DVD of your activities and sell it? Schools might buy your songs to use as issue-based material in education. Audience members might buy it for entertainment.

- This book is part of Vidya's sustainability. All profits will go to keeping the work alive.

- Although we generally don't believe that charging for performances is a good idea as it might exclude those who need it most, there may be occasions when you can organise a fund-raising performance and open it to the general public.

- In some cases the community may support you in a small way. Vidya successfully ran performances where everyone paid the very small sum of one rupee. This tiny amount, when multiplied by large audiences, can generate significant amounts. This may be especially useful during festival seasons when people would be paying somebody to provide entertainment. Why shouldn't it be you?

VIDYA: We will only survive if we keep learning new skills, if we find the right support, if we overcome conflicts, if we stay unified and if we work hard.

Finally it is worth remembering that relying on one source of funding can be dangerous. If it is withdrawn your whole project is in danger. So diversify if you can and search to gain real independence through your sustainability ideas. It will free you from a dependency culture which can grow from expecting money from other organisations.

In December 2007, Vidya launched a new initiative: VIDYA VIKAS – *the broadening of horizons through knowledge.*
Vidya purchased 5 computers through the income generated from Vidya Dhara to teach basic computer skills and provide theatre training free of charge to children from slum communities across Ahmedabad. Classes are held daily and are taught by volunteers from the slum community and Vidya's group members.

Survival and sustainability are vital for you to continue your valuable work. But remember it is the work for change which is vital. Don't lose sight of your original aims as you spend time generating new income. Be imaginative and try to link the two together.

KEEP ON 4

The Future

The time has come to put down this book. We hope it has been useful and we hope that you have learned that the future is yours. This book can only point you in a direction like a compass. You have to make the journey yourselves, and each journey will be different.

> **VIDYA happiest moments...**
> Dipti: I went to Canada. Even if I had worked my whole life, I would have never been able to go outside – people are proud of me because I went to Canada for my work in development – other people who are wealthier would look down on me before, now I can stand in front of them and hold my head up high.

Of course you might come back to this book to renew your ideas. You might keep it in your bag, or your pocket so that you can refer to it when you need to. And perhaps in a few years you will write a book about your experiences.

We don't know what the future will hold but we leave you with some possible ideas for the future. You might like some, or all. You might not go in these directions. Just remember this book has pointed you forward to your work for change. Have a good journey.

Start work in other towns or areas, but make sure they have their own identity. If they are clones of your work they are not true to their communities

Give birth to other projects like yours

Can you think of a time when your work will no longer be necessary? When the goal is that you are not needed?

Start consultancy work for new groups

How institutionalised do you want to become? Part of a government body? A large NGO? How independent can you be if you are in the pay of a large organisation?

You are asking for change. How much do you want?

As members of your group get older, how will you adapt the tasks for them in the group?

THE END
But We all know it isn't.... .

If you want to contact us for more help or information then we can be e-mailed at:

Manisha Mehta - manishasmehta@hotmail.com
Mojisola Adebayo - mojisolaadebayo@hotmail.com
John Martin - j.martin@pan-arts.net

And please don't forget....
You are not alone!

Here are some Colleagues

There are groups and companies across the world which are using Theatre for Development. We have gathered some contact details here. Perhaps there are some near you. Perhaps you can contact them for advice, training or collaboration:

AFRICA

Botswana
SwitchLife Arts for Development
Contact: Shaun Chitsiga
Address: P.O. Box 1717, Selebi Phikwe, Botswana
Tel: (267) 72492753
Email: shaunchitsiga@yahoo.com   Website: www.switchlife.page.tl

SwitchLife employs creative media and the performing arts in projects for social transformation and community cultural development. and is actively involved in local educational, community and social change projects.

Burkina Faso
L'Atelier Théâtre Burkinabé (Burkina Workshop Theatre)
Contact: Prosper Kompaore (director)
Address: University of Ouagadougou –
01 BP 212 Ouagadougou 01, Burkina Faso
Tel: (226) 50 34 03 09
Mobile: (226) 70 20 63 95
Website: http://www.atb.bf/atb.html

L'Atelier Théâtre Burkinabé promotes Theatre for Development and Forum Theatre in Burkina Faso and elsewhere The company acts as a reference centre and has around 100 companies in Burkina Faso regularly using Forum Theatre. The organisation has connections with companies in Niger, Senegal, Chad, Mali, Togo, Benin, Cameroon, R.D. Congo, Guinea Bissau and Madagascar.

Egypt
Contact: Dahlia Sabbour
Address: 4, El Nakheel Street, Mohandiseen, Cairo, Egypt
Tel: (+2012) 311 3976
Email: dsabbour@yahoo.com

Dahlia uses the various games and techniques of the Theatre of the Oppressed to target communities of people who seek to come together through theatre as a way of increasing and heightening their awareness of themselves as creative beings who share common interests, issues and challenges.

Kenya
Kenya Performing Arts Group (KPAG)
Contact: Odak Onyango
Address: Kenya Performing Arts Group
Kenya Cultural Centre, Harry Thuku Rd,
P. O. Box 356-00200, Nairobi, Kenya
Tel: +254-20-242032   Fax: +254-20-242032
Email: Infokpag@yahoo.com   Website: www.kenyaarts.com

KPAG is a Modern Dance and Physical Theatre Company based in Nairobi. KPAG believes in the "development of the art form itself" which in return encompasses everything.

Mozambique
Grupo de Teatro do Oprimido
Contact: Alvim Cossa
Address: Rua Frei Nicolau do Rosário nº 91/RC-1,
Maputo, Mozambique
Tel: +258 82 4325330   Fax: + 258 21 3418993
Email: gtomaputo@gmail.com   Website: www.gtomaputo.com

This Theatre of the Oppressed Group is a cultural association bringing together more than 3000 actors and activists; works on HIV/AIDS, drugs, health, human rights, corruption, and democracy.
Hopangalatana
Contact: Carlos Alberto Chiribdza
Address: Av Amed Sekou Toure, 2733-r/c-1-flat 3
Maputo, Mozambique
Tel: 258 82 4406530
Email: carlos.chirindza@gmail.com
Website: hopangalatana.blogspot.com

Nigeria
Theate for Development Centre (TFDC)
Contact: Ilse van Lamoen
Address: Octopus. Faculty of Arts, Ahmadu Bello University
P.O. Box 399, Samaru. Zaria, Kaduna State, Nigeria
Tel: +234 (0) 69 550205
GSM: +234 (0) 803 703 7441
Email: info@tfdc-ng.org   Website: www.tfdc-ng.org

TFDC pursues social development by sharing with people inside and outside the academic context, participatory development strategies as developed and studied in ABU's Department of Theatre and Performing Arts and put into practice by members of the Nigerian Popular Theatre Alliance (NPTA). TFDC aims to: generate, analyse, and share knowledge on participatory development approaches, especially Theatre for Development (TFD), Participatory Video (PV), and Participatory Learning and Action (PLA).

South Africa
DramAidE
Contact: Professor Lynn Dalrymple
Address: DramAidE offices, University of KwaZulu Natal
George V Avenue, Durban, 4001
Tel: 031 201 7995 and 083 653 2053
Fax: 031 201 7995
Email: lynndal@iafrica.com   Website: www.dramaide.co.za

Based in the province with the highest HIV prevalence rate in South Africa, established in 1992, the DramAidE project uses drama to engage young people to communicate effectively about issues relating to sex, sexuality and HIV/AIDS. DramAidE aims to equip young people with increased knowledge about HIV/AIDS and the skills to inform and communicate with others about sexual health.

Interactive Human Development
Contact: Manya Gittel
Address: PO Box 1973, Saxonwold,
Johannesburg, 2132
Tel: +27 (0)83 232 1374
Fax: +27 (0) 866841352
Email: manya@InteractiveHumanDevelopment.com
Website: www.InteractiveHumanDevelopment.com

Manya Gittel is a professional facilitator and trainer with 22 years experience of facilitating, training, teaching and people-development and empowerment related endeavours. She currently works in both the NGO and corporate sectors, using the techniques of Theatre of the Oppressed.

Phakama
Contact: Caroline Calburn
Mobile +27 82 735 1376
Email: mwmonto@mweb.co.za, Website: www.projectphakama.org

Project Phakama is a collaborative arts organisation producing work based on the combined personal experiences of young people from all over the world. In any site, using any available material and any artistic form, they explore and test issues that are relevant to them

PST Project (Problem Solving Theatre)
Contact: Emma Durden
Address: 38 Burnage, 125 Currie Road
Durban, South Africa
Tel: +27 (0) 826736662 / +27 (0) 312015594
Fax: +27 (0) 866172798
Email: pstproject@magicmail.co.za / emmadurden@magicmail.co.za
Website: www.pstproject.co.za

PST was established in Durban in 2006, although partners have been working together since 1997. It uses theatre to find ways to address social problems within communities, workplaces and other organisations. It has worked on health-related issues, particularly with HIV/AIDS and also on environmental health, stress management, substance abuse and suicide. We work in English and Zulu, sometimes using professional actors to communicate through theatre, and sometimes working in communities to train others in drama skills so that they can become the catalysts for change within their own environments

South African Drama for Life
Contact: Warren Nebe
Address: Wits University, Johannesburg
Tel: (011) 717-4651
Email: Warren.Nebe@wits.ac.za

This programme supports existing organisations already dedicated to HIV/ Aids education through drama and theatre. It is dedicated to empowering young people to take responsibility for the quality of their own lives within the context of HIV/Aids. The programme aims to explore the conceptual, theoretical, pedagogical and ethical practices and inter-relationships within the applied theatre field including: Theatre for Development, popular theatre, community theatre, Theatre of the Oppressed and Theatre in Education.

The Themba HIV&AIDS Organisation
Contact: Eric Richardson or Sweetness Buthelezi
Address: 58 Jorissen Street, Braamfontein,

Johannesburg. P.O. Box 32705, South Africa
Tel: +27 (0)11 403 9367 / 7222
Fax: +27 (0)11 403 9333
Email: eric@themba.org.za; info@themba.org.za
Website: www.themba.org.za

The Themba HIV/AIDS Organisation has been delivering interactive performances to schools, community based organisations and businesses in Gauteng since February 2002. The focus of its process is influencing behaviour to prevent the spread of HIV. Themba also provides training for people in community based organisations, schools, and youth correctional centres. Training is interactive and participatory.

Senegal
Kaddu Yaraax Forum Theatre Company
Contact: Christine Casset
Address: BP 22919 , Dakar Ponty
Senegal
Tel: 00-221-77-561-78-29
Email: diol6@yahoo.fr. Website: www.kadduyaraax.com

Forum theatre practitioners focused on issues around literacy, poverty, education, environment etc. They also have collaboration with public service providers and development partners.

Sudan
Centre for Theatre in Conflict Zones
Contact: Mr. Ali Mahdi Nouri
Address: Centre for Theatre in Conflict Zones
Sudan Centre of the ITI, PO Box 1988
Dairat elMahdi Gamhoria St.
Khartoum, Sudan
Tel: +249 (183) 78 14 19   Fax: +249 (183) 77 16 21
Email: alimahdi@sudanmail.net

This is a partnership between ITI Sudan and an ITI workshop series: "My Unknown Enemy" in several conflict areas of the world.

Tanzania
DramaticFreedom
Contact: Joy Borman
Address: PO Box 25218, Dar es Salaam, Tanzania
Tel: +255 783 629 714
Email: info@dramaticfreedom.com
Website: www.dramaticfreedom.com

DramaticFreedom provides support to NGOs using Theatre for Development in East and Southern Africa. It has expertise in HIV prevention education, gender equality and stigma. There are many specialist services that DramaticFreedom provides to its clients; working with teams to create a purpose-specific drama, activities or games that can be used immediately; giving advice to NGOs detailing the adoption of a strategic approach to the integration of drama and Theatre and Development into the broader programme of regular work and training.

ASIA

India

Jana Natya Manch
Contact: Molosashree Hasmi
Address (postal only): Jana Natya Manch, J 147 R.B. Enclave, Paschim Vihar, New Delhi 110063 India
Tel: 91-11-2526 4822, 2335 6966
Email: jananatyamanch@gmail.com
Website: www.jananatyamanch.org

Janam's street theatre journey began in October 1978 and it has played a significant role in popularising street theatre as a form of voicing anger and public opinion through plays on price rise, elections, communalism, economic policy, unemployment, trade union rights, globalisation, women's rights, education system, etc. This form of theatre has become a vital cultural tool for workers, revolutionaries and social activists. Street Theatre addresses topical events and social phenomenon and takes them straight to peoples' places of work and residence.

Janasanskriti
Contact: Sanjoy Ganguly.
Address: 42A, Thakurhat Road,
Post-Badu, Kolkata-700128, India
Tel: 0091 33 25264540 or 0091 33 25260170
Website: www.janasanskriti.org
Janasanskriti uses its own brand of interactive theatre in West Bengal to tackle a multitude of social issues. Open workshops and festivals also occur regularly.

Abhinaya Theatre Research Centre,
Plathara, Venkode P O
Thiruvananthapuram 695 028
Kerala, India
Tel: +91 472 3208088,   Mob: +91 9387224599
Email: abhinayatheatre@gmail.com, www.abhinayatheatrevillage.org

We are an independent centre for training, practising and research without imposing any philosophies, as we believe time will prove the existence and relevance of any philosophy. As a socially responsible theatre collective we intervene in issues of social and political importance through our medium. We propose to establish a Theatre Village, in the outer skirts of Thiruvananthapuram, with theatre school, traditional/modern performing space, cottages, research wing, library, studios for sculptors/painters/musicians, space for the artistically inclined marginalised sections of society and community farming.

Jaya Iyer – New Delhi
Email *indianajonesiyer@vsnl.net*   *pravah@vsnl.com* mail@pravah.org
Freelance theatre for development practitioner, training and directing forum and other plays

Nepal
Aarohan Theatre Group
Contact: Sunil Pokharel (Artistic Director)
Address: Aarohan-Gurukul Theatre,
Gurukul, Baneshwor
Kathmandu, Nepal
Tel: (00977 1) 4466956, 2101332
Fax: (00977 1) 4477709
Mobile: (00977) 9851034419
E mail: gurukul@wlink.com.np   Web: www.aarohantheatre.org

Pakistan
Interactive Resource Centre (IRC)
Contact: Mr. Mohammad Waseem
Address: 102 - B, Nawab Town,
Raiwind Road, Lahore, Pakistan
Tel: 0092-42-5313038-39
Fax: 0092-42-5313040
Email: waseemmohammad@gmail.com   Website: www.irc.org.pk

IRC was formed in 2000 to explore new avenues for community mobilisation and development and to assist people in their struggle to regain collective power and strength through different forms of arts like interactive theatre and media.

Punjab Lok Rahs
Contact: Tahir Mehdi
Address: Flat 8, 3rd Floor, HB1,
Awami Complex, New Garden Town,
Lahore, Pakistan
Tel: 0092 42 5940166, 5886454, 300 9454421
Email: rahs.lhr@lokpunjab.org or tahir.mehdi@lokpunjab.org

Lok Rahs started as a group of enlightened young people that cherishes a society that has gender equity, democratic values, respects all humans and offers equal economic opportunity to all, and believes in organised and conscious efforts to realise this dream. Theatre is its working medium. Rahs' canvas is very wide and has dealt with subjects like child marriage and women's right to marry of their free will It has staged plays against arms race and military dictatorship. Rahs draws inspiration from Punjab's indigenous theatre tradition.

Tehrik-e-niswan
Contact: Sheema Kermani
Address: GF 3, Block 78,
Sea View Apartments, D.H.A. 5,
Karachi, Pakistan
Tel: 92-21-5851790 and mob: 0333-2155736
Email: tehrik@hotmail.com
Website: www.tehrik-e-niswan.com

Tehrik-e-niswan means the Women's Movement. It was initiated in 1979 as a Feminist group by Sheema Kermani. It is a Cultural Action Group using Theatre, Dance, Music and Video Production to provide good aesthetic entertainment and to create awareness of Women's Rights and other Human Rights issues. Tehrik presents a variety of styles- classical, musicals as well as realistic and modern plays.

MIDDLE EAST

Palestine
Theatre for Everybody Group
Contact: Hossam Madhoun
Tel: 00972599746033
Email: jhtheater@hotmail.com

The Theatre for Everybody Group is the outcome of years of working toward creating an alternative theatre in the Gaza Strip. The members are theatre makers who believe in theatre as an artistic production as well as a way of creating awareness in society towards its main problems; they believe that through plays they can contribute to change in attitude and preconceived ideas. The Theatre for Everybody Group stimulates people to question themselves, their beliefs and their behaviour.

ASHTAR
Contact: Edward   Muallem
Address:P.O.Box. 2127, Ramallah
Tel: 970-2-2980037
Email info@ashtar-theatre.org   Web: www.ashtar-theatre.org

"At Ashtar, we aim for theatre to be a tool for change to serve cultural and social development, and to promote and deepen the creativity of the Palestinian Theatre"

SOUTH EAST ASIA

Philippines
Philippine Educational Theatre Association (PETA)
Contact: Ms. Gail Guanlao-Billones
Address: PETA Theatre Centre, 5 Eymard Drive,
New Manila, Quezon City, Philippines 111
Tel: (63-2) 410-0822 / 725-6244
Fax: (63-2) 721-8604
Email: *peta@petatheater.com* or *gailgb2002@yahoo.com*
Website: *www.petatheater.com*

PETA is an organisation of creative and critical artist-teacher-cultural workers committed to artistic excellence and a people's culture that casts away shackles and fosters both personal fulfilment and social transformation. Since 1967, it has evolved from a small core of theatre enthusiasts into a large cast of characters with a shared artistic, aesthetic, ideological vision and mission: theatre in the service of the common good.

Thailand
Makhampom Foundation
Contact: Pradit Prasartthong (Secretary) or Richard Barber (International Program Director)
Address: Makhampom Foundation
55 Soi Inthamara 3, Samsennai,
Phayathai, Bangkok 10400, Thailand
Tel: (662) 6168473
Fax: (662) 6168474
Email: *makhampom2@hotmail.com*, *inter@makhampom.net*
Website: *http://www.makhampom.net*

Makhampom is a social organization that works in the medium of theatre for community cultural development (TCCD). They produce contemporary Thai theatre, integrating traditional art forms with modern techniques and social issues, and adapting to the popular theatre styles of each audience or community and conduct theatre workshops and performance projects in the community or the school.

Vietnam
Contact: Phan Y I y
Address: 43 Hoang An A, Le Duan,
Hanoi, Vietnam
Tel: +84 904 666 002   Email: *phanyly@gmail.com*

Phan Y Ly facilitates groups of children, young people and adults using a wide range of creative processes and techniques including movement, music, drawing, experimental theatre and film to create dialogue within and between individuals, leading to new types of awareness and action. Ly is also the founder and artistic director of SameStuff Theatre - the first independent experimental theatre group in Vietnam.

THE CARIBBEAN

Trinidad and Tobago
Arts-in Action (AiA)
Contact: Marvin George
Address: Arts-in-Action
Centre for Creative and Festival Arts (CCFA)
University of the West Indies (UWI)
St. Augustine, Trinidad and Tobago
Tel: (868) 663 0327 (AiA)
Fax: (868) 663 2222 (CCFA)
Email: arts.inaction@sta.uwi.edu
Website: under construction

Facebook: http://www.facebook.com/pages/Arts-in-Action/22676910435
Arts-in-Action seeks to extend the work and mission of the Department into communities, primary and secondary schools and institutions throughout Trinidad and Tobago and the Caribbean Region. The philosophical basis of our work has been that the arts have an indispensable role to play in the process of social and attitudinal change and development.

Caribbean Playback
Contact: Tracie Rogers
Address: 36 Lloyd Street
Sunshine Avenue
San Juan, Trinidad
Email: Caribbean.Playback@gmail.com

Jamaica
Alternative Theatre
Contact: Pierre Lemaire
Address: Edna Manley College
jamaicalternativetheatre@gmail.com
jamaicalternativetheatre.page.tl
tel: 001 876-470-8460

A new company based at The Edna Manley School of Drama, aiming to create non-commercial theatre around social issues and to empower community members to create their own work.

SOUTH AMERICA

Argentina
Teatro Foro
Contact: Ada Dorrego
Address: 14 de Julio Street,
1620 Boulogne (1609), Buenos Aires
Tel: 54+011+4737-7185
Mobile: 54-011-15-5752-8372
Email: ada_sinh@yahoo.com.ar or adasinhache@hotmail.com

Brazil
Estrela
Contact: Juila McNaught da Silva
Address: Rua do Sodré 444 - 1°
Centro,   40060-240
Salvador, Bahia.
Tel: + (55) 71 3322 3854
E-mail: estrela@atarde.com.br
Website: under construction

Estrela aims to advance education and intercultural understanding between Brazil, Britain and other countries, focusing benefit on disadvantaged youth and communities in Brazil. The company has bases in NE England & NE Brazil (Salvador).. Estrela use a variety of Brazilian popular art forms, such as capoeira, afro-Brazilian dance & percussion, street theatre as well as creative media (DVD & photography). They also run Participatory Arts Educational workshops

Pressão no Juízo
contact: Claudio Rocha / Mariana Amorim
Address: Rua do Apolo 161,
Caixa Postal 74, CEP: 50030-220,
Recife Antigo, Recife,
Pernambuco, Brazil.
Tel: (55) (81) 4104-0282
Email: mariana.pressao@gmail.com , pressaonojuizo@yahoo.com.br
Website: www.pressaonojuizo.kit.net

Pressão no Juízo believes in the construction of another reality in Northeast Brazil. They aim to contribute to the release of people that have been submitted to inhuman treatment. They use Theatre of Oppressed methodology with marginalised groups and have been accumulating experiences working with homosexuals, transsexuals, and the elderly, afro-Americans, and people 'out-of-law', children that suffer abuses or any kind of violence, disabled people, and others.

CTO – (Centre for Theatre of The Oppressed)
Contact: Julian Boal
Address: Av. Mem de Sá, 31 - Lapa
Rio de Janeiro -
Tel: (21) 2232-5826 / 2215-0503
Email: ctorio@ctorio.org.
www.ctorio.org.br
www.theatreoftheoppressed.org (international website)

The CTO provides workshops and seminars in the methodologies of Theatre of The Oppressed and was founded by the seminal figure Augusto Boal. "Theatre of the Oppressed is the Game of Dialogue: we play and learn together. All kinds of Games must have Discipline - clear rules that we must follow. At the same time, Games have absolute need of creativity and Freedom. TO is the perfect synthesis between the antithetic Discipline and Freedom. Without Discipline, there is no Social Life; without Freedom, there is no Life"

Chile
Compañía de Teatro Pasmi
Contact: Iván Iparraguirre
Address: Pedro Mira 790,
San Miguel, Santiago.
Tel: 56 2 310 5911
Email: teatropasmi@pasmi.org
Website address: www.pasmi.org

founded in 1994 with members from Peru, Chile and Australia. PASMI works in the marginalised sectors of society, and promotes respect for human rights. Our work is focused in three main areas: Theatre FOR the community (Issue-based shows produced and toured by PASMI); Theatre created WITH the community. Current projects include work with: male prisoners, young people with schizophrenia, and women survivors of gender violence.

This book is written primarily for people working in developing countries where there is little or no infrastructure or support for theatre for development. Consequently we have not listed in detail those companies who work in countries where such support exists, as their experience may well be substantially different. However there are sometimes possibilities for international collaborations or you may be able to get advice by email from such people. Here are a few:

UK. British Council: *These offices exist in many countries and have access to local and British theatre makers who may be able to help. Contact: search for your nearest office at www.britishcouncil.org*

United States of America
Vivian J. Dorsett - *Applied Theatre Specialist.*
Email: *vivian_dorsett@yahoo.com*

Mark Weinberg, Jenny Wanasek   Email: *contact@center-for-applied-theatre.com www.centerforappliedtheatre.org*

Canada
Yolisa Dalamba   Email: *yolisa@rogers.com*

Australia
Milk Crate Theatre-
director@milkcratetheatre.com www.darlinghursttheatre.com

France
Compagnie Mots de tête -
Email: *motsdetetecompagnie@yahoo.com*
www.motsdetetecompagnie.com

Slovakia
Divadlo bez domova
Email: *patrikk@mac.com   www.divadlobezdomova.sk*

Divadlo z Pasaze
Email: *divadlozpasaze@yahoo.com www.divadlozpasaze.sk*

Sweden
Bim de Verdier
Email: *bim_de_verdier@hotmail.com www.bimdeverdier.se*

United Kingdom
Action Space Mobile
Email: *contact@actionspacemobile.org www.actionspacemobile.org*

Geese Theatre Company
Email: *mailbox@geese.co.uk http://www.geese.co.uk*

Small World Theatre
Email: *info@smallworld.org.uk   www.smallworld.org.uk*

Ali Campbell – *workshop leader*
Email: *a.m.campbell@qmul.ac.uk*

The Lawnmowers Ind Theatre Co
Geraldine Ling
Email: *info@thelawnmowers.co.uk*   *www.thelawnmowers.co.uk*

Cardboard Citizens:
mail@cardboardcitizens.org.uk
www.cardboardcitizens.org.uk

Acknowledgments

The AHRC Research Team – Ralph Yarrow, Frances Babbage, Franc Chamberlain

And special thanks to all the Vidya Group members and all our administrators, interns, volunteers and students

The Games and Exercises in this book have been adapted from years of working with wonderful artists and reading their work. They include:

Mike Abrams, Peter Badejo, Juma Bakari, Mita Banerjee, Clive Barker, Faye Barrett and Clean Break theatre company, Peggy Batchelor, Augusto Boal, Ali Campbell, Shahana Chatterjee, Emilyn Claid, Sara Clifford, Adwoa-Shanti Dickson, Kees Epskamp, Eugene van Erven, Amanda Evans, Nic Fine, Anna Hermann, Jaya Iyer, Adrian Jackson and the Cardboard Citizens theatre company, Kwesi Johnson, Chris Johnston, Keith Johnstone, B. V. Karanth, Ian Solomon-Kawall, Raymond Keane from Barrabas, Ziki Kofoworula, Petra Kuppers, Tig Land, Jacques Lecoq, Fiona Macbeth, Freda Martin, Zakes Mda, Nancy Meckler of Shared Experience, Mrs. Lila Mehta, Prof S.P. Mehta, Govardhan Panchal –"Rangapari Vrajak", Kailash Pandya, Ms. Krishma P.Dave, Jon Petter, Chrissie Poulter, Tim Prentki, Annie Ryan and the Corn Exchange theatre company, Barbara Santos, Mallika Sarabhai, Simba, Mr.N.D.Solanki-IPS, Nirali Jhveri, Biraj Jhveri, Bhavin Mehta, James Thompson, Bruce Tuckman, Anna Wallbank and Jeff Banks of Theatre Resource, Tim Wheeler and Mind the... Gap, Denise Wong, Sheron Wray, Ashtar Theatre Palestine, Angel Exit, the Fortune Group, Leap – confronting Conflict, Palama Theatre, the groups on Eugene van Erven's video–"Community Theatre"..., and of course the members of the Vidya company

To name just a few!

Want to find out more?

Books that might help you

Although this book tries to cover every step of the path it is always good to read how other people work, how they think about the work, and what their experiences are. Here are a few books we think are worth reading to make your Theatre for Development even richer:

Aston, *Elaine. Feminist Theatre Practice: a handbook.* (London: Routledge, 1999).

Babbage, Frances, *Augusto Boal* (London: Routledge Performance Practitioners Series, 2004).

Baim, Clark, Brookes, Sally, & Mountford, Alun, *The Geese Theatre Handbook: Drama With Offenders and People At Risk* (Winchester: Waterside Press, 2002).

Barker, Clive. *Theatre Games.* (London: Methuen, 1989).

Benedetti, Jean, *Stanislavski and the Actor* (London: Methuen, 1998:).

Bicât, Tina & Baldwin, Chris. *Devised and Collaborative Theatre: A Practical Guide* (Ramsbury, Crowood Press, 2002).

Boal, Augusto, *Games for Actors and Non-actors*, trans. Adrian Jackson. (London: Routledge, 1992).

Boyd, Neva Leona, *Handbook of Recreational Games* (Chicago, IL.: Fitzsimmons, 1945; reprinted New York: Dover, 1975).

Burgess, Thomas de Mallet & Skilbeck, Nicholas, *The Singing and Acting Handbook: Games and Exercises for the Performer* (London: Routledge, 2000).

Callery, Dymphna, *Through the Body: A Practical Guide to Physical Theatre* (London: Nick Hern Books, & New York: Routledge, 2001).

Chamberlain, Franc, *Michael Chekhov* (London: Routledge Performance Practitioners Series, 2004).

Eldredge, Sears A., *Mask and Improvisation for Actor Training and Performance: The Compelling Image* (Evanston, IL.: Northwestern University Press, 1996).

Fanon, Frantz, *The Wretched of the Earth* (Penguin Modern Classics 2001)

Frost, Anthony and Yarrow, Ralph, *Improvisation in Drama* (London: Palgrave, 2007).

Johnston, Chris. *House of Games: Making Theatre from Everyday Life.* (London & NY: Routledge, 1998)

Koppett, Kat. *Training to Imagine: Practical Improvisational Theatre Techniques to Enhance Creativity, Teamwork, Leadership and Learning* (Stylus Publishing 2001)

Kozlowski, Ron, *The Art of Chicago Improv: Shortcuts to Long-Form Improvisation (*Portsmouth, NJ: Heinemann, 2002).

Lamden,Gill, *Devising* (London, Hodder & Stoughton, 2000).

Martin, John, *The Intercultural Performance Handbook* (London: Routledge, 2004).

McCarthy, Julie. *Enacting Participatory Development: Theatre-based Techniques.* (London: Earthscan, 2004)

Mda, Z., *When People Play People; Development Communication Through Theatre* (Zed Books 1993)

Murray, Simon, *Jacques Lecoq* (London: Routledge Performance Practitioners Series, 2003).

Plastow, Jane & Boon, Richard. *Theatre and Empowerment: Community Drama on the World Stage* (Cambridge University Press 2004)

Potter, Nicole. Movement for Actors. (NY: Allworth, 2002.)

Poulter, Christine, *Playing the Game* (Basingstoke: Macmillan, 1987).

Rosenberg, Helene. *Creative Drama and Imagination: Transforming Ideas into Action* (Thomson Learning 1987)

Simon, Eli, *Masking Unmasked: Four Approaches to Basic Acting* (New York: Palgrave MacMillan, 2003).

Spolin, Viola, *Improvisation for the Theater* (Evanston, IL.: Northwestern University Press, 1963; London: Pitman, 1973).

Van Erven, Eugene, *Community Theatre: Global Perspectives* (Routledge 2000)

Wa Thiong'o, Ngugi, *Decolonising the Mind* (James Currey Ltd, 1986)

The Authors

Manisha Mehta, director of Vidya Educational and Charitable Trust is a multi-dimensional person with skills and passions for theatre, music, live media, theatre for development and business management. She has worked on projects with UNICEF on Women's Empowerment, Gujarat AIDS Control Society, the Ministry of Human Resources Development and the MacArthur Foundation and as Programme Coordinator for Darpana for Development. Using Forum Theatre to discuss women's issues and girl child literacy in the slums has been a struggle. However, looking back at where VIDYA began, where it is today and where it is headed tomorrow, Manisha can honestly say that this struggle is very close to her heart, it embodies her identity and her personal struggle to have her presence acknowledged.

Mojisola Adebayo is an actor, writer, teacher, workshop leader, researcher and director working in theatre in Britain and world wide. She specialises in interactive theatre for social change in areas of conflict and crisis, as well as working extensively on new writing, physical theatre, devised work and adaptations of classic texts. In 20 years of being a performance practitioner, she considers working with Vidya to be her greatest achievement. She would like to take this opportunity to personally thank Augusto Boal, and all those who have taught her so much.

John Martin is the founder and artistic director of Pan Intercultural Arts in London, dedicated to using the arts for social change. Its work deals with violence, racism and trauma in the UK and this methodology has been used to establish groups in many other countries. John trained as an actor and dancer and has directed over 70 productions worldwide. He is also a writer and trainer and uses these skills now to bring the possibilities of empowerment through theatre to University students, refugees, victims of crime, slum dwellers, social workers, psychologists, impoverished villagers in developing countries and those affected by war. He knows that theatre can change lives.

Other contributors : Members of the Vidya company, Adwoa-Shanti Dickson, Laurie Miller-Zutshi, and special thanks to Naomi Everall for her wonderful illustrations

Pan announces the launch of its new force

theatREscue

a core of trained Theatre for Development workers ready to travel to areas of human or natural disaster where help is needed. They will be able to provide post-traumatic support through drama and creative exercises to restore people's ability to interact constructively within a community. They will also provide medium-term training to local workers to use theatre as a tool to view problems and begin to find solutions.

theatREscue's members have worked in post-tsunami and post-cyclone situations as well as in war and post conflict zones.

For more information contact
theatREscue@pan-arts.net